Second Chance with my Cowboy Ex
A SMALL TOWN SWEET ROMANCE

JULIA KEANINI

PICKLED PLUM PUBLISHING

Copyright © 2022 by Julia Keanini

All rights reserved.

No part of this book may be reproduced in any form or by any electronic or mechanical means, including information storage and retrieval systems, without written permission from the author, except for the use of brief quotations in a book review.

Lyle

Because you made my dream our dream, here we are. On the ride of our lives. And I wouldn't change a minute of it because I get to copilot life with you. <3

One

"BLUE, NO!" shouted nearly every voice in the crowded ranch home as the adorable, overgrown puppy executed his grand plan, his big brown eyes intent on the huge, delicious mud pie cake that sat precariously close to the edge of the table. Blue made a beeline for it, undeterred by the chorus of humans calling after him.

Logan watched with wide eyes from the other side of the living room as the giant puppy leapt forward but was thwarted when Logan's mom tackled him gently to the ground just before he reached the table. Meanwhile Logan's brother Brooklyn, usually called Brooks, deftly lifted the cake out of the straining pup's reach and deposited it far out of reach on top of the refrigerator. It was truly impressive teamwork. Logan guessed that's what came from a family who ranched together.

Holland, Logan's sister and the youngest of the large Ashford clan, collapsed dramatically back into the couch behind her. "That was too close," the girl sighed, shaking her head. She'd inherited her dramatics from who-knew-where, considering both of Logan's parents were as level-headed as they came.

"We have at least a dozen desserts," Jackson, the brother just younger than Logan, said in his ever-logical way.

"Yeah, but that one's my favorite," Holland argued.

"Mine too," Ben, one of their ranch hands, piped up.

Logan shot the hand a glare and saw all six of his brothers doing the same. Logan guessed he wasn't the only one who'd noticed Ben watching Holland a little too closely. The girl was too beautiful for her own good. Or at least Logan's good. He'd always felt the need to guard his baby sister; all the brothers had. But ever since their dad had died the year before, Logan had felt the need to step into his dad's shoes in every way. Including protecting his dad's baby girl.

Ben closed his mouth and shrank back into his chair. Good. The last thing Logan needed was to worry about a hand getting too close to his sweet, naïve sister.

Logan leaned back into his own seat as he rubbed his full but still flat belly. Most of his friends and classmates had started putting on weight now that they were in their mid-thirties, but working side-by-side with his ranch hands and performing the manual labor needed to keep a ranch going day in and day out had served his physique well. Even though he ate nearly as much as the beautiful horses they cared for.

But today, even his hard-to-satisfy appetite was at capacity, considering they'd just finished the gargantuan Thanksgiving feast his mom and grandma had labored over. He didn't know how anyone who'd eaten the same incredible meal could be concerned about dessert.

"So brother," said Memphis, another of Logan's brothers, as he pulled up a chair next to Logan and draped an arm over his broad shoulders.

Logan fought the urge to groan. Anytime Memphis began a conversation with the term 'brother,' it never bode well for that particular brother.

"How about getting a move on with dessert?" Memphis asked in a nonchalant tone that didn't fool Logan in the least.

"Why would I want to do that? I thought we were all enjoying a leisurely family meal." Logan intentionally drew out each word, knowing he was driving Memphis up the wall. But it was fun to see the man squirm. Especially considering Memphis had flaked on him the day before when he'd promised he'd train their newest hand in his specialty, cutting.

Memphis tapped the fingers of his free hand on his jean-clad thigh. Probably playing some piano piece unconsciously. Once upon a time he'd been a virtuoso, but he hadn't played since their dad had passed. He wouldn't say why, but refused to touch the instrument. Logan knew their mother had been the only one to get through to Memphis and learn the real reason behind his quitting something they all enjoyed, but since she'd stopped pressing him the rest of them had as well. Sadly, the grand piano in their sitting room was getting dusty. No one played much now that Dad had gone.

"It's just that I'm supposed to meet up with—" Memphis began.

Logan interrupted him with a groan. "Really? On Thanksgiving?"

Logan was no monk—he'd done his fair share of dating. Heck, he had a date scheduled that Saturday night. But with Memphis it was different. It almost seemed as if he couldn't spend any time alone, and that worried Logan. It was Thanksgiving . . . couldn't the man take one night off and just enjoy time with his family? Logan was especially concerned because he knew Memphis's reputation was beginning to concern their mom. She tried to ignore whispers about her sixth son's playboy ways, but even their saint of a mother could only put up with so much. This was the kind of thing Dad would have taken care of, so Logan realized it was up to him to curb his brother's habits.

"Just stay here tonight," Logan declared, crossing his arms

over his chest to convey to his brother that the discussion was over. But Logan should have known it wouldn't be so easy.

"Why?" Memphis asked, eyes narrowed.

"We're only together for this one night. Phoenix has to leave at six am tomorrow." Logan hoped that would be sufficient reason for his brother.

It had been a near miracle that Phoenix had been able to join the family, but their brother had moved mountains—or maybe just an overzealous coach—by explaining that their father had died at this time last year and they all needed this time together. The typically unemotional man had been touched . . . at least touched enough to allow Phoenix thirty-six hours off. It had only worked because the Salt Lake Lightning, unlike the many other teams who were playing today, didn't have a game until Sunday.

"Not my fault Nix plays pro ball and has to keep a crazy regimented schedule," Memphis responded with a lazy shrug of one shoulder.

"Just stay home." Logan was sick of trying to make his brother see reason. If he couldn't understand why he should be here by now, he never would. So Memphis could be upset but as his older brother and technically his boss, Logan was putting his foot down.

"Why?" Memphis asked again, his voice petulant.

Logan was about to blow his lid. He was typically pretty chill, but lately Memphis had been getting under his skin. He was irresponsible and refused to see beyond his own pleasure. Logan had tried to ignore it, reminding himself that they were all dealing with grief in their own way. Besides, Memphis was still just twenty-four. But enough was enough. Twenty-four was old enough to man up when it was needed. And right now it was needed. Logan didn't want to see his mother's face if Memphis walked out of that house in the next few minutes.

"Memph," Orlando, the brother just older than Memphis, dragged a chair to his other side. "Last Thanksgiving has some pretty tough memories for Mom," Land whispered, just loud enough for the three of them to hear.

Orlando shouldn't have to remind Memphis of this. They'd all been there, at that tragic dinner. When Dad had collapsed and only after an ambulance had raced him to the hospital did they all find out he'd been battling prostate cancer. He'd told no one, not even his wife, who'd sat in stunned silence as the doctor spoke to them.

They'd only had days with him after that. Awakening in the hospital bed, he had tried to explain his reasons. The cancer had been too far along for any kind of treatment by the time he'd finally gone to the doctor. That hadn't surprised Logan. His dad avoided the doctor, preferring to greet a plague head-on before seeing the person who could cure him.

Dad had figured if he was going to die anyway, it should be on his terms. He wanted to go back to the ranch, work every moment that he could, love hard on his family without them worrying if he was going to drop at any second, and be the man his wife needed.

They'd swallowed their frustration as they spent their last moments with the patriarch of the family. But Logan wished he'd known. That he'd had more time to ask his dad questions. Not about the ranch—his dad had left all of that in perfect order—but about life. About family. About being the kind of man that his father had become. If he'd known that Thanksgiving dinner was going to be their last one, he would have gone on fewer dates, stayed home with his dad more. He would have spent every waking moment with the man.

But maybe that was why Dad had kept it from them. He'd wanted his life to be normal for as long as possible. And looking back, Logan now saw the signs. He recalled his father bending over in pain, then straightening and saying it was nothing. Logan had never pressed the issue, so he'd been as blindsided as the rest of them.

"Stay here for Mom," Orlando continued in his quiet, measured voice. His soothing tone could put even their most spirited horses at ease.

Memphis nodded once. He finally seemed to get it.

Logan shot his brother a smile of gratitude before standing and taking a couple of steps away. Memphis was staying. That was all that mattered. And yet Logan found himself still annoyed with his self-absorbed younger brother, so he decided to take himself out of the situation before he did something he regretted. Mom would be sad if Memphis left, but that was nothing to how she'd feel if her sons got in a fight.

Logan glanced around the room, taking it all in. Holland, Brooks, and Austin had joined Grandma and Mom in the kitchen. The three of them were gently pushing the older two out of the way, insisting they sit down rather than doing all the dishes after preparing the entire meal.

Grandpa sat on a couch, telling stories of the good old days to his audience of Jackson, Phoenix, and the hands who'd joined them for the holiday dinner. The local employees had gone home to their own families, but six of them were too far from home to travel or didn't have anyone to share the meal with, so they'd been welcomed to the Ashford table. Logan couldn't remember a family get-together in his home that had only included their immediate family.

When he and his siblings were little, the old ranch house—Logan still called it that even though it had been remodeled and now rivaled the gorgeous homes in those magazines Holland loved to thumb through—was typically full of Logan's dad's family. But when his three brothers each had their own broods, it became challenging to gather everyone together. They still managed to see one another on Christmas day, a giant chaotic mess of an event, but Thanksgiving was a little more relaxed, with Grandma and Grandpa flitting from one family gathering to the next. This year, though, his grandparents had decided to stay with Logan's immediate family for the entire meal, the loss of their son drawing them together.

Logan decided to join the cleaning crew in the kitchen. He needed to check on his mom anyway. His siblings had done their best to get Mom away from the dishes, but she was still hovering nearby, probably watching for an opening to jump back in and help. Mom had always worked even harder than Dad. And that was saying something, considering their father had built their thriving ranch with his own two hands. But when Dad signed off for the day, Mom kept cooking, cleaning, and mothering. And she was up before Dad every morning to make sure he had a home-cooked breakfast that would stick to his ribs. Mom would never say she worked harder, only that she worked alongside their father. Logan knew they'd been true teammates.

Even without Dad, it was difficult to keep Mom away from any work that needed to be done. When Logan edged past her to dry and put away the clean, wet dishes, he had to laugh at her audible gasp.

"I was just about to do that." His mom, Morgan, held out her hand for the dishtowel Logan had whisked out from under her.

"I know," Logan said with a wink, turning his attention to the mountain of dishes that Brooks had washed and Holland had rinsed. Austin was on leftover duty and was playing the Tupperware version of Tetris to squeeze the massive amounts of food into the fridge.

"Hmph," Morgan responded as she swatted toward her oldest son. Logan laughed but maintained his place, carefully positioned to block her attempts at taking over.

His siblings in the kitchen saw the exchange and joined in the laughter.

"See, Grandma knows how to take a hint," Holland said, pointing a wet finger toward their grandmother, who'd taken a seat at the dining table that was still crowded with untouched desserts. Her eyes were closed as she leaned back precariously in the chair.

"Austin, help Grandma move to a less dangerous seat," Holland commanded as the woman swayed dangerously to the side.

Austin forced the fridge door shut on the overabundance of leftovers and went to do their sister's bidding. She sure was bossy for being the youngest. Or maybe she was bossy because she was the youngest. They'd never know.

Austin showed Grandma to an empty spot on the couch and headed back to the kitchen, his blue eyes trained on Morgan.

"Oh no, you don't," Mom said as Austin re-entered the kitchen. She held out a warning hand as he approached.

"You should get off of your feet too," Austin suggested mildly, knowing a demand was pointless.

"I'm not an old woman who needs to be coddled," she retorted, backing away and trying to snatch Logan's dishtowel.

"I heard that," Grandma yelled from the living room.

"You aren't either," Mom tried to amend, but judging by the crease in Grandma's forehead she didn't buy it.

"Austin, if you value that beautiful head of hair you sport, you won't take a step closer," Mom warned.

Logan had forgotten Mom was also the scarier of his parents. None of them had liked to upset Dad, but they never crossed Mom.

Austin ran a hand through his honey-brown curls. "I think I'm going to go check out the desserts."

"Smart move," Mom muttered as she hovered behind Holland and Brooks, looking for an opening.

Holland hip-checked Mom—she was the only one who dared to go head-to-head with their mother—and Mom took a tentative step back.

"Just let me finish up the big pots," she pleaded, trying to wedge her way in between Brooks and Holland again.

Holland shook her head as Brooks handed her another soapy plate. "Why don't you go check out the desserts as well?" she asked Morgan sweetly.

Mom groaned but surprisingly did as her daughter asked. Logan couldn't help grinning as he saw someone win a power struggle with Mom. Although heaven help them all if mother and daughter decided to team up.

Logan noticed most of the family and hands were beginning to drift toward the dessert-laden dining table. Along with the mud pie cake there were three different kinds of pumpkin desserts; pecan, apple, cherry, and blueberry pies; and a gourmet vanilla bean souffle Brooks had added to the mix.

Brooks had been in culinary school when Dad had passed— he'd been the one exception to Dad's college rule. Although each of Mitchell Ashford's children had known they wanted to come home and work on the ranch eventually, when Logan turned sixteen Dad had made a rule that they all had to go to college. Not only did he feel the extra education would help them in life, but he knew the time away from home was important. So they'd attended various universities around the US, most of them to play football, and Holland was still in the process of getting her degree from Boise State, although she attended remotely. She was the only one Dad had allowed to remain at home through her university years. When Holland hadn't wanted to move out after graduating from high school, Dad hadn't had the heart to push his baby girl out of the nest. So as always, Holland had gotten her way and attended school through the internet.

But with Brooks it had been different. Dad could be stubborn, but he knew his children and he saw Brooks' incredible ability in the kitchen. When Brooks had proposed his plan to attend culinary school instead of following the four-year university route of his older brothers, Dad had jumped on board. And Brooks had thrived . . . until Dad's death. Brooks and Dad had both been quiet, taking in the world more than adding their voices to it.

They seemed to see one another in a way that no one else could, so Brooks had lost more than a father that day. He'd lost the man who truly understood him.

Mom had tried to get Brooks back to school and he always said he'd return eventually. So she stopped pressing. Logan had no idea how she did it. She'd lost her other half the night Dad had died, but still she saw beyond her own grief and noticed each time one of her children was struggling. And they'd all struggled. Mom had been busy, that was for sure. Logan had a feeling she'd continue to be just as busy for years to come.

Brooks finally scrubbed the last dish and handed it to Holland, who ushered her brothers out of the kitchen to join the revelry in the dining room. Logan waited for his siblings to pile their plates high before digging into the desserts himself. It was funny how quickly his appetite got a second wind when the desserts were right in front of his face. He scooped up an extra helping of blueberry pie. It had always been his favorite.

"Thank you for making these, Grandma," Holland said, pointing with her fork to the pumpkin pecan rolls that had been their dad's favorite. Everyone else ate them, and they were delicious, but no one hogged them the way Dad would have. Grandma only made them on Thanksgiving and Dad had often been found sneaking a few away for a snack he'd bring out after the others had gone to bed.

"It wouldn't be Thanksgiving without them," Grandma responded with a sad smile.

Moisture pricked behind Logan's eyes. They'd all promised today would be a day full of celebration. Dad would have wanted it that way. As quiet as he was, he was a huge fan of large gatherings. It was probably part of the reason he'd had so many kids. He always had a party with him. So they'd done this for him. It was for themselves too, but this felt like the best way to honor the man who meant so much to each of them.

Blinking, Logan willed the tears away. No one was crying that day. Far be it from him to be the weak link.

"No it wouldn't," Mom finally agreed after clearing her throat. It was obvious they were all battling emotion.

"They're really good," said Harvey, one of the newer ranch hands, around a mouthful of pumpkin roll. With that the emotions that had been building in the room eased a bit. He had no idea about the underlying conversation, considering he'd never met Logan's father.

"They are," Phoenix agreed as he raised his own pumpkin roll in the air and took a gigantic bite.

Dessert went quickly and soon Grandma and Grandpa saw themselves out, followed by each of the hands, until only Mom and her eight kids remained.

They lounged on various pieces of furniture around the living room, each trying to stretch out. If the rest of the family felt anything like Logan, they were trying to find more room in their bodies to store all of that food. Holland and Mom shared a blanket on the loveseat. They seemed to be the only ones not groaning about having eaten too much.

"Thank you for coming home, Nix," Mom said, looking around the room at each of her prides and joys.

"Wouldn't have missed it for the world, Ma," Phoenix responded.

Logan was grateful as well. It wouldn't have been the same without all of them there. Well, almost all of them. Man, would missing his dad ever get any easier?

Blue's sudden bark was the only warning before a knock sounded at the door.

"Anyone expecting someone?" Mom asked over the puppy's yelps. She pushed the blanket aside to stand but Memphis beat her to it.

If this was his date at the door, so help him. Logan was going to kill his little brother.

Memphis held Blue back with a strategically placed leg as he opened one of the double doors at the entry of the home.

"Blue, come," Land called. Blue immediately responded, trotting over and sitting near Land's feet, though his eyes stayed on the door.

The family couldn't see anything since the living room was behind the door, but they did hear Memphis holding a short conversation with a female before he opened the door wider. A woman who was probably around his age or maybe closer to Logan's walked in and looked around, taking in the family as they all sat watching.

Logan clenched his fists and only refrained from yelling at his brother since his mom was right there. What was Memphis thinking?

"She's looking for Dad," Memphis said. He took a few steps away from the woman as if he was unsure what to make of her.

Oh, so she wasn't Memphis's date. Logan felt only a split second of relief before realizing what Memphis had said. Who this young woman was looking for.

Every head in the room turned to Logan. He stood, knowing his responsibility to his family.

"I—" the woman began and then glanced back toward the door as if she wanted to make a hasty exit.

"I'm sorry to interrupt family time," the woman said as she turned back to the group in living room. Logan could imagine they seemed intimidating, and his first reaction was to put the woman at ease. But why was she here, and why did she want to see Dad?

The woman tugged on the hem of her shirt and Logan began to feel some compassion for her. This couldn't be easy. She must have an important reason to be here or she would have left long ago.

"Come in. Have a seat," Logan offered.

The woman quickly shook her head. "I'm okay right here. I was just hoping to speak to Mitchell Ashford?"

"You've found his family, Sweetheart," Mom said in her kind and welcoming manner even though she had to be feeling unease as well.

"Can I ask your name?" Logan asked since he couldn't very well call the woman 'Sweetheart' the way Mom had.

"Madison," she nearly whispered. She paused, cleared her throat, and repeated more loudly, "Madison."

Logan nodded.

"Can I ask what business you have with Dad?" he continued.

Maybe she was here on ranch business. At eight o'clock on Thanksgiving. Okay, that didn't seem likely. But what other reason could there be?

"I'd like to speak with Mitchell if I could," Madison said, her voice full of uncertainty.

"You can't," Holland spoke up from where she sat. "He's dead."

Leave it to Holland to say it so bluntly. By the way she immediately bit her lip Logan could tell she hadn't wanted to say it but she'd needed that information out ASAP so Madison would stop asking where their father was. Logan understood. That question got almost more painful to hear with time.

Madison's face went white. "What?"

"He died last year," Logan explained since Holland had dropped the news and then gone quiet. He was guessing she was fighting a battle against her tears.

The moment before Madison had entered their home had been somber. With the party element taken out of the evening they were reminded of who was missing. Logan knew their dad wasn't far from any of their minds. And then Madison had come in asking for him. It wasn't great timing for any of them.

"Last year?" Madison whispered.

"You should speak to us, Sweetheart. We'll try to help," Mom offered gently. Only she would be offering help to a young woman asking for Dad even as Mom was mourning him.

Madison shook her head. "I shouldn't have come. I'm sorry." She began to back away.

"It must be important business if you showed up on Thanksgiving," Jackson said.

Madison's backward motion paused.

"It is. Or I guess it was. It doesn't really matter now, does it?" she asked faintly but none of them could answer because they had no idea why she was there.

"It might help you just to let us know why you've come. Or even where you've come from? Have you traveled a long way?" Logan asked, walking toward her with the same slow, careful steps he took toward a nervous horse. He had a feeling he shouldn't just let this young woman go.

"The longest," Madison whispered. She hesitated, but met Logan's eyes and took a deep breath. Before she could say another word, the door flew open again and another young woman entered, pushing her way forward aggressively. She apparently had as much gusto as Madison had timidity.

"You okay, Madi?" the woman asked.

"I asked you to stay in the car," Madison responded.

"You were taking forever. When I saw that big lug stand up, I thought you might need some backup." The woman pointed to where Jackson was standing right in front of the window, easily noticeable from outside.

"Big lug?" Jackson muttered, but Mom shushed him.

"We were just asking Madison why she wanted to speak to Mitchell." Mom's soft voice broke through the tension, offering an olive branch.

"Where is Mitchell?" the woman asked, looking around the room with a hand on her hip.

"Dead," Madison whispered.

The other woman's eyes went wide.

"What?" she gasped. She rushed to Madison's side and drew her friend into a hug.

Logan needed some answers. Why would Madison be mourning the death of his father? A man she had obviously never met.

"Who are you?" Jackson asked the woman before Logan could say anything.

"Ruby," she said, glaring at Jackson. "Madi's best friend."

Logan's mother made her way across the room to where both of the young women stood. "Why are you here?" Mom asked, gently touching Madi's arm.

Madi bit her lip and then looked to Ruby.

"Madi's mom died a few months ago and we found this in her personal effects," Ruby said as she took Madi's purse and dug out a piece of paper that had seen better days.

Even from across the room Logan recognized his dad's handwriting. His stomach dropped. Why had Madi's mother kept a note from Dad?

"Mitchell is her dad," Ruby said as Mom knees began to buckle.

Logan ran the couple of steps to where his mother stood and held her up before she could fall.

"That can't be true," Jackson responded immediately.

"That's what the note says," Ruby countered.

Jackson's long legs ate up the room in a few strides and he snatched the note from Ruby.

They all watched in breath-holding silence as Jackson read.

"That's not what this says," he finally declared.

An audible breath of relief filled the room.

"It's implied," Ruby argued.

When Jackson said nothing more, Logan felt his body tense.

There was no way. His father would have never. He looked at his mother in his arms. His father had been head over heels for this woman. There hadn't been a day of their lives that Mitchell Ashford hadn't looked at his wife with adoration.

Madi had to be in her late twenties to early thirties, putting her right smack in the middle of Mitchell's eight children. There was no chance. Logan wouldn't believe it. But he couldn't take the note from Jackson and read it himself. His mom needed him more. She would literally fall without his supporting arms, and he would never let that happen.

"I'm so sorry." Madi stumbled over her words. "If I'd known he was no longer here . . . "

She shook her head.

"You did nothing wrong," Ruby affirmed as she held her friend close, snatching back the note from Jackson's hands.

"I have to go," Madi blurted and dashed toward the door, Ruby just behind her.

"Wait!" Logan called out but they were out the door before he even finished the word.

What had just happened?

"What did the note say, Jacks?" Austin asked immediately, and all eyes turned to Jackson.

"It was a note to her mom. It said he'd be there for her, and he was sorry about what happened, but she could count on him," Jackson said quietly, as if he didn't want to tell them that truth.

"But nothing about him actually fathering Madi, right?" Logan had to know.

Jackson nodded.

"It was your father's handwriting," Mom finally spoke.

"That doesn't mean anything," Austin replied.

"Then why didn't Dad tell us about Madi?" Holland asked the same question that had been plaguing Logan. "Why didn't he tell Mom?"

Mom blinked rapidly and seemed to be struggling to catch her breath. Logan hated this. His mother had borne grief with such grace. But now this? How much was one woman supposed to endure?

She suddenly pressed her eyes closed for a few moments and then opened them, focusing on Logan.

"We don't know anything, Mom. But I'll get to the bottom of it," Logan promised.

Mom tried to smile but it was broken. "I don't think we'll like what you find."

"Mom," Logan said, shaking his head. He knew his siblings were hanging on their every word.

"She has his nose, Logan," Mom finally admitted. Tiredly she withdrew herself from Logan's arms and walked toward her bedroom.

That was what had been bugging Logan from the beginning, why he'd felt uneasy from the moment Madi had walked in. Mom was right. She had the Ashford nose.

Two

THREE DAYS EARLIER

LAKE FOUGHT the urge to rub at her eyes even though they felt grainy and raw. She guessed that's what crying for weeks on end would do to a set of eyes.

She glanced over at her mother who sat by her side. They both faced the attorney who was about to read the last will and testament of Lake's husband.

Lake's hands went numb even as she thought the words. She wasn't supposed to be here, in her husband's attorney's office, just days after his funeral. This wasn't supposed to be how her life went.

Granted, Lake's life had already taken way too many twists and turns long before Fred had died. She wished all of her tears the last few weeks could have been accounted to her grief over her husband's death. But it had been about so much more. Especially after she'd found out *that woman* had been in the car with him. That they'd died together. And the worst part was that Lake would never know why. Why, after Fred had promised he'd never see her again, was that woman in the car with him?

And just like that the numbness was gone, replaced by the fiery fury Lake felt whenever she thought about the two of them together. Fred's last moments were spent in *her* company. And for that Lake wasn't sure she'd ever be able to forgive her husband. To ever truly mourn him.

But, as she had each and every time she remembered that truth, she shoved it away. Locked her emotions in a box that couldn't ever be opened. Not if she wanted to be a good mother to her two darling daughters. Both of them were grieving the death of their father, their grief unmarred by knowing what their father had done. And it would stay that way. Forever. Those girls would never feel this pain that pierced and shattered Lake's heart.

On the other side of Lake sat the man whom she tried not to blame for all that had happened. Fred had been his own man.

But he had changed so much in the months following his mother's death, when he'd started med school and begun working for his father. The Fred who had shyly asked Lake out in high school was as sweet as boys came and had only seemed to grow sweeter with time. And they had been so in love. So they'd married during their second year at Boise State.

But soon after the wedding Fred's estranged father, Stanley, had entered their lives. The renowned pediatrician who'd taken superb care of every child . . . except his own. He'd met Fred's mom during his own time at Boise State. But when graduation neared and med school beckoned, he'd left his young wife, along with one-year-old Fred, without a backward glance. He had always taken care of them monetarily, but beyond that he had been completely absent. He hadn't attended one baseball game, school event, or graduation. Not even a phone call on birthdays.

But for some reason when he'd appeared at Boise State, offering to pay off both Lake's and Fred's college expenses, he'd been completely forgiven. Especially when he'd added med school to the offer, saying he could think of nothing he'd like more than to have his son join him at his thriving practice.

So Fred had followed in his father's footsteps. The man he'd once claimed to abhor.

Lake had never understood it. With each step that Fred took to become more like his father, he withdrew further from Lake. But she'd held on. Borne him one daughter halfway through med school and another during his residency. She'd given all that she had, figuring if she worked twice as hard at their marriage it would make up for Fred's lack of effort. He claimed he gave all he had to his career, so what else could she ask of him? Lake longed to say she wanted what her father gave to her mother, but that wouldn't have been fair. They weren't her mom and dad.

But Fred said he was trying. And at least he wasn't leaving her the way his dad had left his mom. Wasn't that enough?

It had been. Almost, anyway. Until that woman.

"I think we should begin," Fred's attorney said, clearing his throat as he shuffled some papers.

Lake knew she should remember his name. He'd said it enough times. But a fog had surrounded her ever since the phone call about the car wreck that had stolen her husband from her.

Stanley fidgeted as if he had better places to be. And maybe he did. Lake never could figure out if Stanley really cared for Fred, or if he'd just liked the appearance of having his son work for him. One thing she did know was that Stanley didn't care for her in the least. He'd made it plain that even her daughters weren't worth his time.

Lake wrapped her arms around herself, suddenly cold. Her mom leaned toward her and gently put an arm around her shoulders, rubbing her hand up and down Lake's arm.

What would Lake have done without her parents? She honestly didn't know. Her mom had been with her every moment since the phone call, walking with her through every step of her grief. And her dad had been there nearly as much until after the funeral, when he'd had to return to work.

"Frederick Hollowell's last will and testament," the attorney began.

Lake let out a single, gasping sob before swallowing back the rest. The grief was so overwhelming she felt she was choking on it.

"He started with the practice," the attorney began.

Stanley crossed one leg over the other, shifting away from Lake and her sadness.

"Because he had worked there less than ten years, he owns nothing. Per your agreement," the attorney said, nodding at Stanley.

"What?" Lake couldn't help but ask.

That wasn't what she'd heard. The reason Fred had insisted on working with his dad was because they were to have a fifty-fifty partnership of the practice. "It was better than anyone else would ever offer," Fred had said.

Stanley nodded and stood, gathering his briefcase.

"Um, sir, we actually still have more to go," the attorney stated.

"Anything more about my practice?" Stanley asked.

The attorney shook his head.

"Then you can send my attorney anything else relevant to me," Stanley said, striding toward the door without a backward glance.

Lake couldn't believe what she was seeing. Did he really care so little?

She shouldn't be surprised. When Lake had found out about her husband's affair with one of the nurses at the practice, she'd been too upset to even talk to Fred, but she'd gone to Stanley, begging him to fire the nurse. Stanley had just looked at her as if she were a problem he wanted out of his office. His words would stay with Lake forever. "Sachia is a good nurse. I'm unwilling to hire a new one just because you have a personal dispute with her."

Lake had shouted words she wasn't proud of. Something about the apple not falling far from the tree. And then a few four-letter words she'd never say in front of her daughters.

And she'd made plans to leave Fred. She figured an affair was the last straw. But suddenly he'd become repentant. He'd told Lake he needed her, begged her not to break up their family. He'd promised it would never happen again—he'd even fired Sachia for Lake.

And perhaps that's what made the pain so raw. The car accident had happened when they were still slowly working their way back to one another after his infidelity. It had only been four months since Lake had found out. It had been long enough for Lake to decide to forgive Fred, to try again, but not long enough to reestablish trust.

The sound of the door closing behind Stanley shook Lake out of her thoughts. This was all too much. How was she supposed to continue? Every moment of living, every breath she drew, felt like a fight. And she was so tired of fighting. But what else could she do?

"It'll be okay." Her mother gently patted Lake's shoulder and Lake realized she'd slumped over when Stanley walked out with her financial security.

She'd been counting on that residual income. Fred had assured her after med school that if anything happened to him she'd be taken care of. But after the accident she found out he hadn't had an insurance policy. She wasn't sure why, unless he figured they wouldn't need it because of the money from the practice. But now . . . what had Fred done?

"I don't understand," Lake finally said to the attorney.

"When your husband signed on to work for your father-in-law, the contract stated that he would earn part of the practice every ten years until Dr. Hollowell retired. So after ten years he'd get ten percent, twenty, twenty percent, and so on and so forth until the elder Dr. Hollowell retired and your husband would get fifty percent," he explained.

"But Fred's only worked there for six years," Lake whispered, the reality of what was happening hitting her.

The attorney nodded. "I'm sorry," he said, shifting slightly. His tone said he wasn't done being the bearer of bad news. What more could he have?

"Your husband kept a personal bank account," he continued.

Lake nodded. She didn't like it, but he'd said it was his way of keeping his investment expenses separate from their family accounts. They had a joint account that Fred deposited money into every two weeks when he was paid, enough to cover their family's expenses. It had been nearly four weeks since the last deposit, so the family account was practically empty now. But in the last few months, Fred had rained lavish gifts on Lake, so she was sure that his personal account had to have a good amount of money. It had to have money. Especially now that she knew the practice would give her nothing.

If she wasn't grieving and so utterly angry, Lake knew she would have felt so stupid that she was in this position, but right now she didn't have the bandwidth to feel anything but those first two emotions. She really should know more about their finances, though. Or have worked and earned her own money. But Fred had been resistant whenever she brought up the idea of working outside the home. When he'd been in med school while she was home with a baby, it had seemed impossible and after that she'd felt unmarketable. Who would want to hire a mother with a decade-old history degree and no real work experience?

But Fred had said they'd be okay. She'd be okay.

"Dr. Hollowell made a few investments in the months before his death," the attorney continued, pausing to clear his throat again.

Lake closed her eyes. This was it. Her last hope.

"They didn't go well," he said.

Lake heard herself gasp but she felt so displaced that it didn't even feel like it came from her throat.

"How much is left?" Lake whispered. She felt incapable of speaking at a louder volume.

"Not much," the attorney said, his voice quiet.

Not much. This was what her husband, the man who'd promised to care for them, had left Lake had to live on. Jobless, prospectless, needing to provide for her children.

Lake's throat stung and she thought for sure she would cry. She was destitute. Her children were destitute.

But she held her chin high as she listened to the rest of the will. The toys Fred had insisted on buying were rattled off as Lake's property and she considered what she could get for his boat and jet skis. Each item only equaled a few more weeks to feed her children. She didn't have the luxury of considering what selling those things would mean to her husband. She had to do this, to survive for her children's sake.

But even with all of the toys and her car—his had been totaled in the accident although she'd get a settlement from the insurance company, another tally mark in the money she'd be able to save up to take care of her family—she didn't have much.

But she wasn't destitute. Things would be rough, tight, difficult. But they weren't penniless. Maybe she'd been stupid to not know what was going on before, but now she did, and she'd make the best of it. She would figure it out. For her girls.

She had to get a grip on the emotional side of things. The fact that Stanley was sure to give them nothing after Fred devoted six years of their lives to the practice. Not to mention that they were family. The fact that Fred had been with the woman he'd promised to never see again. The fact that she was a widow at thirty-five. She needed to seal all that away.

She didn't have time or energy for those wounds. Her girls needed her.

The attorney finished reading and her mother watched carefully as Lake stood and, like the robot she was trying to be, walked herself out of that office.

She was grateful to know she wasn't destitute. But she still needed a job, ASAP. They had rented their home because Fred had claimed the market wasn't quite right for them to buy, but now she wondered if he'd said so because they didn't have the money. But they'd lived in a gorgeous lakefront rental. It was way out of Lake's budget now. Maybe it had always been out of their budget. But Fred loved looking the part of a successful doctor. He felt he deserved things because of how hard he worked.

But where would she find a job? And a cheaper rental? Not to mention that the holidays were right around the corner. And childcare? Her girls were pretty self-sufficient, but she couldn't leave her ten and seven-year-old at home alone for hours every day.

She had friends, but did they know of jobs? They all worked on charity functions together, but real work? She doubted they knew about that kind of stuff. And cheaper? That word wasn't in the vocabulary of the ladies Fred had pushed her to befriend. The wives of other doctors and lawyers, along with those who'd made their fortunes as influencers.

"Mom," Lake breathed, falling into the comfort of her mother's arms in the lobby of the attorney's office.

She couldn't believe the mess she was in. How could she have been so blind in every way? She'd put her trust in this man. Had he deserved it, or was she to blame for being lazy? Maybe it had just been easier for her to let Fred take care of it all. Would her daughters have to pay for her mistakes now?

Lake lifted her head from her mother's shoulder and dried her eyes. She didn't deserve the luxury of falling apart. She needed to buck up, get to work, and figure it out. For her girls who had done nothing wrong. She would do anything for them.

"I think," Lake heard her mother say softly and she leaned closer, desperately hoping her mother had the solution. Because Lake was out of them.

"You need to come home," she continued.

Lake watched her mother with wide eyes. Lake had left Blue Falls so many years before and had returned rarely. It wasn't because she didn't want to visit her childhood home, but it almost always became a fight. Fred needed to stay in Boise because of work, while Lake wanted their girls to spend time in their hometown. So if she went back it was often without him. But they already spent so much time apart, the reasons she stayed in Boise built up, and in the end Lake hadn't been back to Blue Falls nearly enough. Fred had looked on the town that had raised them with such indifference, bordering on contempt. She hadn't understood it. Blue Falls had always held a place in her heart. It was home.

You need to come home, Lake replayed in her mind.

Her mom was right. It was time to go home.

And suddenly Lake was filled with a peace that had evaded her for years. This was right, for her and her girls. They needed home.

Three

THE SUN WAS JUST PEEKING over the mountains north of the Blue Falls Ranch as Logan drove from one of the stables toward the northeast side of the property where he'd built a home a few years before.

As his truck jostled over the rough dirt roads Logan thought about turning left toward the old ranch house where his youngest siblings and mom lived. He hadn't seen Morgan since she'd retreated to her room on Thanksgiving night, but Brooks had told Logan the time wasn't right yet. Mom wasn't ready to talk. Logan ached to comfort her but he knew that wasn't his typical role in the family. When Logan came in, they all knew it was time to problem solve and Mom didn't want to problem solve yet. She was still licking her wounds, at least according to Holland.

So Logan had stayed away. But it was now Monday morning and he'd had enough of absence. Sure, he didn't go up to the old ranch house every day, but he typically checked in at least a few times a week. He'd kept away long enough and if Mom wasn't ready to figure things out yet, that was fine by him. He could be a comfort too. At least that was what he was telling himself.

But it was still early. Mom was surely busy with her own work and Logan really didn't have much spare time at the moment. He needed to clean up after helping muck out the stables because he would be meeting with a realtor in an hour and a half. Some of the land just west of the ranch was going up for sale soon and Logan wanted to get a jump on it. The past few years had been good for them and it was time to expand. It had always been their dad's plan to buy this land if the acreage went up for sale so Logan intended to follow through with his dad's wishes. So much of Logan's life felt like that: finishing what his dad never got a chance to do. And although he didn't mind it, he began to wonder if he'd ever live his own life again.

Granted, his life was the ranch the same way his dad's had been. So maybe this was his own life? Who knew? Honestly, it didn't bug him all that much. His dad had carved out a nice little life for himself.

Logan refused to think about their visitor on Thanksgiving night as he remembered his father's legacy. He knew what she'd said and what some of the others thought, but he refused to believe it of his father. Madison may have the Ashford nose, but there had to be some other explanation. His father was nothing if not loyal and he'd been madly in love with Mom. Like any couple, they'd had their rough patches, but Dad never would have strayed. It wasn't the kind of man he was.

So Logan would remember his father's character as he knew it and he'd figure this whole mess out as soon as his mom was ready for him to start digging. There had to be another explanation. There had to be. So Logan would not mar his father's memory by thinking any less of him until they found that explanation. For now, his dad was always the man Logan had thought. And Logan was sure, when all was said and done, his dad would still be that man. At least he was almost sure. He hated that a tiny part of him wondered what if? He sternly shushed that part and turned his thoughts back to his own life.

As much as Logan loved what he did and who he did it with,

there was a certain itch he couldn't quite scratch. Something wasn't quite right and he had quickly realized what it was. Dad's life had been complete because he'd had Mom. He had his kids. His family.

Meanwhile Logan was doing this alone. That was what felt so wrong. It wouldn't feel like he was just stepping into his dad's shoes if he had his own family walking this path with him. Of course he had his siblings and Mom, but it just wasn't the same. Logan had always assumed that by age thirty-five he would have been married with at least a few kids underfoot. But apparently it wasn't meant to be. Dating as a rancher could be tough. He thought about his most recent date a couple of nights before. The woman had been pretty, a niece of someone at church who thought Logan would be perfect for her. But the spark hadn't been there and Logan, after his years of dating experience, knew it was best to end it with that one date when there was no spark. It was hard enough to keep dating even with a spark.

Most of the women in town had no idea just how much work went into ranching. They saw the pretty horses and Logan's beautiful house that backed up to the stunning pond and were sold. But then they'd date Logan and see what ranching really meant. Waking up before the sun, especially in the winter. Long, hard days of manual labor that brought Logan home late, dusty, and often downright dirty. That part didn't appeal to many women. Not that Logan had ever met anyone he'd actually wanted to settle down with. If that had been the case he would have felt more sorry for himself. But usually he was ready to say goodbye to any woman he dated even before she was. All he had to do was play up the worst side of ranching and he could easily drive them away.

No, that was a lie. He had met one woman who'd been happy to live the ranch life even with all its downsides. One woman who'd loved the land of Blue Falls Ranch nearly as much as he did. But . . . well, that was long ago and it was no use dredging it up now. Especially since that woman had married another man.

Logan shook thoughts of her away as he drove up his long driveway, gazing at the glistening pond just beyond the gray stone of his home, and parked his truck in his three-car garage. He shrugged out of his trucker jacket and work boots before walking into his pristine kitchen.

One luxury Logan allowed himself was a cleaning company that came once a week to do the type of cleaning Logan never found time for. The dust from the ranch seemed to spread through his house if he didn't stay on top of those tasks, but with his work there was no way he could keep up. So a cleaning crew it was. And Logan mentally thanked them every time he walked into his lovely home, especially his mostly white kitchen. How Holland had ever talked him into a nearly all-white kitchen was beyond him. It was nice looking, especially with the light wood butcher-block countertops, but it wasn't practical for ranch life. Well, unless he had a cleaning crew.

Logan pulled off his socks, shooting them into his laundry basket before peeling off his shirt. It would never cease to amaze him how sweaty one could get even in the dead of winter.

After a quick shower and a few minutes in the kitchen to put together a sandwich full of Thanksgiving leftovers, Logan wrapped his lunch in a paper towel to make for easier eating as he drove and hopped back in his truck.

His heart rate ramped up as he realized what he was doing. This land would be Logan's first major change to the ranch his father had left behind. He was adding to the family legacy and a small measure of pride welled within him. He imagined Dad would be looking down with pride as well.

He started to back down his driveway when a pounding at his window caused him to jump and slam on his brake, stifling an unmanly squeak of alarm.

Austin stood just outside of the truck, his mouth wide open with laughter.

Logan thought about just driving away but sighed and unlocked the doors. Not only did Austin get in, but Jackson and Land piled in as well. He'd been expecting Jackson to meet him out at the property—he took care of all of their business transactions—but three of them?

"All of you? Who's actually doing the work around here if you all are bumming a ride with me?" Logan asked, although the question wasn't all that serious. They had enough hands-on staff to take care of all of the work if need be. Plus Logan had left his supervisor Brandon in charge and he trusted Brandon not only with making sure everything got done that day, but really with his life. Brandon and Logan went way back, since growing up in Blue Falls together as kids.

"When they heard I was coming out to meet you there was nothing I could do to shake them off. Austin kept reminding me he was on the board, after all," Jackson pointed out from the backseat.

"Dang, skippy," Austin piped up.

The board had been his dad's idea. Having eight children, his dad knew that giving the ranch to Logan after his death wouldn't be fair. But he also hated the idea of his beloved ranch being divided up into eight different parcels. So he found an in-between solution. When each of his sons turned thirty they had a choice: they could either take their six-hundred-acre share, about a tenth of the ranch, and do what they wanted on their own land, or they could join the ranch's advisory board. Each sibling who decided to stay with the ranch got a seat on the board and an equal say on the future of the ranch.

The everyday tasks of the ranch pretty much remained the same because those had been assigned according to their strengths. Logan headed things because he was the oldest and thus had the most experience, Jackson took on most of the business side of things, and Austin oversaw their horse breeding program. Phoenix didn't do much right now because he was in SLC playing ball, but when he was around he typically oversaw the hands. He was a people person through and through. Land never strayed from horse training and Memphis . . . well, Memphis did whatever the heck he wanted even though he was nearly as good with the horses as Land. Brooks now oversaw the hands since Phoenix wasn't around. Brooks hadn't quite found his place on the ranch yet, probably because his passion lay in cooking, but Logan was giving his youngest brother time and space to figure things out.

Holland had her hand in whatever she felt like in the moment, but typically she was with Land or Austin because she adored all living things.

But those roles didn't have to be permanent. Anytime a sibling wanted to take their six-hundred acres and run, they could. So far, though, no one had chosen to do so. Jackson and Austin had both signed on to the board on their thirtieth birthdays and built homes near Logan's. Each of them had an acre that backed onto the pond, enough space to call their own but close enough that they could drop in on each other whenever they wanted. Like they just had to get a ride with Logan to meet with the realtor.

Phoenix, although he was still just twenty-nine, had plans to start on his own home in the coming months and had told Logan he'd be joining the board as well. Land too was committed to following his brothers' path, claiming he would have no idea what to do with his own six hundred acres. Memphis, on the other hand, was sure he would choose to go off on his own. But Logan doubted that would actually happen. If anyone needed the security of family it was Memphis. Brooks and Holland were both too young to commit either way, neither knowing the true paths their lives would take, so here they were, with a board of three currently and plans for others to join.

Logan and his brothers took their board positions seriously. Because buying this land was their first major decision, it made sense that they'd all want their say. Logan just hadn't realized they'd all be showing up at this first meeting with the realtor.

"You do realize you all have your own trucks, don't you?" Logan asked as he drove down the dirt road that would take him to the ranch's west entrance.

"We're saving the planet by sharing yours, bro," Austin said with a grin.

"More like saving your own gas," Logan muttered. Austin was notorious for being cheap.

Jackson and Land laughed from their seats in the back.

The truck was quiet for a few minutes before Austin cleared his throat. Logan felt what was coming before Austin said a word and although he didn't really want to talk about it, he also realized that maybe some of his brothers would need to. So he let Austin go.

"What do we think of this girl?" Austin asked.

"Her name is Madison," Land clarified.

"Right, Madison. Do you think she's telling the truth?" Austin turned first to Logan and then back to Land and Jackson.

"I don't know about her, but I'm not a fan of that loud friend of hers," Jackson scowled.

"You mean the one who stood up to you and called you a big lug?" Land teased, causing his brothers to break into laughter. Count on Land to lighten the mood.

"I think Madison is telling her version of the truth," Logan finally spoke. He had a feeling they were all waiting to hear what he had to say.

"What does that mean?" Austin asked.

"The truth can be multifaceted. The only truth we can tell is the truth we know. Madison has that letter, the only information she's been able to find about her father. That's her truth. We know more. We know our dad: the man he was, the husband and father he was. That's our truth." Logan hoped his brothers understood. He didn't want to discount Madison. Logan believed she was sincere in her reasons for coming. But he also didn't want to mar their memory of their father.

"I hope she comes back," Land said quietly. "I feel like we ran her off."

"I think we did the best we could, considering the circumstances. If anyone's to blame for making the situation tense, it's that friend of hers," Jackson responded, crossing his arms and slouching in his seat.

Land smiled knowingly in the rearview mirror, catching Logan's eye. It was pretty funny that Madison's friend was still a burr under Jackson's saddle even days later.

"Do you think she'll want a piece of the land?" Austin wondered.

"I think that's a worry we can save for another day," Logan said, hoping to shut down the conversation. They'd speculated enough about Madison for one day. Especially considering how little information they had.

"So what are we thinking about this land?" Jackson asked, thankfully on the same wavelength as Logan.

"It looks good from what I've seen," Logan replied.

"But it will be a board decision on whether we buy or not," Austin said, seeming to feel the need to flex his position.

Logan guessed he could understand. Austin was the most recent to join the board and might be anxious to prove his place.

"Yeah, but why are you here, Land?" Jackson asked the brother too young for the board.

"Memphis was bugging me," Land admitted.

Logan let out a bark of laughter. So even the saintly Land had his breaking point.

"We know this acreage almost as well as we know our own. We all know we're buying," Jackson said when they'd all finished laughing with Land.

"But it will be a board decision," Austin reiterated stubbornly.

Jackson rolled his eyes as Logan slowed to park next to the Land Rover already on the property. It looked like Avery was doing rather well for herself. Good for her.

"Hey boys," Avery said as they all spilled out of Logan's truck.

Logan noticed that the woman made eye contact with each of his brothers but tried to hold his a little too long. Logan had wondered if this was going to be an issue. He'd dated Avery about ten years before and they'd broken up amicably, mutually realizing they were wrong for each other. And according to the Blue Falls grapevine Avery was dating one of the sheriffs in town. So what was with the longing glances?

Suddenly Logan was grateful his brothers had decided to tag along.

He shared a look with Jackson—he was sure his brother had noticed Avery's attempt to keep his attention—and Jackson responded with a slight nod, understanding Logan wanted him to take over this meeting. It made sense anyway. If anyone knew the value of this land and how much the ranch could afford to put into it, it was Jackson.

"That was awkward," Land said after they'd all gotten back into Logan's truck.

"Do you think Avery hoping she has a chance to mother Logan's babies will help us get that land?" Austin asked with a smirk.

"Shut up," Logan shot at his brother with a roll of his eyes.

Austin laughed as Land patted Logan on the shoulder.

"We all have those exes," Land said in solidarity.

"Yeah, but only Logan's is in charge of whether we get the land Dad dreamed about us one day owning. If he doesn't let her down easy . . . " Austin piped up unhelpfully.

"Her clients will be making the decision—the Hartfields. Thankfully they love Logan," Jackson said.

Logan let out a sigh of relief. The Hartfields did love him.

However, they weren't exactly fans of Austin or Memphis, who'd dated two of their daughters. Oh, the joys of living in a small town.

"Avery was helpful. We got to see the lay of the land. We know our offer and for now we're the only ones putting one in. I'd say we're in good shape," Jackson added.

They were. This would work . . . Logan hoped. If this went sideways because of Avery's crush due to a few months of dating back in his twenties, Heaven help him.

"Well, I'd still start praying for God's help on this one," Austin replied.

That wasn't a bad idea. Logan sent up a quick prayer and promised to say a more meaningful one that night.

Logan made quick work of the drive back and dropped his brothers off at the ranch office before making his way to the old ranch house. It was just after lunchtime and although he'd had a sandwich as his second breakfast, he missed the one his mom served to all of the ranch hands and his brothers every Monday morning. His growling stomach told him that if he got to the old ranch house in time to eat some of the leftovers he surely wouldn't mind.

"Knock, knock," Logan called at the door before letting himself in, Blue immediately underfoot. His pseudo knocking was more of a greeting than an actual wondering if he'd be let in. None of the kids actually knocked on their mom's door. Maybe one day, when they'd all moved out, they would feel the need to do so. But for now Mom wanted them all to know that her home was their home, even if they had their own houses across the ranch.

"In here," Holland called out. Logan followed her voice and found Holland and his mom at the kitchen table, sharing some kind of creamy soup that smelled like Heaven.

Blue abandoned Logan, opting for a spot under the table

where he was probably hoping someone would drop him a scrap or two.

"Grab a bowl and a hunk of bread," Mom directed.

Logan didn't have to be told twice. His long legs strode across the kitchen and he eagerly tore off a piece of his mom's famous sourdough before finding a giant bowl. His mom hadn't specified the size.

He came back to the table with the bowl and bread and Holland burst out laughing.

"She didn't ask you to bring a serving dish," she said through her laughs.

Mom sent Logan a soft smile but it was clearly strained. Some of the heaviness that had surrounded her in the months after Dad's death had returned. Logan hated that she was mourning him or what they had, or . . . Logan wasn't sure what exactly his mother was mourning, but she was obviously grieving again.

Morgan filled the serving dish, as Holland had called it, with the delicious soup before handing Logan a spoon and motioning for him to dig in.

As he scooped up his first bite, he couldn't help but notice how full his mom's bowl still was.

"This is amazing," Logan said after the first taste, careful to clear his mouth of food before speaking. His mother couldn't stand bad table manners. "I was hoping for second breakfast leftovers but this is even better."

"The boys were hungry this morning so Holland and I made our own meal. I had so many leftover herbs after Thanksgiving, so I decided to throw them all into a creamy stew," Mom explained.

Only his mother could throw together a dish like this. It was no secret where Brooks got his cooking skills.

"We missed you boys at breakfast, but how did the meeting with Avery go?" Mom asked.

Logan nodded. "Fine. Not much can be hammered out until

the property actually goes on the market, but I think we're in good position to get it."

"I should hope so. If you can't get that property, what was the point of dating Avery?" Holland teased.

"Years ago."

"She still holds that flame high and proud," Holland laughed.

Wait, Holland had known Avery still had a thing for him? Had Logan been blind to it? Probably. He tended to overlook things he didn't want to see. And he definitely didn't want to see Avery pining over him. He rubbed a hand over his frustrated face. Whatever. Holland was probably exaggerating things. And he wouldn't have to see Avery all that often. He'd make sure Jackson was the front man for the sale. Yeah, that should totally work. With a sigh of relief, Logan looked up at his sister and mom.

He was more than ready to stop thinking about Avery.

Logan was about to bring up what he'd come here to say. To let his mom know he was here. He wanted to not only problem solve but comfort her. But Holland sent him a barely perceptible shake of her head before saying, "Mom was just telling me about the fight Mrs. Green and Mrs. Blunt got into over bananas."

She spooned in another mouthful of stew, her way of telling Logan he should keep his mouth full as well. Logan could see that his little sister was warning him to stay away from all talk of Thanksgiving night. And he got it. His mom wasn't ready to talk about it yet. They didn't have to talk for him to be a comfort to her. He'd just hang out and show her he was here, whenever and however she needed him.

"It wasn't an actual fight," Morgan clarified as Holland disagreed vehemently.

Logan watched his mother and sister laugh together, and although the moment was sweet, it was only then that he realized what a burden he'd left to his little sister. Not that their mother was a burden, but her grief was. And Holland had been working day in and day out to make sure she kept smiling.

Sure, Holland had told Logan to stay away, but he shouldn't have so readily listened to her. Clearly Holland was wary about leaving their mother alone after their encounter with Madison. That meant she was spending nearly twenty-four/seven with Mom. It couldn't be easy, considering Holland was already carrying a full course load in her virtual studies, not to mention she typically had a pretty busy social life. Holland had sacrificed so much.

And now that Logan had figured that out, he'd do his best to help, even though he and his brothers were needed on the ranch. Maybe they could each take a day or two off but they'd have to be cautious or Mom would undoubtedly sniff out what they were doing and put a stop to it. She wouldn't want to be their project. Still, Logan couldn't leave this on Holland's shoulders, nor should Mom be left with time to be lonely.

He wasn't sure yet exactly what to do, but he knew he had to do something.

So for now he laughed through the story, especially at the part where Mrs. Green yanked the bunch of bananas out of Mrs. Blunt's hands. He could just imagine the spunky eighty-year-old woman's eyes snapping as she made off victorious.

But the thought that he needed to help his mother, to have someone else around to provide companionship through her grief, never left his mind. He needed to find a solution ASAP.

Four

LAKE TUCKED a lock of her dark brown hair behind her ear as she breathed in the crisp air that reminded her of football games and fall carnivals. It was late November, so winter was closing in but Lake was enjoying the last vestiges of fall. She had missed autumn in Blue Falls. There was nothing like it.

Not that there weren't things to love about Boise weather. It was pretty similar to Blue Falls, though in Lake's hometown the sun seemed to shine a little brighter on the sunny days and the air just felt so clean and fresh. She fought the urge to twirl in the morning sunshine. All of this right here . . . it smelled and felt like home.

She looked at her daughters who were following her up to the elementary school where she'd be dropping them off for their first day of school in Blue Falls. She hoped they'd one day feel the same about her—and now their—hometown as well.

The transition to moving back to Blue Falls had been surprisingly easy . . . maybe a little too easy. Lake was still waiting for the other shoe to drop. But things had gone so smoothly that the girls were going to start school a few days before Lake had planned. They'd moved home over Thanksgiving weekend and she had assumed they'd take a week to get acclimated before starting school. But both girls were getting a little stir crazy just hanging out at home, helping their mom move things into the room she'd occupied as a kid and a guest room down the hall. It was a pretty simple task since most of their belongings had been either sold or moved into storage.

The girls, Delia and Amelie, had looked at all of this as a grand adventure. They didn't even mind sharing a room since they were getting to move to a new town and into their grandparents' home. Thankfully they adored not only their grandparents but also their aunt, Lake's youngest sister Grace, who still lived at home.

Of course they had moments of missing their father, but an unforeseen positive of their dad working so much was that the girls didn't notice the hole he'd left as much as if he'd been a more involved father.

But Lake had noticed. The more time she spent with her own father, the more she was reminded of what a dad should be. And Fred, as much as she didn't like speaking ill of the dead, hadn't been that kind of dad.

The girls seemed to understand that as well. Some nights they couldn't fall asleep because they wished their dad could tuck them in, but those nights had come while he'd been living as well. Lake had dried their tears, but not nearly as many as she had anticipated. The girls missed their dad but they also understood their need to move forward and move on. Probably better than any adult would. Kids really were so resilient.

"What's my teacher's name again?" Amelie asked as she skipped up the sidewalk that led to the main entrance of Blue Falls Elementary School. She was too excited to move without bouncing.

"Mrs. Seger," Lake responded patiently even though Amelie had asked the same question nearly a dozen times. She knew that

Amelie understood who her teacher was but asking the question was a way for her to deal with her anxiety.

"Mrs. Seger," Amelie repeated as if she were hearing the name for the first time.

Delia smiled up at her mom with their shared secret. At breakfast this morning Delia had grown tired of that question when Amelie had repeated it for the third time and had been about to admonish her. Lake had taken her aside and explained what Amelie was feeling and how she was processing. Delia had admitted she felt some anxiety as well, and now every time Amelie asked the question it seemed to serve not only Amelie's nerves but Delia's as well. Her girls were so good for one another.

For a moment she allowed herself to wonder what her life would be like right now if she'd continued having children as she'd wanted to. She had always imagined herself as a mother to at least four kids since that was the size of family she'd grown up in—with maybe even more. But after Amelie, Fred had said enough. He'd claimed pregnancy was too hard on Lake's body. She hadn't agreed; in fact she'd told him so. But he claimed superior wisdom as a doctor and that was that. Every time Lake brought it up again Fred had reminded her that they'd already discussed this and had come to a conclusion. When Lake had voiced her concerns about said conclusion Fred would somehow change the subject or leave the room. He was skilled at getting his way.

Lake sighed. She missed her husband, she really did. But she'd also put up with a lot. It was hard to mourn the man while she was still so unsure of what their marriage had meant to him because he'd been found with Sachia. And the reminder of that one fact made it much easier to remember all of the bad about Fred.

And remembering the bad did help when it came to controlling her emotions. If she ever began to wonder how she'd face life as a single parent, she'd remind herself of all she'd already done alone. Fred had been pretty absentee over the years, so she was reassured that she could continue on. So for now remembering Sachia in the car with Fred was actually a blessing in disguise . . . maybe. No, Lake wouldn't go that far, but she would say that allowing herself to remember how distant and difficult Fred could be was helpful in her mourning process because control of her emotions was exactly what she needed. She couldn't allow herself to break down every time she thought of all she'd lost in that car accident.

She shook aside thoughts of Fred and Sachia, even her anger that flared up anytime she remembered the two of them together. This walk up to the elementary school was about her girls. And she had a fun fact to share with Amelie.

"Mrs. Seger was actually Aunt Grace's teacher when she was your age," Lake told Amelie as she opened the front door to the school.

"Lucky!" Delia exclaimed as Amelie beamed.

Lake had just been reminded of that detail this morning as she was waiting for the girls to put their coats on so they could leave. Grace had arrived home from her overnight shift at the Heathcliff Resort where she'd started working just after high school. She worked the front desk at night for now but hoped to move up into management one day.

When Grace had seen the girls up and at 'em she'd asked Lake where they were going and then explained that Mrs. Seger had been one of her favorite teachers. This not only excited Amelie, but put Lake's mother heart at ease.

She was especially reassured since Delia's teacher, Emily Brown, had been one of Lake's friends back in high school. To know that both of her girls were in good hands meant everything to Lake at this vulnerable time.

"Lake!" Emily was waiting at the front desk as Lake entered the office, her girls following closely.

Emily opened her arms and Lake welcomed the embrace. Glancing behind Emily, Lake recognized at least half of the faces in the room. It was wonderful to be home.

"This is Delia," Lake said as she pulled out of the hug and ushered her eldest forward to meet her new teacher.

"I'm Mrs. Brown," Emily said, smiling at Delia. She leaned forward to add in a conspiratorial whisper, "I've always loved the name Delia."

Delia ate it all up with a wide grin.

"And this is Amelie," Lake gently nudged her younger daughter.

"Such pretty names!" Emily exclaimed.

"For pretty girls," Mrs. Forrester piped up from behind the front desk. She'd been there since Lake's elementary school days almost thirty years before.

"This is Mrs. Forrester." Lake introduced the woman who'd made school feel like home for so many of Blue Fall's youth.

"Good morning, ma'am," the girls chorused in unison.

"And polite. Oh, you two will do so well here," Mrs. Forrester said warmly, causing both girls to beam broadly.

Lake felt another piece of her soul come to rest. This was what they needed. She felt it in her core.

"Can I take you both to your classes?" Emily asked the girls.

They looked to Lake for permission and she nodded with a smile.

The girls each took one of Emily's hands as she led them out of the office. Lake watched until the door shut completely behind them before turning back to the office ladies.

"Good to be home?" Mrs. Forrester asked.

"You have no idea," Lake said, walking up to the desk where Mrs. Forrester waited with the girls' paperwork.

"Well, it's good to have you all back. I was sorry to hear about Fred. We're all here for you," she whispered the last sentences as though trying to keep from attracting the attention of everyone else in the office.

"Thank you," Lake replied almost as quietly.

"I know Emily feels the same way, but I'm sure she didn't want to bring their dad up in front of the girls," Mrs. Forrester added.

"Thank heavens for that. And for both of you," Lake said sincerely.

She'd forgotten what it was like to be so understood. It was like Blue Falls was the only common ground any of them needed. Since the town felt like one giant family they sometimes bickered like siblings—or, more precisely, distant cousins—but when it came down to it, just like in a family, Blue Falls was supportive of any and all who needed it. Including long-lost community members like Lake.

Mrs. Forrester patted Lake's hand before handing her a pen to fill out the forms.

"Oh, Lake," came a shrill voice from behind her and Lake fought the urge to ignore it. She'd know that voice anywhere, even though it had been over a decade since she'd last heard it. Here came one of those members of the Blue Falls family Lake wished she could avoid forever. But didn't all families have those?

"Avery," Lake said with a forced smile as she turned to greet the woman who'd called her name.

The only negative aspect to Mrs. Forrester was the fact that she was Avery Forrester's aunt. Lake never understood how the two could be related.

"I was *so* sad to hear about Fred!" Avery exclaimed at full volume. Every head in the office turned to look at the two of them.

"It was sudden," Lake replied. It was her go-to response. Should she say she was sorry too? Avery hadn't actually expressed condolences, she'd just said she was sad.

"He was such a good man," Avery said in a knowing tone.

Lake guessed Avery did know Fred pretty well, considering she'd dated him for a year before his attention had shifted to Lake.

But Lake wasn't sure she could agree with Avery. Fred had had his good points, but she was still stinging from the revelation of his partner in death, not to mention the loneliness of her marriage. And the way Avery spoke made Lake wonder if Sachia was the only other woman Fred had been with. Right now she could believe anything of him. No, it was better not to respond to Avery's strange comment.

"I should probably get back to this," Lake said, turning to her paperwork. She was incredibly grateful that her kids were safely in their classrooms already.

"If you ever want to exchange memories I'm always here." That was definitely the most awkward offering Lake had received since Fred's funeral. Yeah, she would not be taking Avery up on that anytime soon.

But Lake had been raised to be polite so she felt the need to respond somehow. She hadn't yet acknowledged Avery's previous statement either.

"Thank you," she finally said, not sure what else she could truthfully add, as her pen ran across the paper. She needed to get this done and get out of there.

She'd known coming back to Blue Falls would have its downsides and Avery Forrester definitely wasn't an upside. But for every Avery Forrester there were a dozen Emilys, Mrs. Forresters, and others who were ready to step up and support her. Lake would take it.

"I THOUGHT YOU'D BE NAPPING," Lake said as she opened the front door and found Grace lounging on the couch in front of a reality television show. She didn't seem to actually be watching it because her attention was on the phone in her hands.

Grace had a weird sleep schedule, thanks to her night job. She didn't like sleeping the entire day away so she would split her rest: napping for a few hours after her shift and then sleeping a few more hours before her next shift. That way she had most of the day to live a normal life.

"Today's my Friday, so I'm going to hang out with Holland," Grace said, naming her best friend as she held up her phone where she must be making plans.

"But today is Wednesday," Lake replied, slightly confused. She was still getting used to Grace's schedule.

"I get Thursday and Friday off and then I'm back on for Saturday," Grace explained.

"Ahh," Lake replied as she headed to the kitchen to grab some breakfast. "Are Mom and Dad at work?"

Her parents owned and ran a hardware store that had been in the family for generations. For the last few years, Mom had been cutting down on her hours, but she still went in about once a week. Or she had until lately, when she'd missed quite a bit as she devoted herself to helping Lake and her girls. Lake wouldn't be surprised if her mom took this opportunity while the girls were in school to check in on things.

"Yup." Grace nodded. "How did the girls do at school?" She joined Lake in the kitchen, leaning against the gray and white marble countertop that their dad had recently installed for their mom's fifty-fifth birthday.

Lake grinned. "Amazingly. Emily was there to greet them and Mrs. Forrester was great as always."

"Of course she was." Grace grinned back as she grabbed an apple from the countertop and took a big bite.

Lake knew she should probably eat something as well but ever since Fred's accident it had been hard to eat much of anything. She'd learned that if she was able to stomach the idea of eating anything, she should try it. Today the only thing she thought she might be able to swallow was marshmallow cereal.

She poured herself a bowl as she went on. "I ran into Avery Forrester as well." Her whole family knew there was little love lost between Lake and Avery.

"That must have been interesting," Grace said around another bite of apple.

"You could say that again. She offered to 'exchange memories' about Fred," Lake said in an incredulous tone. She wasn't one to gossip often but that had been too much. She had to share.

"What?!" Grace's eyes widened. "Do you think she's trying to claim some of Fred through his death?"

"I have no idea," Lake said, pressing her lips together in annoyance. She hadn't even thought of it like that but it made sense.

"So what did you say to that?"

"Thank you?" Lake replied.

Grace burst into laughter and Lake had to join her. It really had been so weird.

"That woman needs help," Grace said.

Lake had to agree. Avery had taken every opportunity to needle Lake back in high school and it seemed like some things didn't change. Who would use the death of a loved one to try to get under someone's skin? Evidently Avery.

The doorbell rang, letting them know Holland had arrived.

"I'll let you two catch up," Lake said, lifting her bowl of cereal off the counter and turning toward her room.

"You don't have to leave on our account," Grace protested as she headed toward the front door. "Mom always hangs out with us."

Lake chuckled, imagining their mom just hanging out with the twenty-year-olds.

Lake waited as Grace opened the front door. She should probably at least say hi. Holland had been a fixture in their family for nearly all of Grace's life. Lake had dated Holland's oldest brother just about the time both girls were born. Their families had always been close but those two little girls were joined at the hip as soon as they could walk. Lake and Logan's relationship had come to a close but they'd remained friends because of their families, along with the fact that Fred and Logan had been really close back then.

And Lake really did love Holland.

"Holland," she greeted warmly.

Holland rushed across the kitchen to smother Lake in a gigantic hug. Thankfully Lake had had the presence of mind to set down her bowl of cereal when she saw Holland coming. She returned the hug just as enthusiastically, squeezing tightly before Holland finally let go.

The cute little tow-headed blonde was now a beautiful bombshell of a woman. Holland's thick locks cascaded down her back and she looked adorable in her jumpsuit.

"I couldn't believe the news about Fred. We wanted to come out for the funeral but we didn't hear until the day of the funeral and I had this exam I couldn't miss and the boys have the ranch," Holland explained in a rush, but Lake held up a hand.

"Don't worry about it. I'm glad you didn't. It was actually really small. Basically our families and his closest friends in the city," Lake said. As she said the words, she realized it hadn't been Fred's closest friends—the people who'd attended were his only friends. He hadn't kept in touch with anyone from Blue Falls for years. In fact, even though it was the hometown for both of them, Lake's last few visits had been taken alone. Fred had always found something to keep him in the city.

"But you came home for Dad's funeral. We should have been there for you," Holland said.

Lake had come home. But that had been different. Mitchell Ashford had been a pillar of this community. It wouldn't have felt right to miss the funeral of a man who had been such a big part of her childhood and a good friend to her family up until his death.

Things with Fred were different. As Lake had planned the funeral she'd imagined how awkward it would be for their two worlds, Boise and Blue Falls, to collide. Logan, Jackson, Austin, and the rest in a room full of Fred's country club cronies—she couldn't imagine anything worse. Besides, it wasn't like Fred had been a good friend to any of the Ashfords as of late.

So Lake had kept funeral details under wraps until the last minute, hoping to keep the Blue Falls friends and family away. Not because she didn't want them there, but because she knew she and Fred didn't deserve them there. She'd even felt guilty that her family had taken so much time and effort to be there for Fred and her, considering Fred hadn't seen any of Lake's relations in at least a couple of years.

"Really, don't worry. You're here now. That's what matters," Lake said genuinely.

Holland gave Lake another hug.

"We are. All of us. If you need us, we're here," Holland promised and Lake believed it.

"Thank you," Lake replied before shooing the girls into the living room. "I'm sure you have better things to do than offer condolences."

"Actually, I'd love to speak to both of you. I could use all the advice right about now and with the way gossip travels in this town, everyone will know about our late-night Thanksgiving visitor soon enough." Holland took a seat at the kitchen table.

Grace joined her immediately.

Lake hovered uncertainly.

"Are you sure?" she asked. She wanted to be there for Holland but this sounded like a private matter. She didn't want Holland to feel obligated to include her just because she was there.

"Yes," Holland insisted, patting the seat next to her.

So Lake took it.

Holland began to describe how Madison had shown up, what she'd said, and the fallout afterward.

"Your poor mom." Lake mourned with all of the Ashfords as she put an arm around Holland's shoulders. The sweet girl looked ready to break.

"But you know your dad would never do that, right?" Grace said from Holland's other side.

"It's what I want to believe."

"So believe it," Grace urged.

"It's just so hard," Holland said as she buried her head into Lake's shoulder.

Anxiety bubbled in Lake's heart because she knew what she had to say. She could understand what Holland was feeling, or at least some of it, all too well. It was almost like God had placed Holland right here with Lake, a woman she hadn't been close to in years, spilling her heart because God knew that Lake could help. Even if it scared Lake to her core to reveal such honest truths. Things she'd hoped to keep buried forever. But what good was her pain if she couldn't use it? It was time her own suffering helped someone else.

"What I'm about to say cannot leave this room." Lake needed to extract this promise from them. Her girls could never know. She trusted Holland and Grace with this, but others? She needed this vow.

Both women nodded, Holland looking up at Lake expectantly and Grace frowning in concern at her sister's tone.

"Fred wasn't alone when he got into that wreck," Lake said as she held Holland a little more tightly, probably more for her own comfort than Holland's.

"What?" Grace's eyes latched onto to Lake's intently.

She'd been at the funeral. No one had uttered a word about Sachia. Lake wasn't sure how Stanley had done it but he'd covered up everything. The small amount of news coverage never mentioned a second person in the car. Lake wasn't sure what Sachia's family had been told or if Stanley had paid them off, but the secret was somehow safe for now.

"Only Mom and Dad know. Seriously, no one else, even our family, can hear about this." Lake had to be sure Grace wouldn't say a word.

"I promise," Grace assured her.

"Fred cheated on me about five months ago now." Grace let out the smallest of gasps before covering her mouth. Holland froze.

"We worked through it. Or at least I thought we had. It was tough but I thought I'd finally forgiven him. He promised never to see her again."

Lake bit her lip. Could she say it?

"But she was in the car with him when he died?" Holland supplied in a whisper.

Lake nodded.

"No," Grace uttered in a broken whisper.

Lake didn't blame her. It was shocking, frustrating, unforgiveable, so many things.

"So I kind of understand where you're coming from, Holland. Except our situations have one big difference. Over the years Fred turned into a man who would hide things from me, keep secrets to get his way, and manipulate me if I got in his way. It wasn't hard for me to believe he'd cheated. It didn't stop it from hurting like the dickens, but his character wasn't above that. I saw the signs long before he had actually cheated." Lake hadn't realized all of this until the words were on her lips, but she knew every word was true.

"Your dad. There was nothing in his character that would indicate him doing this, right?" Lake asked.

Holland didn't even hesitate before she shook her head.

"So believe that about him. There are always two sides to every story," Lake added.

Holland nodded. "Thank you," she breathed. "I prayed before coming here that I would receive some comfort and you brought it. I honestly can't thank you enough. Especially for sharing your own story. I swear I will take it to the grave."

Lake smiled. It was a little dramatic, but that was Holland for you.

Grace grinned around Holland's head, surely thinking the same thing.

The women sat marinating in their conversation, their shared grief, for a few moments before Holland physically gave herself a little shake. She was ready to move on.

"Where are your girls?" she asked, looking around the kitchen.

"At school," Lake said with a wry smile.

"I thought they were starting next week." Holland gave Grace, who'd surely told her the news, a puzzled look.

"We thought so too, but they were ready today, so we decided not to wait," Lake said.

"Good for them. That's one thing ticked off the to-do list. But you still need a job, right?" Holland asked.

Just how much had Grace told Holland about her situation? Lake raised an eyebrow in the direction of her little sister, who just shrugged. Everything, apparently.

"We're still working on that. Mom and Dad could give me part-time work at the store at least until someone quits, and then maybe they could take me on full-time, but I think I should try to find something else. I'm already asking so much of them by living here," Lake revealed. Might as well be transparent, since Grace would undoubtedly fill in any blanks she left.

Holland nodded as she seemed to consider Lake's words.

"How about the ranch?" Holland asked.

Lake cocked her head in confusion. The ranch? "What about the ranch?"

"We always need help."

"Yeah, ranch hands." Lake laughed. "Pretty sure I'm not qualified for that."

"You are pretty dang strong," Grace teased before joining in Lake's laughter. Doubtless she was imagining barely five-foot Lake as a ranch hand.

"We have other needs too. Let me ask Logan," Holland offered.

"That's okay. If it's not a true need—" Lake began.

"She doesn't want a pity job," Grace finished.

"What if I promise it isn't that? I'll ask Logan if we need any help. If we don't, you just keep looking," Holland provided.

That didn't sound too bad. Lake did love the Ashfords. She'd feel comfortable with them. And maybe they could even work something out so that Lake could pick up the girls after school and bring them to work on the one day a week her mom went to the hardware store. She had been trying to figure out how they would manage that. But she didn't want them to extend a job to her as a favor.

"Only if I'm truly qualified. And I'd go through the normal interview process," Lake asserted.

"Of course," Holland replied.

If the Ashfords could really use her, that would be a dream come true. Maybe it would be a little awkward working for a man as rugged and handsome as Logan Ashford—a man she'd dated once upon a time—but Lake would be fine. She was a grieving widow, for gosh sake. Okay, maybe 'grieving' was a little strong of a word. She was a confused widow. That sounded more like it. She was far from ready to look at any man twice. And Logan had always been so kind, even while breaking it off with her, that she couldn't imagine a better boss.

"You have a deal," Lake said before she could back out.

Right now she had no other offers. And beggars couldn't be choosers, or so she'd been told.

"Yes!" Holland cheered and even Grace clapped her hands together.

Lake was going to work for the Ashfords. Maybe.

Five

LOGAN HUNG his hat on a post in Midnight's stall before he began brushing her down after the morning's brisk ride. Logan didn't often get involved with exercising their horses anymore, but it was good for him when he found time to do it. It helped ground him, remind him of what they were doing on the ranch and why.

Midnight's fiery yet sweet disposition made her one of Logan's favorites. Along with the fact that he'd been there the morning she was born seven years earlier. There was something almost spiritual in witnessing a birth and Logan had been blessed to see many of them. At least equine ones. He didn't plan to view the human type until . . . would he one day find a woman he wanted to have children with? If he'd asked himself that question ten years before it would have been a resounding yes. Logan had never imagined himself as anything but a husband, father, and rancher. In that order. And yet he'd only accomplished one of those feats. Maybe this was what God had planned for him. And who was he to thwart God?

"Seems like some awful deep thought happening in this stall,"

Morgan said as she leaned against the top of the stable door, her chin resting on her arms.

"Midnight has always been the best listener," Logan replied over the crooning of Luke Bryan in the background.

Dad had loved all kinds of music and had jumped at the chance to install a state-of-the-art sound system through the main barn. Now a variety of music played all day in memory of the man.

"Except you weren't speaking to the horse," Mom pointed out.

"Sometimes the best listening happens without any talking," Logan replied.

Morgan cocked her head as she considered his words. "You might be right, Son," she said with a half-smile that didn't quite reach her eyes. Logan missed his mother's true smiles and wondered when they would be back. Did she really believe this of their father? Or was she just lonely? Logan wished he could make things right in his mom's world.

"This was one of your dad's favorite songs," Mom said, gesturing to the speaker overhead.

"Dad had like five hundred favorite songs," Logan joked.

Mom chuckled. "That he did. He only loved you kids and the ranch more than music."

"And you, Mom. Always you." Logan couldn't let her forget that.

"Yeah. I used to think so, anyway. But . . . ah, I'm just so angry with him. How could he leave something like this with no forewarning?" Morgan asked as her arms flew into the air.

Logan didn't blame his mom. He'd wondered the same thing. There had been days between Dad's first collapse and the day he'd actually gone, days when Dad knew he would be dying soon. Yet he'd said nothing.

"Maybe it wasn't his news to share?" Logan offered the only solution he'd come up with.

"That he has a ninth child out there in the world?" Mom shook her head.

"You don't truly believe that, do you?" Logan asked with a concerned frown. There were lots of messed up things in this world but this wasn't one of them. He knew it in his soul. His mom had to feel that as well, didn't she?

"I don't know what to believe, Logan. And if your dad had given us any sort of head's up we wouldn't be in this mess," Mom said quietly but fiercely.

Logan saw that she was hurting so he let her stew. She needed to think through what she'd just said rather than hear arguments in support of Dad.

"I know that man loved me. I know it. And yet right now I'm so frustrated that it's easier to think the worst of him," Mom finally admitted, her expression struggling between anger and grief.

Logan was almost finished brushing out Midnight's mane.

"That's understandable."

"He wrote that letter. We all saw his handwriting. So he knew what this is all about. He knew. And he told me nothing. His wife." Tears welled in Morgan's eyes and Logan pushed his way out of the stall to wrap his arms around his mother.

She let Logan hold her as she crumpled against him and silently wept into his chest.

And now Logan felt resentment toward his dad. Not that Dad would blame him. If anyone ever made their mother cry there was heck to pay. Even from heaven Logan could feel wrath toward him for making Dad's sweetheart cry.

"I miss him. I'm so angry with him. But I want him to be here to make this all right," Mom said into Logan's chest.

He nodded. Dad was gone way too soon for all of them. Things wouldn't feel completely right for a while. Maybe never. Grief was sticky, messy, and often downright horrible.

"I do too," Logan murmured.

He noticed a few hands, along with Brandon, starting in their direction before making quick U-turns as they noticed what was going on between Logan and his mother.

Everyone respected Mama Ashford enough to let her mourn in peace.

"I'm getting your shirt all wet," Morgan finally said with a watery smile as she pulled out of Logan's hug. She sniffled as she wiped her tears away.

"As if I'd care about that," Logan said with a wave of his hand.

"I know you don't. Thank you, Son. I needed that."

"I'm here. You know that, right, Mom?" Logan asked. He had to be clear.

"I do. You kids are the only thing that's felt right through all of this. You dad may have left me with this mess, but he also left me with the eight most wonderful humans on the planet. He was smart in doing so," Morgan said with a shaky laugh.

Dad was quite the cunning man. But Logan didn't think he'd have planned things out this way. He would have never chosen to leave them all so early in his life.

But like his mom, Logan was also grateful for the legacy of family his dad had left behind. Because that was what mattered when you left this world. The ranch was nice, but the parts of Mitchell Ashford that had really mattered were his family.

"I'd better get back up to the house. Holland should be back from Grace's soon and she'll be wondering where I went off to." Morgan wiped away the last remnants of her tears.

That was why his mom was wandering around the stables. Holland had left. As she should have—Holland deserved to have a life. But his mother was probably looking for some human interaction. That house was really too big and lonely for her while they all had their daily tasks.

Maybe it was time to finally hire some cleaners for the old ranch house. When Logan had hired the crew for his own home he'd tried to talk Mom into enlisting them as well but she'd bucked against it immediately. Why would she need a bunch of strangers to clean her own home? What would she do all day?

But cleaning people in the house would make it less lonely, wouldn't it? Then again, Mom really would hate strangers being around.

Logan decided to broach the subject once more. This time he'd try to do so with some care. He tended to be as gentle in conversation as a bull in a china shop.

"So I was thinking," he started before his mom could walk away.

Morgan met Logan's gaze, eyebrows raised. Well, so much for approaching this gently.

"Can I finally hire those cleaners for you? You could surely use some help keeping that big house clean."

"I told you how I feel about a bunch of strangers in the house," Morgan said with a shake of her head.

But she hadn't said no. So Logan was hopeful.

"Wouldn't it be nice to have another set of hands to help with some of the work?" he pressed.

Morgan pursed her lips as she thought.

"I guess one person wouldn't be too bad."

Yes! Logan wanted to celebrate but he wasn't there yet.

"But I don't want it to be a stranger," Morgan clarified.

Dang it. Logan quickly scanned through a mental list of his mother's friends and acquaintances and came up with no one.

But he got it. His mom wanted more than a cleaner—she needed a friend. Someone like Holland. But Logan couldn't ask Holland to quit school to help their mom out. He knew she'd be willing. But he couldn't do that to her and Mom would never stand for it.

"Every friend begins as a stranger," Logan pointed out.

"Your smooth words won't work this time, Logan. I know what you're trying to do. It's the same thing Holland is doing. You see how lonely your mother is and want to fix it."

"No, it's not—" Logan began but his mother shushed him.

"The problem is you both are right. I am lonely. It *is* getting harder to clean that big old house. I could use some company as I prepare meals. Part of me is frustrated that I didn't take on some help at the house years ago when your dad suggested it. Most ranching outfits have house help, he'd pointed out. But I was too prideful. This was my house. I could care for it and for all who lived in it on my own. Little did I know how empty that house would one day feel," Morgan admitted.

Logan felt a mixture of pride at his mother's honesty and extreme sadness that she felt that way. But then Morgan's eyes began to sparkle.

"Maybe if I had some grandkids running underfoot . . . " she teased and Logan knew everything would be okay. His mom was sad but she'd get over it.

"Logan!" Holland's voice called out from the front of the stables.

"Back here!" Logan called back.

"Oh hey, Mom," Holland greeted as she approached them.

"Hey, Sweetie. Did you have a good time with Grace?" Mom asked.

"Always," Holland said before turning to Logan, confusion written all over her face. She'd come to the barn to find Logan and had found her mom with him. That wasn't a typical sight.

"If you're wondering what I'm doing here, I thought I'd take a little wander while you were out," Morgan clarified, showing that she still could practically read her children's minds, a trait that had always scared Logan in high school. Heck, it scared him now.

"Nice," Holland said as she turned back toward their mother. "And how's that wander treating you?"

Morgan shot a glance up at her eldest. "Quite well, thank you," she said with a smile, the closest thing to her real smile that Logan had seen since Thanksgiving. He was going to count that as a win.

"Great," Holland said before turning on her heel to face Logan. "I actually have a question for you. Could we use any help around here?"

Logan raised an eyebrow. That question had him nearly quaking in his boots. What was Holland up to now? She was known for taking in strays, animals as well as people. Logan would never forget the boy she'd brought home for dinner during her junior year of high school. He was the scruffiest person Logan had ever seen—and he'd seen some rough-around-the-edges characters working at the ranch. But this guy—or boy, since he was still in high school—had long shaggy hair, unkempt facial hair, fingernails nearly an inch long, and smelled as if he hadn't bathed in months. Holland had told the family before he'd come that his parents often worked late and she wanted to show him the kindness of a home-cooked meal. No one could begrudge her that so they welcomed him to dinner. And afterward he tried to steal one of their horses. Thankfully he was an ineffective thief so Dad hadn't pressed charges. But none of them, including Holland, were very sad when he and his parents moved out of town a few weeks later.

"Who are you saving now?" Logan asked, crossing his arms with a sigh.

"I hate it when you do that." Holland pointed a finger toward Logan's arms and then waved said finger in a circle.

"What?" Logan asked.

"That intimidation thing where you puff your chest out and look kind of like a gorilla." Holland scowled.

Mom spat out a laugh.

"I don't look like a gorilla. Do I?" Logan turned to his mother.

"Well . . ."

Logan rolled his eyes. "Back to my initial question." He jutted his chin out to complete the picture. If Holland wanted to antagonize gorilla Logan, she was going to get him.

"I'm not saving anyone. In fact, she made me promise that if we don't actually need her I couldn't try to talk you into giving her a job," Holland said as she dragged a tennis-shoe-covered toe through the remnants of hay on the ground.

"Who?" Logan asked again, dropping his arms. He was getting a little tired of playing gorilla Logan.

"Lake," Holland said.

Logan fought to keep from showing any kind of emotion. Who knew what would play on his face at the thought of Lake?

"Lake Johnson?" Logan clarified before clearing his throat.

"Or Lake Hollowell, as she's been known for the last fifteen years since she got married. Weird that you'd call her by her maiden name," Holland said with a smirk, her blue eyes dancing with mirth.

"It's just—I'm just—" Logan glared at his baby sister. "That's how I knew her since we were friends back in high school."

Logan folded his arms again. He'd felt better that way.

"Friends." Holland giggled, making air quotes with her fingers. "Oh, you were more than friends if I recall correctly."

"Were you even born yet?" Logan shot back.

"Not my fault you're so old," Holland retorted.

"So Lake needs a job?" Morgan asked, drawing the conversation back to the matter at hand.

Thank goodness for his mother. Logan was still reeling at the news that Lake was home. No one had told him. He still felt guilty for missing Fred's funeral. They hadn't been close in years, but they'd been friends once upon a time. And he'd been Lake's friend as well. He should have at least been there for her. But they'd gotten news of the funeral just hours before it began.

It had taken longer than Logan would have expected for news of Fred's sudden death to reach Blue Falls, and when it did no one knew funeral details. Logan hadn't expected Lake to reach out to him personally, and she hadn't. Had that stung? Could that have been part of the reason he hadn't attended the funeral? It was only a two-hour drive. He could have figured out how to leave the ranch for a day. But he hadn't. And for that he felt terrible. He really should have put his own feelings aside and gone. Who cared if he'd heard the funeral details from his mother, who'd heard from Lake's mother? He didn't need an engraved invitation to be there for his friends.

It was just that it had been so long. He hadn't seen Lake since his dad's funeral and it had been much longer since he saw Fred.

Maybe that was it? He remembered feeling resentment toward Fred when he hadn't bothered to show up at Mitchell's funeral, while Lake had gone out of her way to be there. Fred hadn't been home in years and hadn't reached out to Logan for many years before that. The last time they'd seen one another was at a bar maybe seven years ago. And even then they'd barely said hello. Logan had a hard time reconciling the man in a suit on the other side of the bar with his childhood friend, but he'd expected Fred to show up when it had really mattered. Yet he hadn't. Was that why Logan hadn't made the effort? That was surely petty and Logan hoped it wasn't the case, but he couldn't be sure.

At the time of Fred's funeral a mare had been about to give birth. The foal was fathered by a stud that could mean big things for their ranch, and he told himself that was the reason he shouldn't leave the ranch long enough to go to the funeral. And it very well could have been. But that didn't stop guilt from creeping in. If he could help Lake now, he would.

Holland nodded.

"I didn't even realize she'd moved home," Logan said, trying to focus on Holland and the discussion once more. He didn't like the way his thoughts seemed to drift whenever Lake was involved.

"She didn't want to make a big to-do about it. But I'm sure you'll be hearing the news from other sources soon enough since her girls started at Blue Falls Elementary this morning," Holland replied.

Logan smiled as he remembered the adorable little girls who'd trailed after Lake at his dad's funeral, both the spitting image of their beautiful mother.

Whoa, Buddy. Where had that come from? Sure, Lake was beautiful, but those thoughts needed to be put away immediately. She was a widow grieving for her husband, the man she'd chosen to date as soon as Logan had broken up with her back in high school.

"What brings her back?" Morgan asked.

"Grace told me some stuff but I'm not supposed to share. Basically, Lake had no other option but to come home," Holland answered.

Logan frowned. No other choice? That made no sense. Fred had been a pediatrician with a thriving practice in Boise. There had to be some sort of mistake. Grace must have exaggerated Lake's circumstances.

But if they were okay financially, why was Lake searching for a job so soon after her husband's death? There had to at least be insurance money or something. None of this was making sense to Logan.

Then again, it wasn't his business. What was his business? Lake needed a job.

Suddenly the puzzle pieces fell into place. His mother needed companionship. Lake needed a job. His mother loved Lake and he was pretty sure vice versa.

"Well, I think we've got a job for her," Logan said as he met his mother's eyes.

Morgan seemed take a second to catch up before a true, genuine smile covered her face.

"With me?" Morgan asked, her smile lighting up that stable.

"Lake hasn't been around for a while. Would you consider her a stranger?" Logan teased. He couldn't help it. It was so nice to see his mother back to herself even if just for a moment.

Morgan swatted at Logan but didn't stop smiling. "Lake is

better than I could have ever imagined. If she'd want it." Morgan looked to Holland.

"I'm lost. What's the job?" Holland glanced from her mother to Logan.

"We were just discussing how nice it would be for Mom to have some help around the house. That way you could concentrate on school more and Mom wouldn't be the only one cooking and cleaning up there," Logan explained.

"Hey, I help," Holland replied before frowning. "Okay, I kind of help," she clarified.

Morgan laughed. "It's alright. I've never asked more of you. You've always been so busy and I know you do everything you can. But what do you think? Do you think Lake is desperate enough to want to spend all day with me, cooking and cleaning?"

Logan hated the insecurity he heard in his mother's tone. He knew she was stepping out of her comfort zone, asking for help.

"That's a silly notion and you know it, Mother," Holland said with just the right amount of seriousness. Logan should have known his sister would know exactly how to handle this. "She'll be thrilled! I can't wait to tell her. Should she start tomorrow?"

"Maybe give me a day or two. I want to get used to the idea first," Morgan replied.

"You're going to clean the house before you let Lake come over and help you, aren't you?" Holland asked, her eyes narrowed.

Logan's head spun to look at his mother.

"It's just such a mess right now. I don't want her seeing—"

"The whole point is that she's supposed to help you with that mess," Logan sighed. "She can start tomorrow." He spoke in his firmest voice, trying to overrule his mother, but should have known that would never work.

"I'll be elated to have her. She can start in two days' time," Morgan countered, her eyebrows raised in challenge toward her son.

Logan knew when he was beaten.

"Two days sounds great," he muttered.

Holland laughed before stopping abruptly. "Shoot. I forgot. She made me promise you all would interview her for the job. She didn't want to get it based on our personal relationships."

But that was precisely why Lake was getting the job: because his mother felt comfortable with her.

And because you'd love to see her around more often, an annoying voice whispered from the back of his mind. He'd be ignoring that voice.

Morgan chuckled. "Well, if she insists. She can come up tomorrow to the offices for the interview. Then she can start the next day."

"I'm not telling her that last part. She has to think this is all on the up and up," Holland stated.

"It is on the up and up," Logan argued.

"Of course it is, darling." Morgan patted Logan's arm.

Holland wrapped an arm around her mother's waist and led her out of the stable as they started talking a million miles a minute. Logan couldn't hear much of it, but gathered that all of it had to do with how exciting it would be to have Lake here.

They needed Lake and Lake needed them. What was shady about that? Logan was still a little confused but realized he'd never understand the female mind so he let it go.

But with his confusion gone only one thing remained. Lake would be there the next day. And then the next and the next after that, assuming she took the job. Logan would be seeing the woman he'd always deemed the one who got away . . . every day.

Things would be different now, though. They weren't high school kids. She was a widow with two children, while he was a bachelor rancher who couldn't seem to find the right woman for him. They had too much baggage. Too much time had passed. She'd been his friend's wife. It was all too messy. And Logan would do well to remember that.

Six

"MOM, YOUR HAND IS ALL SWEATY," Delia complained, tugging her hand away from Lake's as the two of them and Amelie walked up to school together.

It was only day two at their new school and Lake had wanted to drop them off closer than just the curb. She thought the walk in the cool November air would also help to calm her nerves a bit, but evidently her sweat glands didn't get the memo and the thought of her interview at Blue Falls Ranch had her more nervous than she cared to admit.

Lake wiped both of her hands against her pencil skirt and took her daughters' hands again.

"It wasn't *too* sweaty," Amelie said sweetly.

Lake fought the urge to laugh at her youngest. Amelie had reached an age where she didn't like to be laughed at, even if it was because she was so cute. Lake often found herself smothering her laughter where Amelie was concerned.

"Thank you, Sweets," Lake said as she swung both of her arms, trying to relax not only the girls but herself. She really shouldn't be so anxious over this interview. It was just the Ashfords, some of the kindest people she'd ever met. But it felt monumental. This would be her first job as a grownup, her way of providing for her children all on her own . . . well, if she got it. What if she didn't get it?

And her palms were back to being sweaty. She dropped the girls' hands before they could point it out.

"There's Eloise!" Delia pointed out a girl walking up to the school with a couple of other kids who looked just like her. "Bye, Mom." She didn't even glance back at her family before running to her friend.

"Oh, and there's my new friend Lara." Amelie also started forward but paused, turning to look up at Lake. "Thanks for walking us to class, Mama." Then she was off, dashing toward Lara and her mom.

Come to think of it, Lara's mom looked rather familiar.

"Lake?" Lottie, Lara's mom, waved a hand.

Lake waved back enthusiastically. She hadn't seen Lottie in years. They'd only been a year apart in high school and had been pretty close back then. Lake knew that Lottie had taught school in San Francisco for a bit before moving home to help with her family B&B . . . and then had married one of the most eligible bachelors in the nation, Leo Heathcliff. Even though Leo was a billionaire he still worked as the town sheriff and, according to Lake's mother, the little family was loved by all. Even the extended Heathcliff family, who had once been shunned by locals for encroaching on the town with their gigantic resort, had been accepted and were now considered Blue Falls residents through and through.

Lottie bounced a baby carrier she wore over her chest and stomach, shushing the sweet little babe whose head just barely peeked out of the carrier. Lake could see a full head of brown hair and a pair of bright eyes.

"Number two?" Lake asked as she pointed to the baby in Lottie's arms.

"Three," Lottie replied with a tired smile. "It really is true what they say. Two kids is like having two kids but three is like having a million."

Lake laughed, suddenly feeling a little gratitude toward Fred. Maybe he'd been right in his assessment of their family. But then again, Lake wouldn't mind feeling like she had a million kids right about now. Especially seeing the adorable little bundle resting on Lottie's chest.

"How many do you have?" Lottie asked.

"Two," Lake said with a grin. "Delia and Amelie. And it looks like Amelie is friends with your Lara."

"They're carrying on a great tradition," Lottie said, pumping her eyebrows. Suddenly memories of late-night milkshake runs and swimming in the Peterson's pond came flooding back.

"They truly are. I just want to start with apologizing, Lottie. I've been terrible about keeping in contact with—"

"I'm going to stop you right there," Lottie said, raising one hand while the other patted the sweet baby's bum.

"First off, it takes two to stop communicating. I am definitely partly to blame for falling out of contact. And two, friends are friends. We didn't hang out for years but I have a feeling that's all going to change now that you're home." Lottie's words were exactly what Lake needed to hear.

The guilt about past friendships had been eating her up. She knew she'd be coming face to face with so many people she hadn't reached out to for years. Heck, she didn't even go on social media anymore. But if they were even a little like Lottie, Lake knew she'd be just fine.

"I'm glad to hear that. I'm going to need all the friendship I can get," Lake said gratefully.

"I was so sorry to hear about Fred. I hope you know I'm here," Lottie said.

Lake nodded. She hadn't until this moment, but Lottie's support meant everything.

"I'm sorry I didn't reach out before. I should have. I thought

I'd talk to you at the funeral, but I didn't even know about it until after the fact," Lottie said.

Lake wasn't surprised.

"Everything was so crazy," she began.

"Don't you dare think about apologizing for that. I was just giving my excuses, poor as they may be."

"Not so poor. You can't go to an event you're unaware of," Lake said.

Lottie laughed. "So now that we both have our ridiculous apologies out of the way, what do you say we hang out some time this weekend? I could really use a break from the kiddos for a minute or a day."

Lake laughed. She remembered those first days of mothering when hours felt like years and minutes like days. But then things sped up big time and you wondered how you were here, a widow with two big girls.

"That sounds amazing. I hope to be starting a job in the next couple of days, but as long as I have some time off I'd love to see you. Maybe get some steak fried chicken?" Lake asked. She'd been missing the hometown favorite something fierce.

"Yes please!" Lottie tried to rub her stomach around her baby.

"We'll catch up then," Lake said with a grin.

"And you can tell me how you're really holding up. I know you're a strong woman, Lake, but you went through some of the worst the world has to offer. You don't have to always be so resilient," Lottie said seriously.

Lake sighed. How could a friend who'd known her so long ago hit the nail precisely on the head?

"Maybe I should be avoiding you," Lake teased.

"You can try," Lottie teased right back.

"See you this weekend," Lake promised before turning back to where she'd parked her car. She nearly began skipping, she felt so good about life. It was almost like Fred—the way she'd lost him and what he'd done—was all part of a past life. She thought about her daughters running to their friends, how happy they appeared to be. The past wasn't gone but it at least felt distant for the time being and Lake would take the reprieve from her anger and grief. It looked like this new start had been exactly what they'd all needed.

"You're a knockout," Holland said as she greeted Lake by her car.

"Is it too much?" Lake asked, glancing down self-consciously at her burgundy blouse and matching pencil skirt paired with a black peacoat and black tights. She'd decided against light colors because she remembered the dustiness that was part of ranch life, but now wondered if she should have worn jeans like Holland was. She'd thought she should dress up a bit for an interview to show she was taking it seriously.

"Not at all. I'm just a little worried about throwing you to the wolves with you all dolled up like that," Holland said as she looked beyond the old ranch house and toward the offices that were equidistant between the ranch house and the main stables.

"The wolves?" Lake stammered, suddenly feeling the urge to wipe her hands against her skirt once more.

"I think Nix is the only one not in on the interview today," Holland replied with a grimace.

Lake was about to complain but reminded herself that she'd been the one insistent on this interview. None of this was Holland's fault.

"Fun," Lake said with about as much enthusiasm as one felt before a dental exam.

"You'll be fine. If anyone can tame the wolves, it's you," Holland said as she offered an arm.

Lake had wisely opted for boots instead of pumps, but maybe

71

she should have reached for her flat boots, not the cute ones with a three-inch heel.

Holland led Lake past the old ranch house as she said, "Mom really does need you. I hope you remember that through all of this. Even when you want to chuck something at Austin's head or hightail it to your car."

"Really?" Lake asked.

"Yeah. Almost everyone wants to throw things at Austin."

"No, the part about your mom," Lake clarified. She tripped over a rock but Holland steadied her.

Lake made a note to herself to only wear sneakers or maybe her cowboy boots to work.

Holland nodded. "She's been lonely with Dad gone but this Madison thing has really shaken her. Oh, and please don't say anything to anyone about that. I didn't tell them I told you. And while I think they wouldn't mind . . . "

"I get it," Lake assured her.

Holland grinned.

"I'm gonna like having you around," she said.

"Only if I pass this interview process."

"Oh, believe me, if you don't leave you'll get the job. Logan is way more worried about our impression on you than your impression on my rodeo of brothers. He's been trying to run off any and all brothers that he could all morning. He's been unsuccessful."

Lake grinned, imagining anyone being able to hold their own against the rugged Logan Ashford. His brothers might be some of the only ones who could.

They were at the pinewood steps that led up to the tiny porch of the ranch offices and Holland continued to lead the way up before opening the front door.

"She's here," Holland called out before issuing the warning, "Everyone on their best behavior."

Holland walked in and held the door open as Lake followed.

Lake wanted to take in the room around her but got hung up on the seven faces that stared back at her. She'd forgotten what a tribe the Ashford clan really was. If she didn't know them so well she would have surely been intimidated. At the moment all she felt was an immense bout of adoration for these boys she'd grown up with and the woman who'd raised them all.

"Mama Ashford," Lake said, hurrying across the room as Morgan Ashford stood to greet her.

Mama Ashford took Lake into her arms and hugged her tighter than anyone else had dared to.

All of the other hugs Lake had received since returning to Blue Falls had always had a little gentleness behind them, as if people couldn't believe that Lake could withstand the force of a real hug. And although Lake was rather small at her barely five foot she had walked through an abundance of despair. She could handle an aggressive hug.

"It's so good to see you, dear girl," Morgan breathed, not making a move to let go. Lake didn't want to either. "I hate that you are enduring the grief only old women should ever feel." Morgan whispered those last words in Lake's ear as if they were a message just for her.

"If you're counting yourself as one of those old women you'd be dead wrong, Mama Ashford. I am so sorry." Lake knew she didn't need to clarify the reason for her words.

"I'm sorry too. But I can't think of anyone I'd rather have with me during this time," Morgan said. Lake understood. There was something about shared grief that could bring people together. Things about Lake that only Morgan would get and vice versa.

"But I don't have the job yet," Lake said, reluctantly pulling away from Mama Ashford to face the wolves, as Holland so lovingly called them.

"Hey boys," Lake greeted the clan, not sure if she should turn to each one individually or not. She quickly decided on not.

"We're not boys anymore." One of the younger brothers sauntered toward Lake. She couldn't believe it had been so long that she couldn't tell the younger Ashfords apart. Of course she knew Austin, Jackson, and Logan. She was pretty sure she would have been able to pick out Phoenix. And she'd seen all of them at the funeral, but they were en masse then, and she hadn't needed to distinguish them. She did remember wondering when the little ones had grown up. Before the funeral, when had Lake last hung out at the ranch? Years before. The younger boys would have still been in elementary school or maybe middle school. But whichever brother spoke to her was right: they weren't boys anymore.

She was going to guess this was Memphis from the stories Grace had told her. He had a bit too much swagger to his confident step and she swore he was flirting even though she had to be at least ten years his senior, and a widow to boot.

"Sit." Lake didn't even need to look to know who was responsible for that command. It was so powerful that Lake had to fight the urge to obey too. Logan Ashford had always been able to control a room. She was sure it was his superpower. Granted, he had quite a few of those if Lake remembered correctly. Including . . . her cheeks got red and she desperately hoped she wasn't blushing as she remembered the Logan Ashford she'd dated.

None of that, she said to herself.

Slowly Memphis took a seat and there was nothing for Lake to do but turn toward that voice. Logan would be the one conducting this interview.

As she turned, Lake's gaze bounced from brother to brother. She was sure Brooks was first, his baby face still a little less sharp than the other Ashfords. Then came Austin's smirk, Jackson's grin, and someone—she guessed Orlando—who smiled sweetly. Phoenix wasn't there so there was only one last face to encounter. She finished turning and there he stood, just as handsome and studly as ever.

Oh heavens. Her stomach took a tumble.

She and Fred had had their issues, but she shouldn't be feeling anything for another man. Not so soon. And yet . . .

"Good to see you, Logan," Lake finally managed as she stuck out her hand with what she hoped was a friendly but detached smile.

There, completely professional. She was proud of herself.

"You as well," Logan drawled, likewise offering his hand, but he and Lake were still too far apart for their hands to meet.

Lake ignored the buckling of her knees caused by his voice with his gorgeous face and broad shoulders and took a step forward.

Only for those poor knees to give out, depositing her flat on her behind.

So much for feeling proud of herself.

Seven

"JUST GO," Brandon directed when Logan had peeked out of the window of the office toward the old ranch house once again.

"Go?" Logan tried to play it cool but knew he was failing. That's what he got for working with one of his closest friends. Brandon had been with Logan day in and day out for nearly every day of the past six years. Although Brandon was a few years younger than Logan, they'd always managed to be around the same places at about the same times, whether for football, t-ball, or Peterson's Pond. But it was when Brandon had moved back to town after retiring from the rodeo circuit that their friendship went from friendly to brotherly. Since then Brandon had been one of those men Logan could count on, come what may. He'd been a rock when the brothers had all fallen apart in their own ways after their father's death.

"Didn't you date Lake back in high school?" Brandon asked instead of answering Logan's lame attempt to act as if he didn't care that Lake was working her first day on the ranch.

"Yeah. Like twenty years ago," Logan said as if the relationship shouldn't matter to him. And it shouldn't. Because it *was* twenty years ago and because she'd dated and been married to his friend in the meantime. She was still grieving the loss of that friend. Like Logan should have been doing instead of coveting his wife. Logan was a terrible man and had probably just punched his ticket to hell.

But then the image of Lake with her big hazel eyes and in that curve-hugging skirt popped into his mind. What a way to go.

No. He was stronger than this. Sure, it was annoying to watch his little brothers drool over a woman whom none of them deserved, but Logan had no claim to her. She was Lake and he was Logan. Two separate entities.

What was he even going on about?

He turned away from the window and back to the computer where he was supposed to be approving a contract for the sale of four horses. A ridiculously important thing for their business, and yet . . . his mind was still in the old ranch house with Lake.

"Man, you're old," Brandon muttered.

"And you're like a year younger." Logan wasn't about to hold the title of old all on his own.

"Make that three," Brandon said.

Logan cocked his head.

"I was a freshman when you were a senior," Brandon replied.

That was right. But he wasn't about to let Brandon win. "We were in high school at the same time. Close enough. If I'm old, you're old," Logan said with a satisfied nod and then turned back to the window.

Dang it! He had been supposed to turn back to his work.

Brandon caught his faux pas and fully enjoyed it, according to the smirk on his face.

"Oh shut it," Logan muttered as he finally focused on the computer. Or tried to.

"You might as well go. All the rest of your brothers are there," Brandon said instead of listening to Logan's demand.

Wait, what had he said?

Logan's head snapped up to look at Brandon and he did a slow perusal of the office. Come to think of it, things were pretty quiet in there. He could at least count on Jackson to be here with him. Memphis too, if he was trying to get out of work. Sometimes even Austin and Land. Only Brooks kept to the stables for nearly all of his work hours.

"They're at the old ranch house?" Logan needed Brandon to be clear.

"I saw most of them make their way up at some time or another," Brandon said, his smirk still firmly in place.

Logan growled.

Brandon snorted.

"Stake your claim, man," he said through his laughter.

Logan was too frustrated with his brothers to pay any mind to Brandon. Were they really up at the house? While Logan had fought every urge and instinct all morning?

"Before Memphis does," Brandon added.

Logan whipped his head toward his friend once again. If he kept this up he'd be getting whiplash soon.

"I heard Austin telling him Lake was out of his league but the guy seemed determined to make his move. Austin followed him, saying he needed to see Memphis crash and burn."

Logan stalked out of the office. What was Memphis thinking? The boy was still a cub and Lake was a woman, not one of his conquests. If it meant Logan had to grab Memphis by the scruff of his neck and throw him out of the house, he'd do it.

"Careful, Logan. You look like a man on a mission. You don't want to scare the poor woman off." Brandon was still laughing.

But he was right.

Logan inhaled deeply and slowly let it out. He needed to calm down before he went in the house and acted like some caveman doing something he was bound to regret.

Although he knew he would never regret saving Lake from Memphis. But how he did it? That would be what mattered. He needed to be cool and collected Logan, not the hothead he worked hard to control.

The chilly air that hit his face as he stepped out of the office helped to relax him as he realized it really wasn't all that big of a deal. His initial reaction had been to protect Lake, but he doubted the woman needed any protecting. Not if she had an ounce of the girl she once was still in her.

He remembered one of their outings to the pond. It was a favorite spot of all of the teens in the area and during the summer it was the only place to be. There had been a pretty raucous gathering one June afternoon, the summer before he and Lake had dated.

One of Logan's football teammates, the kind of guy Logan loved to put in his place, had taken one look at Lake in her new swimsuit and decided she was the one for him. The problem was, Parker was the kind of guy who wanted only one thing from a girl.

But before Logan could warn Lake—they were friends long before they dated—Parker had made his way to the side of the pond where Lake and her friends were lying out in the sun and had grabbed her behind.

It took three of Logan's teammates to hold him back, but in the meantime Lake had stood, given Parker one disdainful look, and slapped him right across his face.

The boy had been stunned long enough for Lake to gather her things and start back toward the cars with her friends. But when Parker had started to stalk after Lake, Logan's friends had let Logan loose. Logan had made sure Parker didn't follow Lake then or any other time.

If Lake could stun a guy like Parker, Memphis would be a piece of cake.

But actually, now Logan was hurrying to the house for a whole other reason. He, like Austin, couldn't wait to see Lake put Memphis in his place.

Just as Logan was nearing the back door, he heard Blue's commanding bark and the crunch of gravel as a car pulled up on the drive.

It wasn't uncommon for them to get visitors to the ranch during the day, but everyone typically knew to drive to the office. They wouldn't stop at the house. Who wouldn't know that? Or was the visitor really there to see someone at the house?

Logan decided to jog around the house and head off whoever was there. Most likely it was someone needing the office and Logan would direct them there, where Brandon could surely help them.

The cement path that lined the house had been poured by his dad. His parents had worked together to plant the bushes that ran alongside that path, although at this time of year they were more just branches than full bushes. Beside her family, Mom's pride and joy was the greenery and flowers that surrounded her home. Every time Logan walked this way he couldn't help but remember all the hard work both of his parents had put into the practicality and beauty around him.

Logan jogged past the last of the bushes—the ones closest to the front of the house were evergreen, blocking his view—but froze when he saw the woman getting out of the car parked in his mom's driveway.

Part of him had been hoping she'd come back. No, all of him had. He knew if she came back things could be righted. Mom, along with the rest of the family, needed closure. But he wasn't sure now was the time for this confrontation. His mom was still reeling from just meeting Madison and now Lake was here to witness it all. It wasn't that Logan didn't trust Lake to keep their family drama private, and honestly he'd already heard whispers of Madison's existence in town so it wasn't like it was some big secret, but he didn't want her to have to witness it firsthand.

Unfortunately, it looked like whether his mom was ready or

not, whether or not Logan wanted Lake to have a front row seat to all of this craziness . . . Madison was here.

Ruby got out of the driver's side much more quickly than Madison exited. She looked up, appraising the house before her with a frown.

Madison, on the other hand, kept her eyes focused on the ground just outside of the car. As if she had to just take one step at a time, and anything more would be too much.

Suddenly, Logan put himself in Madison's shoes, just for a moment. She'd found a note. It was her only link to her birth father, and her mother was gone. Logan was guessing Madison didn't have siblings or she wasn't close to them if she was here with a friend instead. So she had no family. But she'd bravely decided to follow her one clue: this note.

Then when she got to the house of the man who could give her answers, he was gone, along with all of those answers. And she had to face the fact that she really was all alone in the world.

Logan felt a protectiveness come over him as if this young woman was Holland. If his little sister had found herself in this situation, what would he have hoped someone in Logan's position would do?

As he watched her staring at the gravel, he knew. Madison needed an advocate. And he was the one to be it. He couldn't count on his brothers and Holland was too worried about their mother—rightfully so—to do the job. But Mom had seven other children to protect her. Madison had no one.

So while he knew in his soul that Madison wasn't his sister, he was going to treat her the way he would have if she were. Besides, she did have the Ashford nose. She was most likely a relative of some sort. But even without her nose she was someone Logan's dad had promised to protect. And now that he wasn't here . . . it was up to Logan. He was just frustrated that he'd taken so long to come to this point.

"Madison," Logan said, his voice strong but kind. He hoped it would have a calming effect on her, considering he could see her hand shaking as she closed the car door behind her.

Ruby had already noticed Logan and had turned her frown toward him but Madison had been so focused on the ground that she jumped at the sound of Logan's voice.

"I didn't mean to startle you. I heard the car when I was out back and thought I'd greet whoever was here," Logan said, speaking slowly because it felt like what Madison needed.

"Are you sure you're here to greet us? Or do you plan to run us off?" Ruby snapped, her hands on her hips.

Logan smiled. He was glad Madison had such a loyal confidant.

"Definitely greeting you. Only a fool would think he could run you two off," Logan replied.

He wasn't sure if it was his smile or his answer but Ruby's hands dropped and she appeared slightly less hostile.

Just slightly.

"I'm not sure why I'm back," Madison said softly, raising her eyes but not quite all the way. They stopped around Logan's chest.

"Yes, you are. You can't leave here without knowing more. Without knowing if this . . ." Ruby paused, looking at Logan and then back up at the house. Logan was going to guess that at least a couple of his brothers were now at the windows. ". . . family is any relation to you. You deserve to know, Madi."

Madison nodded as if trying to convince herself, although Logan would be willing to bet they'd had this conversation more than once before.

"I just feel so badly. I had no idea Mitchell would be—" Madison looked up all the way at Logan with wide eyes.

"It's okay. You can say he's dead. We've had some time to get used to the idea," Logan said as he took a step forward, hoping to close the literal as well as metaphorical gap between himself and Madison.

"And then I ran away last time."

"I imagine it was a lot to take in. I'm guessing you had no idea Mitchell had a wife and eight kids?" Logan asked.

"Especially kids so close in age to me," Madison nearly whispered.

She obviously hadn't realized she'd be accusing a man of stepping out on his family. It made sense, now that Logan thought about it, but he hadn't even considered it. Man, he needed to work on having some empathy.

"And the last thing I want is to bother you," Madison began.

"No. We are fine bothering them if it means giving you some peace of mind, Madi," Ruby interrupted.

"I don't want to hurt their family, Ruby," Madison turned to her friend.

"I know. It's not fair. But this isn't your fault. None of this is your fault," Ruby reiterated.

"And I understand that," Logan interjected.

"You do?" Ruby and Madison asked in unison as they turned to him.

"It took me a minute, but yeah. I'm sure the rest of my family will catch up. Although I bet my mom's already there. She's the best woman in the world," Logan replied, his smile still firmly in place.

"I could feel that the last time I was here. It was why I almost didn't come back. I couldn't bear to hurt her." Madison's voice dropped to a whisper and she wrung her hands in front of her.

"Well, I for one am glad you're back. Because Mom has been hurting and you're the only one who can give us answers as well. If you hadn't come back, we'd have to spend the rest of our lives assuming the best or the worst. We'd never know for sure," Logan said.

"But a DNA test?" Madison offered.

Logan nodded. From the minute Madison left last time Logan had hoped she'd be willing to do this for them.

"Do you want me to leave and come back with one?" Madison asked.

Ruby was already shaking her head no as if she wouldn't allow her friend to agree to this.

"How about this? You come in with me. Come get to know my family. Because even if that test shows Dad isn't your father, I'm pretty sure we're related. You have the Ashford nose," Logan said, trying to offer an olive branch.

"I do?" Madison asked as her hand went to her nose. "I've always liked my nose."

Logan laughed. "Yeah, I guess it's a good one."

"But you don't think your dad is my father?" Madison asked.

Logan shook his head. "I know you didn't know him, but I just can't believe this of him. Maybe if you were older than I was, but Dad was completely and utterly devoted to Mom. I'm not sure why he didn't tell us about you, considering he must have known who you are. We all recognize his handwriting on the note. But I'm going to figure it has something to do with protecting someone he loves. Or making up for someone he loves. Dad has three brothers and dozens of cousins on the Ashford side. Some of them haven't always made the best decisions in life and as the oldest, Dad was forever helping them through things."

Madison pursed her lips. "So you think I might be a cousin?"

"With that nose I think you have to be," Logan said with a grin.

"But not a sister?" Madison asked.

"Is it horrible of me to say I hope not?" Logan ventured.

Madison shook her head. "After seeing the look on your mom's face, I have to say I hope I'm not either."

Logan lifted his arms and gave her a questioning look.

"Should we hug it out?" he asked, his grin growing wider. He already felt like Madison was related to him. Maybe it was the nose or maybe it was her demeanor, but she felt like an Ashford.

"I guess?" Madison said as she warily walked toward Logan and his hug.

"So I have a big family?" Madison asked, her voice muffled, from within Logan's arms.

"Yeah, you could say that. We're an averaged-sized family in the Ashford clan. My dad's cousin Dwight has twelve kids," Logan said as he released Madison.

"What is up with you Idahoans and your huge families?" Ruby asked from a few steps behind Madison. She'd never let her friend too far out of her reach.

"Family is everything. So might as well have lots of it," Logan replied, giving Madison a look to let her know he already considered her one of them.

Madison smiled back and for the first time since Thanksgiving Logan felt that things were going to work out just fine.

Now to convince his family of that.

Eight

"So we're all supposed to welcome her with open arms like you did?" Jackson asked from the barstool he occupied by the gigantic blue island.

Lake loved the colors of the old ranch house. Everything was serene and almost oceanlike with all of the shades of blue, green, and white. The kitchen was mostly pale blue and white, the island a slab of marble that swirled icy blues with streaks of white and even a few threads of gold.

The cabinets were a light pine that matched the enormous table in the eating area. Everything about the old ranch house was large. Probably because at its peak ten people had lived there, with extra room for friends, hands, and extended family to drop by all the time.

"She's scared. She's getting a DNA test. But right now she has no family . . . besides us." Logan ran a hand through his wavy brown locks. Lake had always loved Logan's hair. The color was much lighter in the summer and became almost a mahogany in the winter.

Lake wasn't sure if she should still be in this kitchen. Everyone else here was family. But she'd been tasked with baking bread today and was elbow deep in flour. She guessed she could back out, wash her hands in the bathroom, and wait out the conversation, but she also didn't want to draw any attention to herself. Heaven knew this had nothing to do with her.

"As far as we know we aren't her family either," Austin spoke up from where he leaned against one of the wide kitchen windows that overlooked the front yard and driveway. He'd been spying on Logan, Madison, and Ruby from the moment the car had pulled up. He'd been giving everyone in the kitchen a play-by-play and had nearly choked on his own spit when Logan had given Madison a hug.

Lake, even though she had no right to an opinion, had been proud of Logan. Did she feel the tiniest twinge of jealousy when she'd heard Logan was hugging the girl? Yes. Was that ridiculous? Yes. But when Logan had come in, asking the family to accept Madison as one of their own, all jealousy was gone and pride for him welled up within her. Logan was the best of men.

"She has the Ashford nose," Holland piped up from where she stood next to the other window. She'd grown annoyed at Austin's commentary and decided to see things for herself.

"Plenty of people have the Ashford nose," Memphis argued back.

"Name one?" Holland retorted.

Memphis opened his mouth.

"Who isn't an Ashford," Holland amended hastily.

Memphis closed his mouth.

"So just because she shares a nose with us we're accepting her as one of us?" Jackson stood up and began to pace behind his stool.

"Until she takes the DNA test, yeah. Why not?" Logan asked.

"Doesn't it feel like a betrayal to Dad? This girl is claiming to be his daughter. Meaning he—" Austin began.

"We get what it means," Holland shot back.

This time it was Austin's turn to shut his mouth.

Lake watched as Land's head bobbed from one sibling to another, frustration building in his demeanor. He wanted to solve this, that much was obvious, but he didn't know how.

"Enough," Morgan finally said. "That poor girl has been through so much. She's lost her mother. Came here to find her father and instead found all of us."

"It would be my worst nightmare," Holland muttered.

"Even if she is not a relation, family doesn't have to be connected by blood. Logan is right. We should welcome her with open arms. So no matter what that DNA test says, she'll be treated as one of us. Do you all understand?" Morgan asked sternly, determination in her spine as she sat tall on her barstool.

Lake closed her mouth, realizing it had fallen open sometime during Morgan's incredible speech.

No matter what. So she was saying she'd accept Madison even if she was not related at all or—what would probably be worse for Mama Ashford—if she was Mitchell's daughter.

Lake hoped to one day be half the woman Morgan was.

"Let the girl and her friend in. They're probably half frozen by now. And if any of you are anything besides welcoming, you can see your way out," Morgan declared, meeting the eyes of each of her children.

Holland and Land nodded immediately, the rest of the boys slower to follow but each eventually doing so. Jackson was last of all. The man sure was stubborn. Lake couldn't wait to meet the woman who could tame him.

Logan waited for his mother to finish but as soon as she gave him a look that even Lake could read as *let her in,* he walked to the door, every set of eyes in the room on him.

Logan opened the door, offering those beyond it a wide smile, and stepped out of the way to let them in.

Blue's barking could be heard from the main bedroom where Holland had shut him away as soon as they realized that Madison and Ruby would be coming inside. Coming into a room full of the

Ashford crew was daunting enough. No need to add a rambunctious and ever-curious puppy who was sure to jump all over the newest arrivals to the mix.

Morgan shushed the puppy from the kitchen and his barking dwindled to a pitiful whine. Lake felt badly for just a second but knew Blue would be out soon. They only needed to keep him back there while Madison and Ruby were there, and it was doubtful it'd be a long visit.

The woman Lake had been told was Ruby walked in first. Apparently she was a friend of Madison's but judging by Jackson's animosity toward her she'd already managed to get on the wrong side of at least one Ashford brother.

Ruby was what Lake would call stunning, with a heart-shaped face and long, lean body. She was taller than her friend by half a foot, making her much, much taller than Lake. If Lake had to guess Ruby was probably about five-foot-ten. And in many other crowds she would have probably stuck out, but here in a crowd of Ashford men who ranged from six-two to six-five, she seemed downright petite. The only reason Lake even noticed her height was because she walked in beside Madison.

Madison was equally beautiful. While Ruby kept her striking silver-blonde curls long, Madison had an adorable brunette bob that just suited her face. Ruby's eyes were an unusual shade of light green while Madison's were a bright blue. And of course, Madison did have the Ashford nose.

Lake tried not to gasp when she saw it in person. She would never have noticed if she'd passed Madison walking down the street but now that it had been pointed out to her, it was glaringly obvious.

It wasn't a wonder why this woman had the family in a tizzy. Lake felt for each and every person in that room. They were all in a position they would surely rather avoid.

"Welcome to our home, Madison. I'm sorry that the first time you came wasn't quite the impression we would have wanted to give," Morgan said as she walked forward to meet Madison by the door where she seemed stuck. As if she couldn't quite make her feet take her across the rest of the foyer and into the kitchen where they were congregated.

Morgan took Madison's and then Ruby's hands, leading them to the large island where Jackson, Orlando, and Memphis were seated. Morgan ushered Memphis down a barstool so that the friends could sit next to one another.

"I think the orange rolls are just about ready to serve?" Morgan turned to ask Lake.

So they did know that she was still there. And so far no one had shooed her out. At least now she didn't feel so guilty about not exiting the room earlier.

"They are," Lake said, quickly washing her hands and moving toward the oven, but Morgan beat her there, taking out the ooey gooey deliciously sweet rolls that made the kitchen smell like the best kind of bakery.

"Mom's famous orange rolls," Holland offered when the room went quiet and each person either looked down at their hands (Madison) or started a stare down competition (Jackson and Ruby).

Although Morgan had greeted the women so graciously, she too seemed to need a moment as she took far longer than she should have to serve the rolls.

"They smell incredible," Madison said softly, finally looking up.

"Don't they?" Lake decided to say something because it seemed all the others were tongue-tied. "As a kid I used to try to time my visits with the days Mama Ashford would be making these. Although the baking doesn't stop there. Mama Ashford makes the best cinnamon rolls and cream cheese frosting as well."

"Don't forget her toffee bars or lemon squares," Austin piped up.

Lake grinned. She'd had a feeling her comment on food would loosen the boys' tongues.

"And her beef stew," Memphis added to a chorus of *Mmms* from the others.

"If we start adding all of Mom's savory dishes in as well we'll be here all day," Land said with his teasing grin. The one that had been absent for the past few minutes but was thankfully back.

"I'm Orlando," he said, offering Madison a handshake before turning to Ruby. "But the family calls me Land and you all should too."

Madison accepted Orlando's offering and lost a little of her deer-in-the-headlights look. As if the relief of someone accepting her helped her face to relax as well.

"I'm Memphis," Memphis said from the other side of Orlando and soon the entire family had introduced themselves.

"Sorry it took us longer than we should have to get here," Logan said when Jackson finally gave the women his name. It had almost seemed like he wasn't going to but he gave in at the last moment. "We should have introduced ourselves the moment you came in."

Madison shook her head. "I get that my visit is unprecedented. Let's just say there are only explorations of what we should do in this strange situation, but no mistakes." Her soft smile melted Lake's heart. She was as timid as a rabbit and yet she was here, trying to figure out her life. Lake's admiration for the woman grew.

Morgan plopped a huge orange roll, dripping with frosting, on a plate and handed it to Madison, then dished another for Ruby. Only then did she take the open seat beside Ruby, sinking wearily into the chair. This was taking way more out of Morgan than she would ever let on. That much was easy to see.

"And this is Lake," Logan introduced the last person in the room. Lake hadn't been sure how to acknowledge her own presence and was grateful that Logan had done it for her.

"Not family but here anyway. I'm just the hired help," Lake said with a self-deprecating laugh. It was weird to be in the Ashford home as anyone other than a girlfriend or friend, but now that she had a job there, for which she was supremely grateful, she *was* the hired help.

"You could be family if you'd accepted my proposal," Memphis joked.

The boy had offered his hand in marriage to Lake as he'd introduced himself that morning. Lake was going to go out on a very short limb and predict that this was a typical way Memphis introduced himself. That boy seemed to be as committed to a long-term relationship with one woman as Lake was to her car that she'd just sold.

"You proposed?" Logan, who had been lounging comfortably against the far wall of the kitchen, raised himself to his full six-foot-three, his broad shoulders seeming to overtake the room. "To Lake?"

"Take it easy, brother. Pretty sure with Memphis we all know it was a joke," Austin chided from where he still stood by the window.

"So where are you from? I feel like we hardly know you." Morgan decided to steer the conversation back to Madison and Lake could have kissed the woman, she was so grateful.

All of the attention had turned to her and that felt completely wrong, considering Madison had just met the family. Although Lake was curious about Logan's reaction. Had he been upset about Memphis fake proposing to Lake? It sure seemed like it. She felt her heart begin to race. To be protected by a man like Logan Ashford . . .

Lake drew in a calming breath. She was being silly. If Logan seemed upset, it surely had little to do with any feelings she hoped he had for her and everything to do with the fact that she was now working at the ranch. Flirting with employees was probably frowned upon. Yup, that had to be it. And was Lake really so fickle that she could hope for any kind of attention from a man when her husband had died not even a month before?

A voice from the back of her mind told her she had every right to look at other men, as their wedding vows hadn't stopped Fred from doing much more than looking at other women, but that was petty. Even if Fred didn't deserve her loyalty, she wanted to hold to a higher standard. As an example to her kids and for her own peace of mind. Things had already been such a mess in her marriage, thanks to Fred's decisions, and Lake wouldn't add to them by lusting over her ex-boyfriend and . . . oh Heavens, Logan was now her boss.

Yes, Lake would stay far, far away from the man who could make her heart flip with just a smile. But how would she do that while working for him?

Okay, she wasn't sure how that was going to work. But she had to do it.

"Oregon. A little town close to the eastern border called Willowcreek," Madison said, thankfully shushing all of Lake's errant thoughts. "Lived there my whole life."

Morgan nodded as she leaned forward to look around Ruby and meet Madison's eyes.

All signs of Morgan's exhaustion were gone; she was putting her everything into getting to know Madison.

"Do you have lots of family there?" Holland asked as she moved from her spot at the dining table to the island. All of the stools were taken but she leaned against the countertop on the far side of her mom.

Madison shook her head.

"Hey! You have me," Ruby stated.

Madison looked to her friend and a smile spread across her face. "That's true. But other than Ruby, no. My mom was an only child and my grandparents passed a couple of years ago. And then Mom . . . well, you know about Mom," Madison said softly.

"I'm so sorry for your losses," Morgan offered as she reached around Ruby to pat Madison's hand that sat on the counter.

Lake watched as Madison stared at her own hand, as if she couldn't quite believe Morgan was reaching out like this. When she lifted her eyes to meet Morgan's again, admiration shone in them.

Lake could only imagine the heart-rending pain of losing one's mother. It had been hard enough to lose Fred and she wasn't even sure what she still felt for the man. So much love had been shattered when he'd chosen to have an affair and though Lake thought things were mending, as soon as she heard the news about Sachia in Fred's car, that they had died together, it was as if those months of working on their marriage had disappeared. Lake was right back to being that woman who was ready to demand a divorce. But there was no one left to demand it of.

Her emotions fluctuated wildly. Fury toward Fred for the situation he'd left her in. Guilt for not loving him. Annoyance at loving him. Aching that she wasn't able to properly mourn her husband and the father of her children. Frustration and fear that one day her girls might find out what their father had done.

"I'm so sorry for yours as well," Madison replied in her soft, shy way.

Morgan nodded.

Grief was ridiculously unpredictable. It could be the most isolating thing in the world but then again it could bring people together in a way nothing else could. Lake would never understand it. Nor did she want to experience it enough to understand.

Jackson cleared his throat and shoved his hands into his pockets.

Lake could imagine these displays of affection were uncomfortable for him. He wasn't the most emotional of men, to say the least, but she also knew that the death of his father had hit him hard. It had been the kind of blow some hadn't been sure the Ashford family could overcome. So to have their father's death brought up by the young woman who could tarnish his memory for them? Lake could see Jackson was struggling.

But she really hoped he could also see this from Madison's perspective. She hadn't asked for any of this either. She couldn't help her parentage—though Lake truly hoped her father wasn't Mr. Ashford. She'd been in pieces after Fred's revelation of infidelity, almost losing faith in mankind. Especially because the men in her life at the time were people like Fred, Stanley, and their cronies.

But then she remembered her own father and the way he adored even the ground Mom walked on. She also distinctly thought of Mitchell Ashford. Lake knew men like them existed too. So she'd been able to restore her belief in some of mankind. Just not in Fred. At least not for a few months to come. And then the accident . . . nope. Lake would not spiral again.

Morgan finally released Madison's hand and Lake swore she heard a few of the brothers let out breaths they'd been holding. Why? Because they were worried about their mother? Because they weren't sure about this new young woman in their midst? Because they were worried about what she could reveal about their family? All of the above?

Lake pressed her back against the refrigerator once again, realizing just how out of place she was. She didn't belong in this intimate setting. But where could she go? So far she'd only been assigned kitchen tasks. It felt strange to try to find something to do on her own, considering she hadn't set foot in other portions of the old ranch house for too many years.

"So what are your plans while you're here, Madison?" Austin asked, shifting to press one foot against the wall behind him.

Morgan shot her son a warning glare.

Austin shrugged back at her before Madison had a chance to turn to him as if he hadn't understood what he'd done wrong.

But Lake knew Austin well enough to know he'd have no problems stirring up the waters and making Madison feel at least a bit uncomfortable. He wasn't malicious; he just enjoyed awkward situations.

Madison finally turned and all communication between mother and son had to cease.

"Not much. We're staying at the B&B," Madison supplied.

"The Browns are good people," Morgan said quietly.

Madison nodded. "We like them a lot. They've been very welcoming."

"Have you met Brandon?" Logan asked.

Madison shook her head as she shifted to turn to yet another brother.

"Oh, sorry. That came out as an accusation and I didn't mean it like that," Logan added.

"No mistakes, remember?" Madison said with a true grin. It seemed that Logan was the only one who could bring it out.

"Right." Logan winked and darn it if it didn't make Lake's heart flutter. What was her problem? He wasn't even winking at her.

"Brandon is our foreman here and he's Charlie Brown's son," Logan continued.

"I love that her name is Charlie Brown," Ruby said to no one in particular.

"Isn't it awesome? Her daughter is Charlotte as well but goes by Lottie. Too bad; it would have been so cool to have two Charlie Browns in town," Holland supplied.

"So do we get to call her Christmas trees Charlie Brown's Christmas trees?" Ruby pressed.

"Duh," Holland said in her Holland way.

Ruby laughed. "I think she's putting her first one up today. I can't wait."

"You're in for a treat," Holland said.

"I'd love to meet Brandon one day," Madison said, returning their conversation to its original track.

"I'm sure he'd love to meet you too," Logan replied and then frowned. "Wait, maybe I don't want you meeting him or the other hands. It's hard enough to keep them all away from Holland. But another . . . "

Logan's voice trailed off. It was obvious he'd been about to say 'sister.' And judging by the glares Jackson and Austin were directing at him, it was an unwelcome almost admission.

"Attractive woman on the ranch?" Logan kind of saved himself.

Jackson suddenly stood. "It was nice to meet you, Madison," he said with a gruff nod. "I'd better get back to work but I'm sure I'll be seeing you around."

Lake could tell it pained him to admit that. He would rather have Madison and the issues she'd unearthed far away. But for the sake of his mother and even for the young woman he was wishing away, he was being cordial, almost kind. That couldn't be easy.

"I'd better head too," Orlando said, his demeanor much more relaxed than Jackson's.

"Are you going to check on the Tennison account?" Austin asked Jackson.

Jackson nodded.

"Then I'd better go too." Austin pushed himself off the wall and walked toward the island. "I really do hope you find what you're looking for," he said, tipping his hat. The others had taken theirs off when they'd come in, but Lake was pretty sure Austin even slept in his cowboy hat. She hadn't seen him without it since they were kids.

"Thank you," Madison said sincerely.

That was typical of Austin. He was the first to make a joke at another's expense but also the first to comfort someone in need.

The three men left through the back door in the kitchen, all eyes in the room on them as they did so.

"So Ruby," Memphis said in his smoothest voice, trying to lean around Madison to obviously flirt with her friend. Thankfully the idea that Madison could be his sister kept him from flirting with her.

"Go with your brothers," Morgan commanded immediately.

"I was just . . . " Memphis began.

Morgan pointed toward the back door in silent command.

"Fine," Memphis muttered as he stood and stomped out.

Lake fought the urge to chuckle. Oh that Memphis. He was adorable in a naughty puppy sort of way.

And then it was just six. It still seemed like a big number, but the absence of the four strapping young men made it somehow seem empty. Although the most attractive and strapping of them all was still in their midst.

No. Lake had not just thought that. Corny and ridiculous thoughts be gone, she ordered her brain sternly. She hoped her mental command would be as effective as Morgan's to Memphis had been.

"We should probably get going too. I really don't want to overstay our welcome," Madison said as she stood, Ruby following her example.

"That's not possible," Morgan assured her, turning to Madison with a genuine look of concern in her eyes. "I'm going to tell you what I just told these kiddos of mine. You are now one of us. Like it or not. I'm not sure what my . . . what Mitchell's relationship was with your mother. But it was obvious you meant a lot to him. And if you mean a lot to him, you mean a lot to us," Morgan promised.

Madison's eyes were gigantic as she stared at Morgan in disbelief. Ruby's mouth had dropped open.

"I can't tell you . . . You should hate me," Madison finally managed.

"Because your search for your father brought you to us? Because that's all you've done. Everything else is on other people," Morgan replied.

Holland and Logan nodded in agreement.

These Ashfords were something else.

"It might take a bit, but let us get to know you. Before you know it we'll be loving on you and you'll wonder how in the heck you got dragged into this circus," Morgan added.

Madison's eyes filled with moisture. "I would love nothing more than to have a circus to be a part of."

"Then consider it done," Holland said when it looked like her mother was tapped out for words.

Lake knew Morgan meant every word of what she said, but without knowing who Madison's father really was it was taking all that was in her to speak them.

"I was wondering . . ." Madison paused.

"Just ask, Sweetheart," Morgan prompted.

"I was hoping to get a DNA sample from Mr. Ashford?" Madison asked, her face red.

She didn't need to say why she wanted it.

Morgan nodded and then looked up at Logan.

He left the kitchen immediately.

"Thank you for doing this for us. I'm sure you feel you have enough evidence to know who your father is without the test. We'd be happy to reimburse you," Morgan offered.

Madison shook her head. "I'd want this anyway. I need more proof. But—and I hope you don't take this the wrong way; I am so grateful for the offer of family—but I really hope you all aren't my family. At least not my immediate family. The man I've met through all of you, I just can't see him doing this."

"We can't either," Holland replied quietly. Her hair had fallen on either side of her face as if forming a blonde shield of sorts against the world.

Morgan, Holland, and Logan were putting up the bravest face of them all, but it didn't mean they weren't all hurting at the possibility. Logan had declared he couldn't believe it of his father, but Lake knew some small part of his brain had to be asking what if? And yet even that part of his brain was welcoming Madison into their lives.

Logan came back into the kitchen with a brown hairbrush and went to a drawer near Lake. He opened the drawer, pulling out a small plastic baggie, and threw in a few pieces of hair.

"I guess this is the upside of me still not clearing out all of your dad's stuff," Morgan said with a weak smile.

Lake longed to hug her but stayed rooted in her spot. Morgan would need her support at some point but right now wasn't the moment.

"Do you think this is enough?" Logan asked as he handed the bag to Madison.

"I think so?" Madison replied. "I guess we'll find out."

Logan nodded.

"According to the company we're using, hair samples have only sixty percent accuracy," Ruby said, looking up from her phone as she pursed her lips. She probably didn't like being the bearer of bad news.

"Do you know what might work better?" Logan questioned before he disappeared again.

He came back within moments, a cotton swab in his hand. He dropped it in another baggie before he offered it to Madison.

"I swabbed the inside of my mouth," he explained. "We can see how well you match my DNA."

Lake's stomach turned as she watched Madison look at Logan in awe.

"Really?" she asked.

Logan nodded. "We all need to know the truth. We deserve it." Logan looked at Madison and then to his mother, who had tears in her eyes.

"We do," Madison finally agreed before carefully placing both bags into her purse.

Madison stood. "The place we're using says three to five business days so we should know, at the latest, by the end of next week."

Logan nodded as did Holland and then Morgan.

Madison hesitated for a moment, looking at the Ashfords. "Are you sure you want me to do this?"

Lake worked hard to hide her shock. This woman was offering to give up the possibility of learning who her father was, all for the sake of people she'd just met.

Logan and Holland waited, looking to their mother.

"Yes," Morgan finally said.

Lake gripped the countertop beside her. She honestly couldn't imagine. She'd thought she'd endured the absolute worst with what Fred had done to her. But to see Morgan consider the possibility? Fred had avoided Lake's phone calls and changed his computer and phone passwords. Their marriage had been strained, weak at best. And it had been hard enough to hear the truth then, even when she hadn't been sure she still loved Fred.

But to have what Morgan and Mitchell had had? Lake hadn't even been around for years but knew the affection between them ran as deep as love could flow. Staring this possibility in the face should be unbearable. Yet Morgan was doing it.

Madison and Ruby left quietly, leaving behind a somberness that enveloped everyone left in that kitchen. They sat in silence, the four of them, for several long minutes before Morgan finally took a deep breath.

"This is what we hoped for, right?" she asked.

Logan nodded. "We need this."

Holland sighed.

Morgan bit the inside of her cheek. She'd been strong for so long, but it looked like her composure was failing.

Lake glanced around. Where could she go to give Morgan some privacy?

Morgan stood, hugging both of her children before turning to Lake.

"I think I'll probably just nap for a while and then spend some time in my room. Thank you for coming today, but you can go home now," she said graciously.

The woman was amazing.

Lake nodded as she watched Morgan walk out of the room. Lake remembered even as a young girl admiring the way Mama Ashford seemed to practically float as she walked. It was in stark contrast to her boot-stomping boys.

"I'm going to check on her," Holland said before they'd even heard the door to the main bedroom shut.

She didn't wait for a response before scurrying out of the room.

Logan sighed.

"This . . . this is just a lot for all of us," he said as he gazed down the hall.

Lake wasn't sure if Logan had noticed the familiar way in which he was talking to her. Not as a woman he hadn't had a real conversation with for over a dozen years. But almost as if they were back to where they'd been years before. And she loved it.

"I totally understand that," Lake said from her corner of the kitchen where she'd stayed since the moment Madison and Ruby had arrived.

Logan pushed off of his own wall and started toward the huge dining table that took up nearly half of the gigantic kitchen. He took a seat and patted the spot beside him. The act was so achingly familiar and yet foreign at once. As if his familiarity with her was from another life, one Lake hardly remembered yet missed with all her heart.

Lake wasn't sure why she was making so much of this, but it felt monumental. She could still leave. She should come up with some excuse to get out of the house. She was no longer working, after all. Morgan had told her to go home.

Because if she stayed and took that seat, it would mean she wanted to be there to comfort Logan in this time of need. She'd be staying for no other reason. It was what Logan was asking, surely without even knowing it, and a part of her knew that she should keep her distance. For the sake of appearances—she'd just lost her husband—but mostly for her heart. It was too easy to foresee it being entangled with Logan's once more.

And the biggest problem was that she doubted Logan knew what he was asking. He just wanted comfort from the only other person in the room. She doubted he'd be committing in any way. Why would he when he could have any woman he wanted? Why choose Lake, the ex he'd dumped who was now back in town with no money, no future, and a couple of kids to boot? The best of kids but a burden nonetheless, especially for one who didn't love them.

But no. This commitment would be Lake's and Lake's alone. She was the one who could see this situation for what it was because she wasn't the one who had been crushed by the thought of what Mitchell Ashford might have done. She doubted Logan could see much through his grief. But Lake could see that if she stayed it meant she cared for Logan. She wanted to be that person he turned to in his time of need.

A friend would stay, that little voice argued. However, Lake knew the truth. From the moment she'd seen Logan in the office the day before she had hoped something would be rekindled. That they'd have a second chance. Her heart *wanted* to fall. The silly thing was threatening to give itself to Logan even if he didn't want it.

Logan was the best of men. She'd always known that. He was gorgeous, sure, but that was the least of his many, many fine attributes. So being this close to him, while her hurting, mending heart was so tender, she ached to believe in more than what Fred had given her these past years. And her heart had immediately begun to believe in Logan.

Could Lake do that to herself? Could she stay?

Nine

LOGAN COULD SEE the indecision on Lake's face. A better man would have let her off the hook, taken back his offer. Not made her wade through the extensive emotions that staying alone with him had to be stirring up within her.

But Logan wasn't a better man. He wanted her to choose him. He wanted to see if he even stood a chance with this incredible, beautiful woman.

Even after Fred had started dating Lake, Logan had been sure that she would one day be his again. He'd always had affection for her. He'd been such a fool to break up with her to begin with, but he hadn't regretted it at the time. He'd felt deep down that they were meant to be, but that they'd needed that time apart to grow as individuals. Eventually, he'd believed, they would find their way back to one another.

But then she'd married Fred. And left town. And Logan had told himself that was it; his soul-stirring feelings had been wrong. He should have never let her go. He had moments of terrible regret. He'd worked so hard to forget all he'd felt for her.

But now she was back, and stronger than ever. He'd seen it in the way she held herself when she walked into their office to interview. She hadn't wanted to be there, asking them for a job. But she had. For her children. And because Lake could do whatever the heck she set her mind to.

So how was Logan supposed to resist her? This woman he'd always loved, who was now more beautiful, not to mention stronger and kinder than ever before.

Suddenly a part of Logan awoke. One that was no longer buried in worry over his family's predicament, a part that shook off the bands of what he'd always felt for Lake.

She was grieving. She should have still been married. If the world wasn't such a cruel place, she would still be in Boise, with her family intact, loving and being loved by Fred. How could he be so foolish and unsavory as to take advantage of his friend's death, especially so soon?

Logan felt his stomach lurch. He was going to be sick.

But then she sat beside him.

While he was lost in thought, she'd moved from the other side of the kitchen and had taken the seat he'd offered. He'd been too late in his discovery that he was manipulating the poor woman.

"I—" he began as Lake said, "I want you to know I'm here for your family. For you."

With that Logan was silenced again. His heart was telling his mind to stop, just to feel. To relish in that pull he felt toward Lake, delight in the words that she'd just said. She was there for *him*. Because as his mind was telling him this was all wrong, his heart was convinced it was right.

But then again, his heart hadn't been his best friend over the years, considering he'd never been able to settle down because he'd pined after the woman he'd dated as a teenager. The woman married to his friend.

Logan guessed that wasn't fair to his heart. If any other woman was just as gracious, patient, kind, and hilarious as Lake he would have dropped to a knee immediately. That woman just wasn't out there. Or at least Logan had yet to come across her.

That sick feeling overcame him again. How could he be manipulating Lake? Of all of the damned things he'd done . . .

"I appreciate that, Lake. But—" Logan was going to let her off the hook. Tell her she should go home to her sweet babies and leave the man who was trying to already make his move on a widow. The widow of his friend to boot.

"Oh gosh." Lake's cheeks went red and Logan berated himself for thinking she was adorable when she was embarrassed.

"That's not why . . . " Lake paused, unable to meet Logan's eyes.

"Oh!" she suddenly said.

Lake was the only one speaking because Logan was unsure of what to say.

"I promise I won't tell a soul what I heard here today," she continued, her eyes round with sincerity.

What? Now Logan was lost. Did Lake really think he was worried about her airing their dirty laundry?

"I know I should have seen my way out while Madison was here but I wasn't sure how to do it. Technically I was still on the clock and I hadn't been assigned any tasks other than in the kitchen. I didn't even consider going home. I probably should have," Lake blurted, her cheeks somehow even redder than before.

"Hey!" Logan had to stop her.

Lake abruptly finished her monologue and looked up at Logan, an emotion he couldn't place in her eyes.

Was it fear? That wasn't quite right. Shame? Oh, he hoped not. If anyone should feel ashamed it was him.

"I wasn't going to ask that of you," Logan promised and some of the red drained from Lake's cheeks.

Good.

"I know you would never say anything to anyone. I trust you,"

Logan said, realizing too late how intimate that sounded. "*We* trust you. That is the only reason we asked you to be here with Mom."

Lake nodded, her face nearly back to its typical color and her eyes conveying her relief.

But if Logan hadn't asked Lake to stay to make sure she'd keep her mouth shut, why had he? He couldn't tell her the truth. That he'd hoped she would want to comfort him. That they could have a moment here, just the two of them. That he was counting on her feeling bad for him after all she'd witnessed and would feel the need to stay with him.

But she shouldn't have felt that badly for him. Asking her to stay was milking the situation a bit, because Logan's grief was purely over the fact that he was worried about his mother. And maybe because he missed his father, but he had no doubt in his mind that Mitchell wasn't Madison's father. Had Mitchell kept a secret from the rest of his family, including his wife? Yes. But that was all his father was guilty of. Logan didn't need a DNA test to prove that to himself.

But Logan had wanted Lake to think that he needed her. And then he wanted to see that she would stay. Because she cared.

What a foolish, ridiculous, immature . . . he could come up with many more adjectives but needed to move on. Why had he asked Lake to stay?

Maybe it was the other way around. He wanted to make sure she was okay. She had witnessed quite the scene, and she couldn't be in the best place mentally or emotionally, considering she'd just lost her husband. Yes, as her friend and boss that was what should be happening. That was what a better man would have done. And from this moment on, Logan would try hard to be that better man.

"I'm so sorry that you had to witness all of that. Not because I'm worried you'll say anything, but it was a lot. And you shouldn't have been drawn into it," Logan said. As he spoke he felt better about himself because he sincerely did feel this way.

Lake shook her head. "I'm the last person you should be worried about."

Logan felt shame coil in his belly. Because although he couldn't help but feel Lake's presence in any room, notice how beautiful and graceful she'd been, he hadn't been *concerned* for her until that very moment. He should have thought of her needs long before. But he'd been busy worrying about his mother, Madison, his siblings, and even a little for himself. And maybe in that situation he should have looked out for those immediately affected first, like he had.

But someone should be looking out for Lake, so that was what he was trying to do now. This conversation had to have been a lot for her. Especially while her heart must still be raw. He remembered the month after his father's death. Logan had still been in a downright desolate state. But there Lake stood, working because she had to, even while she still had to be mourning.

The woman was a wonder.

"Well, since you're the only one left in the room, can I be concerned about how you feel now?" Logan asked with a wink.

Lake chuckled at his light manner. "I'm fine. Just fine. But how are you?" She leaned forward with intense sincerity.

Logan shrugged. This wasn't the finest of days for him or his family, but then again he was now sitting next to the loveliest woman he'd ever known, so it wasn't too shabby overall. "I'm fine too," he said honestly. He was surprisingly okay after all that had transpired.

Lake nodded in relief, leaning back as a serene look crossed her gorgeous face.

Logan followed her lead, folding his arms as he relaxed into his own chair. Silence filled the air. But it was nice. The kind of quiet one usually had to seek, but today it was just there.

As they sat in comfortable silence, a thought suddenly came

to Logan's mind, a reminder of something he'd just told himself. Lake was working a mere month after her husband's death. Why? Did she need the work? The idea had been pestering him ever since Holland had first asked for a job for Lake, but Logan had gone straight into fix-it mode and had forgotten that niggling question. He'd brushed it off as none of his business, but now that they were sitting here like this he remembered Lake wasn't just his employee. She was someone he trusted. Someone he cared for. And Logan watched over those he cared for.

But could he ask her?

Lake seemed deep in her own thoughts as she gazed out the window. He shouldn't interrupt her and yet . . . he had to know.

Surely Fred had taken care of her, right? He was a very successful—Fred's own words—pediatrician. So why did Lake need work?

"Can I ask you a question?" Logan finally got up the nerve to ask. If she shut him down, that would be that. Logan could cope with his curiosity and maybe when Lake trusted him more, she'd tell him.

"Huh?" Lake shifted her gaze from the window to him. "Oh, yeah. Sure."

"This isn't a typical workplace question. I might be prying a bit." Logan felt he needed to give Lake one more chance to escape.

Lake gave him a smile that shot warmth right to his core. He remembered that smile all too well. It was the same one she used to give him right before she was going to kiss him. Logan still had dreams about that smile.

Earth to Logan. The woman isn't going to kiss you. That smile means nothing.

He really needed to learn to manage his feelings for Lake better if they were going to do this friends thing. Because that's what they were, right? Logan had officially been friendzoned.

"Gotta say I'm not usually one to appreciate prying. But when it comes to you . . . " Lake's voice drifted off as she rested her elbows on the table and propped her face on her hands, covering the brand-new redness in her cheeks, but not before Logan got a peek at them.

She was embarrassed by what she'd said. Why? What had she admitted? But Logan had no time to dwell on that. He had a question to ask.

"Why do you need to work?" Logan asked, paying close attention to her expressions and body language. He wanted to be sure that if he was making her uncomfortable they could move on.

"Oh, that." Lake relaxed a bit, as if she'd expected a harder question.

Logan made note of that. He could pry even deeper into Lake's life and she wouldn't mind. At least that was the way it seemed right now.

He couldn't help his satisfied smile.

"Same reason most work, I guess? Money." She shrugged as if that explained everything.

But it explained nothing. She shouldn't be hurting for money. Logan hadn't been close to Fred in years but he checked social media every month or so, often enough to see all the ways Fred was spending the money he was making. The last he recalled, Fred had bought a pair of wave runners to go along with the boat in his five-car garage.

"But you have that house," Logan said. He'd seen pictures. It was gorgeous. Right on the lake where Fred used the boat and wave runners.

"Rented," Lake said simply, as if it wasn't a big deal. "Fred wasn't ready to buy. And he . . . well, I let him control the money."

She looked down at the table as if she were ashamed.

Logan couldn't let her feel that way. Before he knew it he was touching her, his finger ever so gently lifting her chin.

A small gasp escaped her lips before Logan realized what he'd done.

This was not keeping space between them. This was not what a friendzoned man should be doing.

He instantly dropped his hand below the table, far from Lake.

"Lots of marriages are like that," Logan said, trying to move past the awkwardness of his actions.

"Not one I'd ever imagined myself in. But Fred felt it was best and sometimes it was easier to let him get his way than fight him on things." Lake let out an exhausted sigh.

Logan had never imagined their marriage to be anything but blissful. Although thinking of them like that had been painful, it would have been torture to think that Lake had endured anything in less than bliss in marriage. They'd been so happy in those early years, back when Logan had seen them more often. What had happened more recently? Had he been wrong to assume his friend was taking care of Lake?

"I know what you're asking, and just give me a minute to berate myself before I answer." Lake said the words with a smile but Logan knew that smile as well. It was the one she used to cover her pain, the same one that had haunted him for years. She'd worn it while he'd suggested she date other guys when he went to football camp for the summer. He had thought it would be best for them to grow on their own. If only he could give Logan of yore a swift kick in the pants.

"No," Logan said. He was not okay with that. "Don't you dare berate yourself. I'll take back my question before I allow that."

Logan knew what Lake did to herself wasn't up to him, but she had to know how opposed he was. If he could stop it, he would.

"Wait until you hear my answer to your question before you make that declaration. If my actions had only affected me they would have been foolish enough, but I have two wonderful, perfect little girls who are trusting me to provide everything. And I was so dumb."

Lake dropped her head again but Logan didn't dare lift it this time. Even if all of him longed to do so.

"I accepted everything Fred said at face value. I never pried. It felt like too much work. He hated it when I pried."

Anger for Fred welled within Logan. He knew it was probably wrong to be so angry at a dead man but he couldn't help it.

"He said that the practice was half his. And it would have been if he'd outlived his father's retirement. But he didn't," Lake began.

Logan watched and listened intently.

"Unbeknownst to me, he signed a contract agreeing that after he worked for ten years he'd get ten percent, and so on until Stanley retired," Lake continued. "But he didn't make it ten years."

Lake's voice broke over those words and Logan ached for her. Fred should have survived long beyond that.

"But his dad will surely honor his agreement to his son's family now that his son is gone," Logan couldn't help saying.

Lake let out a snort. "That's not really Stanley Hollowell's way."

"Meaning?" Logan asked.

"We get nothing. In his mind Fred earned nothing, so why should we take any of his hard-earned practice?"

"You've got to be kidding me," Logan muttered and just barely held in a few choice curse words. Stanley Hollowell had better pray that he never cross Logan's path. The man didn't deserve to be called a father-in-law, much less a grandfather. He was a weasel. Cheating his own daughter-in-law and granddaughters out of money. Who did that?

Logan was beginning to feel desperate for Lake. She had to have been counting on that money. It wasn't fair that now she had to worry about making ends meet while grieving her husband.

"What about insurance money?" he asked.

"Apparently Fred didn't take out a policy. I hadn't even thought to ask him if he had." Lake shook her head as if she was to blame.

"He didn't need you to remind him to care for his family in case of the worst," Logan pointed out.

"It's been a long time since you've known Fred." There was a sadness in Lake's voice that turned Logan's stomach.

What did that even mean? What had he done to her? Logan was now starting to feel grateful that his old friend was already dead. He wasn't sure what he'd be doing to Fred if he'd discovered all this while he was alive.

"He had a personal bank account," Lake revealed.

A personal bank account? Separate from Lake? Logan tried not to judge and failed. He knew plenty of people kept separate banking accounts. But something wasn't right about the way Fred did it. By the way Lake said it he was sure she didn't have one as well.

"We had a family account too. He paid us month to month so that we'd have all that we needed," Lake said, probably thinking she was defending her husband.

But really? She just got money month to month while Fred had his personal account to play with? That must be how he got the boat, cars, wave runners, etc.

"But he made some investments," Lake continued.

He made investments. He hadn't even considered her with those decisions? Logan knew Fred had asked Lake to stay home. Not to pursue a career after she'd gotten her degree because he wanted to go to med school. He remembered Fred sharing that with him. Logan had been annoyed with his friend, but had told himself it was only because he still had lingering feelings for Lake that he cared so much. So he'd taken himself out of the situation.

But years later Lake was enduring not only the loss of her husband but their only stream of income. Would it have mattered if Logan had said anything to Fred back then? He'd never know. And he'd always regret it.

"And they didn't pan out," Lake said matter-of-factly, as if that were the end. But Logan still had so many questions.

"He lost everything?" Logan asked incredulously. How could a man be so irresponsible when he had a family to care for?

Lake nodded, but then paused. "I'm not sure why I'm unloading all of this onto you. I'm sorry."

Logan shook his head vigorously. "No way. I asked. And my only frustrations stem from—" Logan broke off. He had no right to judge Lake's husband. Especially while she was mourning him.

"He wasn't always that way. But then money became so important. And he made all of it. I figured, what harm would it do to let him take care of it since it meant so much to him?" Lake dropped her eyes and bit her lip.

She was blaming herself. Again. This wasn't her fault! Logan had to get her to understand that if nothing else. Fred wasn't here to make things right. Maybe it wasn't Logan's place, but he couldn't bear to see Lake hurting over things that should bring her no guilt.

"He wouldn't have let it be any other way, Lake. You couldn't have changed his mind. Remember that old Mustang?" Logan asked.

Lake shook her head. Not because she didn't remember—of course she did—but because of the silly memories that car dredged up. None of them could forget Fred's old rust bucket.

"He wouldn't let any of us touch it. Even though I knew a heck of a lot more about cars than Fred ever did, he still wouldn't let me near it. I know how Fred got when things really mattered to him. There's nothing you could have done to change his mind about how he wanted to manage his money," Logan said, trying to feign a calmness he didn't feel. Fred deserved a punch to the gut. Hopefully it would have knocked some sense into him.

Lake pondered Logan's words, tipping her head thoughtfully. "I guess you're right," she said, the release in her voice loud and clear.

Logan swallowed a sigh. Thank goodness. At least he'd helped to relieve Lake of one burden.

"He's lucky you aren't angry with him for the position he's put you in now, having to work," Logan added, driving the nail into his point.

Lake let out a single sarcastic laugh. "That's definitely not the reason I'd be angry with him."

What did that mean? But Lake moved on before Logan could question it.

"If we weren't out of options and if I didn't have to work, I wouldn't have come home. And for that, I can only feel gratitude to Fred. The girls and I, we needed Blue Falls," Lake said carefully, her voice thoughtful.

Logan felt a wry smile grow on his lips. He guessed for that he could only feel grateful as well. Blue Falls was certainly lucky to have Lake and her daughters back in town. Logan felt luckiest of all—even if it would drive him crazy to have Lake so close but still out of his reach, he still couldn't feel anything but appreciative. Because Lake in his life, however she was in it, was better than no Lake at all. Two decades of experience without her had taught him as much.

Ten

FRIDAY HAD BEEN an odd and eventful first day working for the Ashfords, so as Lake parked the decade-old minivan—she'd purchased it after trading in her brand new state-of-the-art SUV to get a little extra cash for the move—she wondered what today would bring. Surely it would be calmer, right?

"Good Monday morning, Lake," Morgan greeted exuberantly as Lake entered the kitchen where Morgan was whipping a huge bowl of eggs.

Breakfast was long over on the ranch, but from her childhood experience Lake knew that many of the boys, the Ashford sons and the ranch hands, tended to take a break around ten. Morgan had warned her that they still had their Monday tradition of second breakfast during the break. It would be a fast and furious meal since everyone on the ranch worked long and hard, keeping breaks short. They needed to have all the food prepared well before ten so that as the boys came in they could grab their food, eat like the wind, and get back to work.

"Do you want me to start on some bacon and sausage?" Lake asked as she surveyed the meal. Holland was mixing biscuit dough, a streak of flour on one cheek. So with eggs and biscuits, breakfast meat seemed like the logical choice.

"That would be fantastic. And I wanted to give you a heads up: I hope you don't mind, but I've invited Madison to come and hang out with us whenever she'd like. She said she'd be coming by around ten this morning. I hope that won't be awkward . . . " Morgan's voice trailed off.

Lake stopped her perusal of the fridge and turned to face Mama Ashford.

"Mama Ashford, if this is what you want, I support you one hundred percent. Don't let the jeans and plaid button-up fool you; I am your biggest cheerleader," Lake said.

"You are a blessing, Lake Hollowell. And don't you forget it," Mama Ashford proclaimed as the sizzle of scrambled eggs hitting the hot pan reached Lake's ears.

"What she said," Holland echoed with a wide grin.

Lake turned back to the fridge, trying to shake off the uncomfortable feeling of being called Lake Hollowell. She shouldn't feel that way. It had been her name for the past fifteen years, after all, but after everything that had happened with Fred and then returning home where she'd always been Lake Johnson, it had almost stung her. Almost as if it felt all wrong. But that was silly. It was her name. The name she shared with her children.

But she didn't like the way it tied her to Fred. Not while her feelings for the man were still so muddled.

Lake pulled out a few packages of both bacon and sausages—did she mention these men could eat? Giving herself a little shake, she pushed all thoughts of her last name aside. It was her name. Nothing more, nothing less.

Just as Holland was pulling the biscuits out of the oven and Lake was piling the final pieces of meat on a platter, the back door opened and the sound of boots filled the kitchen.

"It's time," Holland sang as the men greeted Mama Ashford and eagerly began loading their plates.

Lake noticed one of the hands paying particular attention to Holland. He seemed to be much more interested in her than in the meal offerings.

"Fill your plate and grab a seat." Logan pushed the hand, not too gently, down the line of food.

Logan sent Holland a warning glare and she just shrugged her shoulders. It was easy to see the poor hand's attraction was unrequited after Holland's reaction, but Logan didn't seem worried for him, just relieved that his sister didn't seem to care.

"Good to see you back again, Lake," Austin drawled as he paused with his full plate just in front of where Lake stood waiting to take empty plates to the sink.

"Same," Lake said, unsure of how to answer. Austin's tone was bordering on flirty and she would be stupid if she wasn't at least cautious.

"Move along," Logan said to Austin, shoving his brother from behind.

Austin stumbled forward before turning to glower at Logan. "What's your problem?" he demanded.

"No problem, you're just slowing the line down."

"Then go around me." Austin gestured to show how easy it would have been.

"Just go sit down," Logan commanded.

"And if I don't?" Austin challenged, stepping forward so that he was now in Logan's face.

"Both of you, sit," Morgan ordered as she moved between the brothers, waving a spatula.

After one last glare for each other, Austin and Logan separated to find seats at the long table.

"Is second breakfast always this eventful?" Lake whispered to Holland.

Holland seemed to study Lake before answering. "Never," she finally responded before taking Jackson's and Land's empty plates and setting them in the sink.

And just like that second breakfast was already over.

Lake was busy for the next hour or so, washing not only the dishes and the cookery but also sweeping and mopping the floors. The men's boots had tracked in all kinds of debris. And Lake's girls had eaten more neatly when they were toddlers than this bunch.

Mama Ashford had just laughed when she had made the comparison, joking that Lake's daughters probably had had better manners as toddlers as well.

But soon the kitchen was sparkling clean and the three women were just sitting down for a much-deserved rest at the dining room table when Madison entered, Blue trailing behind her. He'd barked when he heard her knock, but as soon as he saw her at the door, he seemed to acknowledge her as family. Blue was already an Ashford through and through.

"Sorry I'm so late. I know ranch life begins much earlier in the day, but I was getting stuff figured out with the DNA tests. I had to go ask Logan to swab with their specific swab, anyway . . . you all don't care about that." Madison shifted on her feet where she still stood near the doorway.

"We love to hear anything and everything about your life," Morgan said with a genuine smile.

Lake had worried that talk of the DNA test would stress Morgan again but she seemed to be doing great. Almost as if she'd come to some sort of conclusion about who Madison's birth father was or maybe just made her peace with everything. Lake guessed Morgan had had the weekend to digest Madison's last visit and had come to terms with the situation.

"Well, I do like to talk. You may regret that invitation soon," Madison joked.

The women all laughed.

"Please have a seat." Morgan offered the open seat beside her. "We just finished cleaning up and decided to take a quick—or maybe not so quick—break."

Madison took the seat. "I knew I should have been here earlier. It's just like me to miss all the work. I promise I'm not lazy. Just lucky with my timing."

The women laughed again and Lake couldn't help but think Madison fit right in, now that she was comfortable here. She had that same self-deprecating humor as many of the Ashfords. She joked enough to make you laugh but never feel sorry for her. It was an art.

"Do you want something to drink?" Morgan offered, leaning forward in her seat as though she was about to stand, but Lake quickly jumped to her feet instead.

"I can get them," Lake said.

Morgan smiled gratefully at Lake. "If you wouldn't mind. My poor back is screaming."

Lake could only imagine what the years of this kind of labor had done to Morgan's body, although she appeared years younger than her fifty-five.

"I'll take a glass of water," Morgan said.

"Coming right up," Lake replied, looking to Holland and Madison.

"Water sounds great," Holland added.

Madison nodded.

Lake left the table and gathered four glasses from the cabinets and a pitcher of ice water from the fridge.

"What were you cleaning up after?" Madison asked while Lake was in the kitchen.

"Second breakfast. We serve it every Monday. It started as a tradition when my dad watched those ring movies," Holland stated.

Lake shot a quick glance toward her young friend. During the last sentence her voice had gone quieter. Lake couldn't tell if she was worried about bringing up Mitchell in front of Morgan and Madison or just missing her dad.

From the way Holland's eyes bounced between the other

women at the table Lake was going to go with her former assumption. Although she guessed it could have been both.

"I've never understood those movies," Madison said, choosing a safe subject as she picked up on the new tension in the room.

"Me neither!" Holland exclaimed. "But the rest of the family loves them."

Morgan spoke up, a soft smile on her lips. "I didn't get them until your dad made me watch them all with him. I'm still not sure how I feel about them, but I know I love him. Love makes us do silly things sometimes."

Lake returned to the table, setting down the stacked glasses and the pitcher. Deftly she filled the cups and passed one to each woman.

"I like hearing you all talk about him," Madison said tentatively as if she was worried she was overstepping.

"We need to do it more," Morgan said, sharing a glance with Holland.

Holland nodded. "It doesn't hurt as much as it once did. But sometimes I think that's worse than when it hurt. I'm scared that the fact that I'm not hurting as much means I'm missing him less."

Madison pursed her lips. Morgan looked down at the table.

"Hurt and missing someone don't necessarily go hand in hand." Lake entered the conversation. She wasn't sure it was her place but Holland shouldn't feel guilt. "Pain from losing someone is supposed to go away with time. It's human nature, thankfully. And the hole they left in our lives might feel a little smaller. But that does nothing to diminish what we felt for them. What we still feel for them."

Holland shot Lake a relieved glance as if those words were exactly what she'd needed to hear.

"I know you're going through it firsthand right now," Morgan said as she patted Lake's hand.

Lake wasn't sure what to say. She couldn't tell them how little she missed Fred at that moment. That anger was too present to feel much else. So she decided it was better to say nothing.

"Did you lose a parent as well?" Madison asked. Lake had forgotten Madison wouldn't know her backstory. Why should she?

"My husband," Lake said, trying to keep her voice even.

"Oh. I'm so sorry. I had no idea," Madison exclaimed and Lake took immediate pity on the poor girl.

"It's fine. I'm coping," she said honestly. That's exactly what she was doing.

"She's coping very well," Mama Ashford was quick to point out.

"Thanks," Lake acknowledged but was ready to move the conversation along. "So those movies started second breakfast?" she asked, returning the conversation to where it had been.

Holland nodded. "Dad loved the idea, but Mom said she could only handle it once a week. So Monday second breakfast was born."

Morgan smiled. "Mitchell loved to start the week this way. Said it boosted morale."

"It would. I could totally use second breakfast every Monday," Madison said as she patted her flat stomach.

"It is nice," Holland agreed. The women hadn't eaten this time, but only because they'd done their fair share of sampling while cooking.

"Although this morning's second breakfast was much more eventful than most," Holland added.

"Yeah, Logan was pretty unhappy with the way that ranch hand was eyeing you," Lake said.

"Oh, Ben is harmless and Logan knows that. No, I was talking about the brawl that almost happened between my brothers. Why do you suppose Logan was so annoyed when Austin flirted with you?" She gave Lake a saucy grin.

"Holland," Morgan warned and Lake could understand why.

To most it would appear that Lake was still grieving her husband. And maybe she was, somewhere under all of the anger. But she had to admit that part of her was curious.

"They don't always fight like that?" Lake asked.

"Logan? Never." Holland shook her head vehemently.

Lake didn't appreciate the way her stomach flipped. Morgan was right. She shouldn't even be considering another man so soon after the death of her husband. And Lake would have never thought that she could or would, until Fred had been unfaithful.

After some thought this past weekend, Lake had realized she'd romanticized the last four months of their marriage after Fred had apologized. As Lake had recalled those days, she realized that even then things hadn't been great between the two of them. She'd considered divorce or at least separation weekly. Fred had been better in those months than during his affair, but he'd never been as attentive, warm, or caring as when they were dating and first married. Lake had told herself no one could stay in the honeymoon stage, but it was more than that. Fred had checked out sometime before his affair. And even when Lake threatened to leave he could never find his way all the way back into their marriage. Lake could feel that he had one foot out the door.

But no matter her feelings for Fred, it was still too soon. Lake knew she couldn't squash what she felt growing within her for Logan, but she could control it. Keep others from seeing it. Finish processing the remains of her marriage first.

What was strangest to Lake was that even at her lowest, when she'd first found out about Fred, she couldn't fathom looking at another man. Yet now, a mere month after his death she was battling what she was feeling for Logan. Didn't that prove that Lake wasn't being fickle or jumping at the first man to come along? That what she felt for Logan was true?

Well, if her feelings were genuine they would last until the time when society, her girls, and her conscience deemed it okay to let out what she was feeling. If Logan reciprocated what she felt. Would he reciprocate?

"Those were worries for another day. "I'd better get to my classes. I have a test tomorrow that I haven't started studying for," Holland said as she stood.

"Holland," her mother reprimanded. Mama Ashford took school seriously.

Holland grinned unrepentantly. "It was good to see you again, Madison. And Lake, try to refrain from making my brothers fight over you."

"Oh Heavens, Holland," Morgan murmured.

Holland just laughed as she left the room.

The rest of the day was relatively uneventful, though very pleasant. Lake, Madison, and Morgan decorated the entire house for Christmas.

"It's later than I usually put them up so let's make quick work of it," Morgan had told them.

And they did. They started with garland and lights on the stair rail and ended with the ten-foot tree that graced the front room.

Lake found she loved working alongside Madison as much as Morgan and Holland. The girl was easy to talk to and even easier to like. And it seemed to Lake that Morgan liked Madison as much or even more than Lake did.

"Be sure to steer clear of that doorway," Madison directed Lake as Morgan stood on a chair to hang a bunch of mistletoe.

"Will do," Lake agreed, taking a step closer to Morgan just in case. She didn't like seeing Mama Ashford up in the air like that. Even Blue seemed to be standing by in case anything went wrong.

Madison had tried to take the job—she didn't want Mama Ashford balancing precariously on a kitchen chair—but Morgan had insisted. She'd put up this exact mistletoe for the last thirty years, and she wasn't about to stop this year.

"Perfect," Morgan said as she got off of the chair and surveyed her work with satisfaction.

"I agree." Madison glanced around the kitchen at the garland and other Christmas décor that covered almost every surface. It looked like Santa's elves had thrown up in the room and Lake absolutely loved it.

"Well, you two have been here long enough," Morgan said as she ushered Madison toward the front door. "And we don't even pay you to be here."

"You've welcomed me like family. Family doesn't pay family for help," Madison said with a grin.

"But you aren't working at all, are you?" Morgan asked and then seemed to instantly realize she was prying. "I'm sorry, I didn't mean to . . . "

"I love that you asked that question. Thank you for caring, Mama Ashford." Madison finally tried the nickname Morgan had urged her to use. It was what all of the Ashford kids' friends, their hands, and pretty much half the town called Morgan. But Madison had been hesitant.

Lake couldn't help but smile for both of her friends.

"My mom left me enough that I'll be just fine for some years to come," Madison said. "She wasn't rich but between what she'd saved, her insurance money, and the inheritance her parents left her that she'd never touched, I've been blessed."

Lake tried to ignore the clenching of her gut reminding her that her husband hadn't taken the same assurances to care for her. Granted, he was taken violently and quickly. He'd had no idea his life would be cut short and maybe Madison's mother had had time to plan. But still, when you loved someone, didn't you do those things, just in case?

Lake really didn't want to make things about money. Honestly, if Fred had acted like he'd cared for her the money wouldn't matter at all, but the money or lack of it now just reminded Lake of how little her husband had actually considered her, her feelings, and her welfare. And even if he hadn't considered her, he should have at least looked out for his children. But he hadn't.

Frustration bubbled within her.

"I'd love to come by again tomorrow if you don't mind?" Madison asked Morgan, her timidity showing just how nervous she was. This was Madison stepping out onto the ledge. Lake sure hoped Morgan would catch her.

"Tomorrow and the next day and the next. In fact, if you'd like to stay here, we'd love to have you," Morgan offered.

Lake should have known Morgan wouldn't just offer a hand. She'd offered all she had.

"Thank you. Truly. I think I should stay at the B&B for now, but I will be here tomorrow to lend a hand with whatever you need. There isn't any more decorating, is there?"

Madison could see not only the kitchen but the front room and the stairs from her spot by the door. Every inch was decorated, including the front doors that each boasted a giant wreath.

"Nope. You all worked a miracle getting it done in one day. It took me four to do it on my own last year," Morgan stated.

"Okay, then, see you tomorrow," Madison said with a wave and a grin.

"See you," Morgan responded and Lake waved as well.

"I like her," Morgan said as soon as Madison was out the door.

"I do too," Lake said, her eyes trained on Morgan for signs of fatigue or grief.

Although Morgan had been as gracious the last time Madison was here, Lake had seen her fall apart after Madison left last time. Today Madison had been here much longer. Surely that had worn on Morgan.

"Stop watching me like a mother hen," Morgan admonished and Lake quickly looked up at the ceiling, pretending to check on a garland.

Smooth.

Morgan chuckled. "I'm in a better place. I was so hurt when we were blindsided by Madison's existence, but this past weekend gave me some good time to think. I realized I trust my

Mitchell. He kept a secret but he isn't the father of that girl. I know it."

Lake blinked, pushing the tears away. She wished she could be half as sure of Fred. But it was because of the husband Fred had been that she couldn't trust him after death. And it wasn't just the affair. Fred had lied to her frequently, anytime it was convenient for getting his way. He had shown time and time again that he would rather Lake suffer than allow anything to harm himself. And he had been in the car with that woman. It was too easy to imagine that he'd missed Sachia and hadn't been willing to tell Lake the truth. He wouldn't have wanted to deal with a messy divorce. He wanted to have his cake and eat it too. Lake wanted to rage at the man but he was dead.

She squeezed her eyes shut tightly before opening them again.

"I believe it as well," she finally said. This wasn't about her. Morgan's realization was huge. "I didn't know Mitchell as well as I would have liked, but he was the kind of man who would have always put his family first."

Morgan nodded before moving to put an arm around Lake, allowing her to rest her head on Morgan's shoulder. "You'll find that man one day too," she said softly.

Lake jumped, her head lifting. She couldn't know. Had Holland told her?

"I don't know everything. I do know that you are hurting now, but not in the way one would expect. I see the anger in your eyes when we talk about Fred. Whatever you are feeling, it's okay. Feel those things. Work through them. Remind yourself that you deserve the sun, the moon, and the stars," Morgan added, putting Lake at ease.

Morgan was right. There was no perfect way to deal with the mess Fred had left behind. Lake was doing her best, at least most of the time. And she would continue to do so. It didn't matter what others thought of her. If her actions were what she and her girls needed, it would be enough. It would be right.

Morgan walked away with Blue, leaving Lake in the silent kitchen for a few moments alone. Morgan always knew just what to do. Would Lake ever be that wise?

Lake was sick of thinking about Fred so she turned her thoughts to Christmas. Her girls had already been making their lists. Lake wasn't sure how she was going to manage them, considering she was making nowhere near the amount Fred had. And the girls wouldn't understand that even Santa had taken a pay cut. She had to at least get the biggest gifts. Somehow, someway.

Last Christmas hadn't been the greatest. Looking back, Lake realized that Fred had been in the middle of his affair. He was working late nights—or at least that's what he had said—but put extra money into the family account and told Lake to buy whatever she and the girls wanted for Christmas. Fred had always been quick to throw money at any problem. Just like Stanley.

Fred had even come home late on Christmas Eve. Lake had swallowed her disappointment during their family traditions of reading the Polar Express and the story of Jesus's birth from Luke. The traditions were important to her, but Fred had missed them with the barest of apologies. She'd done her best to smile and laugh with her girls but after they were in bed she'd sobbed her way through hours of wrapping presents.

He'd had some excuse. A good one, Lake was sure. They were always good ones and Lake had quickly forgiven him because she didn't want contention in the house on Christmas. But she should have expected more from Fred. The sadness from that night was long gone, replaced with fury. How could he have cared so little for them that he would have missed Christmas Eve?! Yet a couple of months later as he begged for forgiveness, not only had he seemed to forget what he had done, but so had Lake.

She blinked her eyes and remembered where she was. The rage that had filled her moments before melted away when the reality hit afresh that the target of her anger was no longer alive.

Even so, she realized that she should reminisce in her own home or in the car. She needed to get out of there before the kitchen filled with Ashfords.

She started for the front door but remembered she'd parked behind the house today. Pivoting, Lake headed for the back door but just as she was about to walk through the mistletoe-infested doorway to the mudroom, she heard the telltale sound of cowboy boots on the back porch.

Sure enough, the back door flew open and in no time at all Logan was there, hat in his hands, pausing when he saw her standing just beyond that doorway.

Were it not for her mistake, Lake would be there as well. In that doorway. Under that mistletoe.

She let out a breath she hadn't realized she'd been holding.

"On your way out?" Logan asked.

There was something about his voice that drew Lake in. Maybe it was the memories. Or maybe it was knowing the honest man he was.

Oh help her, she needed to stop.

Lake finally nodded. How long had she been lost in her thoughts?

"Looks like you guys did some major work today," Logan said, his eyes sweeping across the kitchen.

Lake nodded again. Had she been rendered mute? She needed to say something.

"It's cute, right?" she asked, grimacing inwardly at the lameness of her words. Her brain had apparently quit for the day.

"I'd say better than cute," Logan replied. This time his eyes were focused on Lake.

Lake felt her chest lift with her breath. She felt tight and warm, yet happier than she had in a very long time.

Logan moved to the side, still under the mistletoe but giving her enough room to join him. She knew that wasn't what he was offering. He was letting her leave the house so she could go home. He hadn't yet noticed the mistletoe.

But if he did, would he want to use it? Lake's treacherous heart asked.

He'd been talking about her, hadn't he? She was better than cute. But maybe he'd been flirting in the same lighthearted, noncommittal way Memphis and Austin had.

And she was being foolish. She was in no position to kiss a man. The fact that she'd even considered it showed just how off her rocker Logan made her feel.

Lake looked up so Logan did the same, his eyes widening in realization.

"Oh," he said immediately, stepping as far from the doorway and mistletoe as one giant Logan step could take him.

Well, there was her answer. If he'd known about the mistletoe he would have run. No kissing for Lake and Logan. As it should be.

He had just offered her a compliment and then been a gentleman, letting her pass so she could go home. No unrequited feelings there.

"Have a great evening," Logan said to her back as Lake walked through the now empty doorway and opened the back door.

"Same to you," Lake replied but didn't allow herself another look.

If tonight had taught her anything it was that she needed to take a step away from Logan Ashford. She was feeling too much in way too short of a time. And she was still completely entangled in the web that Fred had woven. She first needed to free herself and her children. To figure out what was best for them. Maybe then she'd be free to have feelings for a man.

Preferably a man who reciprocated them. So it looked like that man wouldn't be Logan.

Eleven

"I NEEDED THIS," Lottie sighed as she took an enormous swig of her diet coke. "I'm going to pay for it later when I can't fall asleep until two am but it is so worth it."

She leaned back into her side of the booth and shot Lake a smile.

"Won't you already be up at two to feed your baby?" Lake asked.

"Don't remind me," Lottie groaned. "Do you remember the days when Friday used to be the start of everything good? Now Friday is just another day of the week. I know I shouldn't be complaining. I am so lucky to be at home with my kiddos. It is literally what I've dreamed of . . ."

"But life is always reality, even when we're living our dreams. There are downsides to every reality and we are allowed to be frustrated with them," Lake completed for her.

Lottie lowered her eyes. "I can't believe I've become that friend. The one who complains while the other one actually has things to complain about and yet doesn't get a word in because I am being ridiculous."

Lake laughed. "That is silly, Lottie. Yes, you've taken like seven seconds to let me know that two am feedings suck. Guess what? They really do suck."

Lottie joined Lake in her laughter. "Have I mentioned how glad I am to have you home?"

Lake glanced around the dining area in Chicken and More, one of her favorite childhood restaurants, taking in the red booths and familiar faces. She and Lottie had already ordered steak fried chicken, the restaurant's specialty, and Lake was eagerly anticipating the taste of her old favorite comfort food. While she'd gotten a few unwelcome stares when she'd walked in, she knew her abrupt return and Fred's tragic death were the talk of the town and rumors were probably swirling. For the most part she'd received smiles of encouragement and she was getting to sit and talk with an old friend.

"I'm glad I came back too," Lake said truthfully.

She was, although circumstances weren't all cupcakes and roses. After her near run-in with Logan under the mistletoe and her feelings coming to a head, Lake had spent all week avoiding the eldest Ashford. It hadn't been too difficult, making Lake wonder if Logan was avoiding her as well. It was probably for the best, even though the idea stung. It was one thing for her to avoid Logan because she felt too much for him, but it was another for him to avoid her because he had picked up on her feelings. Because why else would he avoid her?

"So make me feel better and talk about you for the next seven to ten seconds," Lottie joked.

Lake laughed. "I'll try. My life is pretty boring right now."

Lottie narrowed her eyes.

"I'm serious. The girls are going to school, my parents are being amazing, Grace is being Grace."

"And you're grieving the loss of your husband," Lottie added in a hushed tone.

"Yeah, that too," Lake agreed, glancing away. She wasn't ready to tell Lottie more. She totally trusted her nearly lifelong friend but it had been hard enough to tell Holland and Grace the whole truth, and she wasn't ready to do it again. Especially not in such a public place.

"But you seem to be managing that pretty well," Lottie added.

If only she knew. But instead Lake nodded in agreement. And it wasn't a complete lie. In the ways Lottie would expect Lake to mourn she was doing well. She missed having a father for her children and she was mostly sorry that Fred was gone. But she had a feeling that even if Fred were still on this earth, they'd be going through a divorce right now. And the frustration and rage Lake felt when she considered that had her nowhere near pretty well.

"I did notice you left a huge portion of your current life out though," Lottie whispered as she leaned into the table.

Had Lake?

"Your job. Working with the Ashfords. How is that going?" Lottie asked.

Lake tried to shutter her face, but she'd always been one to wear her emotions.

"What?" Lottie asked, her forehead creasing as she noted the distress on Lake's face.

Lake shrugged. "It's a wonderful job."

"That sounded nearly robotic," Lottie said with a raised eyebrow.

"It is." Lake's voice nearly screeched.

"Lake!"

She knew she was making it all worse but Lottie kept pressing.

"Things are a little complicated. Can we just leave it at that?" Lake asked, her voice finally sounding almost normal.

Lottie nodded but Lake could tell she'd want an explanation soon.

"Speaking of complications . . . " Lottie looked over Lake's shoulder, causing Lake to turn and see what Lottie was talking about.

Just inside the door stood Logan Ashford.

"You've got to be kidding me," Lake muttered as she shrank down into her seat to hide.

"I had a feeling he was the biggest complication of all. Just know, Lake. I am not judging. But you and Logan would make some beautiful babies," Lottie whispered.

"Lottie!" It was now Lake's turn to exclaim. She clapped a hand over her mouth, hoping Logan hadn't heard her.

"You didn't tell me much about Fred, but I know things weren't what they seemed. If you're ready to move on, those who love you won't judge you," Lottie continued.

But that was just it. Lake wasn't ready to move on, was she? Even if she didn't feel badly about Fred, he'd broken her heart enough times that he didn't deserve her loyalty. But it wouldn't be fair to her girls and her parents, who were still working through their emotions and had no idea about Fred's failings. And she was still so angry with Fred. Surely she couldn't start a healthy new relationship before she'd processed that. Not to mention the tiny tidbit that Logan didn't return Lake's feelings.

"Here you go," said Sally, the owner of Chicken and More, as she placed plates heaped with chicken and mashed potatoes in front of the two friends.

"Oh, it smells delicious!" Lottie exclaimed and Lake just nodded because she heard Logan's voice and dang it, she was doing her best to listen to every word.

"We don't have a booth open," Lake heard Jeffrey, Sally's husband and the co-owner of the place, say to Logan. "But you can wait a few minutes for one or we have space at the counter."

"Enjoy," Sally said as she left their table and Lake couldn't help her sigh of relief. Now nothing would keep her from eavesdropping on Logan.

For a woman intent on avoiding him, she wasn't doing so well now.

Lake noticed that Lottie had picked up her fork but held it suspended in midair. "Uh-oh."

"What does *uh-oh* mean?" Lake whispered frantically.

"See for yourself." Lottie nodded in Logan's direction as she dug into her meal.

How could she eat at a time like this? When she'd just said 'uh-oh' in association with Logan?

Lake slowly turned and cautiously peeked her head around the edge of the booth.

Logan had taken one of the chairs in the waiting area, but making a beeline for him was Avery Forrester.

"Did you know they dated?" Lottie asked.

Lake swung her head toward Lottie so abruptly she felt a little dizzy.

"What?" she asked, rubbing her neck.

"Some years back. But word on the street is he broke her heart and she's willing to do anything to win him back," Lottie revealed.

"Hi, Logan." Avery's nasal voice was impossible to miss even if Lake wanted to. But she had no desire to miss a single word of this conversation.

"Evening, Avery," Logan replied.

Even without seeing anything Lake could imagine the slight tip of his hat that Logan would have offered to Avery. What was it about a man in a cowboy hat that could make a woman's knees go wobbly?

"I heard you were looking for a booth. I happen to have one if you want to join me? We could talk about the land deal?" Avery asked hopefully.

"Was she in a booth by herself?" Lake whispered to Lottie.

Lottie chuckled as she shook her head. "I saw her usher out Paul Wilkins, one of Leo's sheriffs, before she hurried over to

Logan. Poor Paul had to take his food to one of the open counter seats."

Lake went back to her position of spying. She was no longer even attempting to keep what she was doing from Lottie. Thank heavens the booths were pretty private, so unless someone made the effort they wouldn't see Lake's asinine attempt at being covert.

"Is she with Paul?" Lake had to ask. Would Avery be that brazen to her boyfriend?

"They've been off and on for the past couple years. Honestly, poor Paul doesn't even seem bothered. I bet Avery hasn't been able to hold back that he's her second choice."

Poor Paul was right. Granted, he was making the choice to stay with Avery, so Lake guessed she shouldn't feel too badly.

From her position Lake could now see Paul's back at the counter, Avery standing in front of Logan, and Logan's broad shoulders. It was hard to make out his face since he had his hat on.

"Aren't you working on the deal with Jackson?" Logan asked.

Lake didn't need to see Logan's face to know that was a brush off. Logan wanted to eat with Avery about as much as he had wanted to get caught beneath the mistletoe with Lake.

"But it concerns you as well, right?" Avery pressed, her voice somehow nasal and shrill at the same time.

Although considering Lake had been speaking just as weirdly a few moments before, she shouldn't judge.

"It does. But I'm here for a relaxing meal. I'd rather not talk business tonight," Logan said slowly, as if considering each word. Being careful not to say the wrong thing.

"Are you going to eat that?" Lottie asked Lake's back.

Lake kept her eyes fixed on the unfolding drama, waving a hand behind herself to tell Lottie that everything on her plate was up for grabs. She couldn't care less about dinner with a show like this one.

"I'm happy discussing pleasurable things as well," Avery remarked.

Lake turned to Lottie to share a silent gasp.

"Oh wow," Lottie said, proving she'd heard Avery's words as well.

Lake quickly twisted back to Logan and Avery and noticed Logan stretch his neck in the direction of where Jeffrey should be, surely wondering if a booth had opened yet.

"You need to save him," Lottie said matter-of-factly.

"What?" Lake whispered, whipping back to her friend and sitting the way one should in a booth.

"He obviously doesn't want to get stuck with Avery. Jeffrey isn't out there to offer the counter seat again. He *needs* you, Lake."

Lake didn't like the way Lottie had emphasized 'need.' It was almost the same way Avery had said 'pleasurable.'

Ew.

"Either you go or I will. I don't have a crush on the man but even I wouldn't subject him to the dinner Avery is offering," Lottie replied. "And if I go to him and he sees you here, his friend, the one who should have saved him . . . "

Lake understood a threat when she heard one.

"I thought you were *my* friend," Lake ground out.

"That's the reason I'm doing this," Lottie said with a wink. It reminded Lake of Logan's wink and how it had flipped her stomach even when it hadn't been directed at her. And then when he had sent one her way, whoo-wee . . .

"You would want him to do this for you. Your feelings aside." Lottie finally made an argument Lake couldn't disagree with.

"It's just right there, Logan," Avery spoke again, a clang of victory entering her voice.

Lake found herself standing, her feet guiding her to the waiting area of their own accord. They knew what they were doing was the right thing.

"Finally!" Lake said as she stopped in front of Logan, just to the right side of Avery.

"Finally?" Avery asked.

Logan nodded, catching on much more quickly than Lake would have.

"I didn't realize you were already here. I was waiting to get a booth for all of us," Logan said to Lake as he hastily stood, the shadow from his hat moving so that Lake could see the gratitude written all over his face.

"Lottie's already digging into her meal. It isn't like you to be so late," Lake said before recognizing her error.

"Why would Logan be trying to get a booth for all of you if he was so late?" Avery asked suspiciously, her eyes darting back and forth between them in displeasure.

Avery was a lot of things, but dumb wasn't one of them. Lake knew it would take some fast talking to get them out of this mess. So she was going to leave the talking to Logan.

"I'm not sure. Logan?" she asked as she bit back a smile. She'd thought this was going to be uncomfortable but she found she was actually having fun.

"I lost track of time," Logan offered. It sounded more like a question.

"So you had no idea what time it was? Even though you were supposed to meet people at a specific time?" Avery asked, skepticism lacing her every word.

"Yup," was all Logan said. Lake watched him bite down on his lip.

"And Lake, you had to have heard Logan earlier. Why did it take you so long to come over? Or Logan, why didn't you take a mosey on down the aisles of booths to check for Lottie and Lake?"

"All good questions," Lake heard herself saying. Seriously? All good questions?

"I was deep in discussion with Lottie," Lake added almost too excitedly. But it was an answer to Avery's question. Almost a decent one.

"And I'm tired," Logan replied.

Lake let out a snort but covered it with a cough.

"Too tired to walk about twenty steps?" Avery asked.

"Hey, weren't you here with Paul? Why is he at the counter now?" Lake wasn't sure where that last burst of inspiration came from, but turning the tables on Avery felt genius.

"Um," Avery said.

Lake put a hand on her hip, waiting for an answer. Logan pulled off his hat and held it in his hands. Lake had always wondered how his waves could stay so bouncy even after being under a hat all day.

She realized she was gazing longingly up at Logan. *Focus.*

Thankfully Avery was too worried about coming up with an answer to notice Lake's most recent mistake.

"We got into a fight," Avery finally said.

"Maybe you should make up with him," Logan offered.

Avery frowned.

"See you later," Lake blurted and grabbed Logan's hand, tugging him toward her booth. They had to move quickly before their story fell apart any more.

She noticed her heart rate had increased but it wasn't until she let him scoot into the booth ahead of her and let go of his hand that she'd realized what she'd done. She'd held Logan's hand. After avoiding him all week she'd undone it with a single gesture. But she couldn't bring herself to regret it. His warm, callused hand had gripped Lake's with a certainty that made her feel comforted and thrilled.

"Thanks for finally showing up, Logan," Lottie said with a Cheshire grin as Lake settled into the booth.

The seat had always felt so wide to Lake before but suddenly there wasn't enough room. If Lake shifted this way her shoulder brushed against Logan's, that way their thighs just barely touched.

Was it suddenly way too hot in here?

"Here you go, Logan," Sally had come up to their table with a glass of iced tea and a plate of the special. "That was quite the show you two put on out there." Sally chuckled before walking back to the kitchen.

"I agree," Lottie added.

"Was everyone watching?" Lake asked, suddenly self-conscious. Between that and the fact that she couldn't stop touching Logan, her cheeks were on fire.

"Just everyone in the restaurant," Lottie said unhelpfully.

But Logan let out a belly laugh and suddenly it didn't seem like such a big deal. Lake felt her cheeks cool but they quickly warmed again as Logan neared her, his lips a mere breath from her ear.

What the heck was he doing? Did he want her to spontaneously combust?

"Am I supposed to swoon and call you my hero now?" Logan whispered into Lake's ear. She worked hard to ignore Lottie pumping her eyebrows from across the table.

"I'd settle for the promise of your firstborn child," Lake replied and then nearly choked.

What was she doing? She was totally flirting. The opposite of avoiding Logan. But she was pretty sure he had started it.

"I think that can be arranged," he said as he somehow moved even closer. Lake fought the urge to close her eyes and focus on feeling the ghost of his lips on her earlobe. She could imagine him moving from there down the soft skin of her neck.

Lake blinked frantically and sat up straight.

"Great, awesome," she chattered as she scooted so far to the edge of the booth that half of her butt was off the seat. But that was safer than where she had been. The fall from there would have hurt so much more.

Twelve

LAKE CAME RUNNING into the old ranch house, her hair in a giant messy bun on top of her cute head with wispies falling every which way. She wore leggings instead of her typical jeans and a puffer coat over a giant t-shirt.

"I'm so sorry I'm late, I tried to call and . . . " Lake looked from Morgan to Holland and then finally at Logan.

Logan had to admit the only reason he was still at the old ranch house was because he'd hoped to see Lake. Things had been awkward between them last week but then the dinner had happened and he . . . well, he didn't want to give Lake the opportunity to keep on avoiding him. He figured he'd see her this morning, acknowledge her head on, and then there would be no point in her trying to avoid him later. He understood that there were many flaws in his logic but that had been his plan, for better or worse.

He understood why Lake was avoiding him. Heck, he probably would have avoided Lake last week as well if she hadn't decided to do it first. There was a tension between them that he was pretty sure she felt as well. Something was pulling them together and it felt wrong. Her husband had just died. He'd been Logan's friend . . . years ago, but still. It was wrong to move in on his friend's wife, well, probably ever. But Logan was going to have to break that rule with Lake. He couldn't stay away from her forever. She was too danged incredible. But he could give it time, give her the time she needed.

But avoidance didn't seem the right way to give time. She worked with their family, and he wanted to be her friend. He was sure that during this time she needed all the friends she could get. So he was here. At the old ranch house, when he should have been in the stable, out in one of the pastures, or at least at the office. By the smug, knowing looks his sister and mother had sent his way when he'd shown up they knew it as well. Heck, even Lake probably knew he shouldn't be there. But at the moment she seemed too harried to care.

"Not a problem, Dear. We were just finishing up some rolls for the church's bake sale tomorrow and then I thought we'd go through some of Mitchell's things," Morgan said.

The three other heads in the room snapped toward Logan's mom. Had she just said . . . ? She'd been avoiding that job for over a year now, but she was finally ready? And wanted to do it with Lake?

Logan glanced at Lake and saw the awe on her face. She knew what she'd been entrusted with as well.

"That sounds amazing. I just have a slight—"

"Mom!" a young voice called from just outside the front door.

Blue sprang to his feet and began barking at the sound of an unknown voice. Morgan hushed him as Lake spoke over the chaos.

"Amelie, I asked you to stay in the car while I spoke to Mama Ashford," she admonished.

"Is that one of your girls?" Morgan asked.

Lake nodded, a grimace on her face.

"They're both out there. Delia had a field trip to the aquarium but suddenly decided this morning she is deathly afraid of octopus...es? Octopi? What is the plural for octopus, anyway?" Lake sounded so distressed Logan felt the need to immediately pipe up.

"Either works, I'm pretty sure," he offered.

Lake let out a sigh of relief as she nodded in Logan's direction.

"I told Delia that there probably aren't even any of those eight-legged creatures at the aquarium. I had no idea but I figured I'd shoot her teacher a text to quickly usher her past the exhibit if there was one. But Delia was adamant that there were and then when Amelie heard her sister was staying home from school she didn't want to go either." All relief had fled from Lake's face as she recounted her stressful morning.

"They just don't understand quite yet that things are different now. Before I used to be able to keep them home any day because I was always home but now . . . anyway." Lake shook her head before continuing, "Typically my mom would be happy to step in, but today is her day to be at the store. Usually she would just stay home or take the girls but she's covering a shift for a cashier that called in sick, so I tried to text you and then called when I got no response."

"Oh, darling, I'm so sorry. I always keep my phone by the charger and I haven't checked it in a few hours," Morgan replied.

Logan would have laughed if Lake weren't so frazzled. They'd told their mom time and time again that a cell phone wasn't like a landline. Morgan could keep the phone on her all the time if she wanted; it didn't have to live by the charger while it wasn't being charged. But Morgan wouldn't hear it, saying that carrying a phone around all the time was a burden she didn't need. Therefore she missed many, many texts and calls. Logan wondered if she'd wear a smart watch if he bought her one. Then at least she'd have some way for people to get ahold of her.

"It's fine. Totally not blaming you. This is my fault. My responsibility." Lake squared her shoulders.

"Well, let the poor dears in," Morgan said, looking toward the door.

"Oh, they're fine. I just need a few seconds to figure out what to do. Grace said she could take them from noon to three so I just need someone from now until noon and then from three to five." Lake put her fingers on her temples as if that would bring the answer.

"Or they could stay here," Logan offered.

Morgan's face lit up. "Of course they can!" she agreed. "I've been hoping for some time with those sweet girls of yours ever since you started working with us and this will be perfect."

"Oh, no. You've initiated Mom's grandma response. There is now no way back unless Logan here starts popping out some babies," Holland joked.

"Popping out . . . " Logan let his voice trail off. It was better just to ignore Holland when she started saying ridiculous things.

"They can't stay here. We are supposed to go through Mitchell's things today. I love my girls but they tend to . . . well, make every job take about ten times as long," Lake replied. "I'll figure something out. Maybe Lottie would take them?" she thought aloud.

"Or Logan can. He's just hanging around here this morning. I'm sure he'd be happy to show your girls around the ranch. Are they afraid of farm animals?" Morgan asked.

"Just octopi, as far as I'm aware. Although that didn't start until this morning, so who knows what else could start in the next ten minutes. But I can't ask that of you." Lake looked back toward the door again.

"Can we come in, Mom? It's cold out here," Delia complained.

Morgan stood, bypassing Lake, who stood uncertainly between the foyer and the kitchen, as she hurried to the door. "Of course you both can come in." She held open the door as two adorable little carbon copies of Lake skipped in.

Blue followed Morgan, first curiously, but when both girls bent down to start petting him, he was immediately won over.

"He's so cute," Delia cooed.

Her sister nodded in agreement.

As they were entertained by the dog, Logan had a few moments to study Lake's daughters. They both had her cocoa brown hair with hints of copper and her wide hazel eyes. Delia's were a little more green and Amelie's slightly more brown. Their exclamation of how cold it was outside was a little hard to believe, considering both girls held their big puffer jackets instead of wearing them. Logan was pretty sure it was just an excuse to get inside but honestly if he were in charge of those girls they would need no excuses. With how adorable they were, how could he resist giving them their way?

"Oh, you two are just darling," Morgan said as she gazed lovingly at Lake's daughters.

"Told you," Holland said as she nudged her brother. She'd noticed their mom's look as well.

"You must be Delia," Morgan said to the taller of the two.

Delia nodded proudly.

"And you're Amelie?" Morgan asked the tiny girl beside Delia.

Logan knew from Lake that her youngest was in second grade but judging by her size Logan would have thought she was at least a grade younger. He recalled Lake had always been that way as well. Tiny but mighty. Logan would venture that Amelie probably took after her mom.

"I am," Amelie replied, her voice nowhere near as small as her stature.

Morgan, as well as the rest of the Ashfords, had met Lake's children a few times but they hadn't been able to spend any significant amount of time together so this was their first true introduction to the girls. Morgan appeared to be on cloud nine.

"I'm sorry you're missing your fieldtrip, but we're so happy that you get to join us here today," Morgan said even though Lake hadn't yet agreed to allowing the girls to stay. But what could she do? When Logan's mom set her mind to something no one could budge her.

"We get to stay here?" Delia asked, her eyes wide with excitement.

"Did she plan this?" Lake whispered, probably to herself, but from his seat at the table closest to the foyer, Logan couldn't help but overhear.

He chuckled inwardly as he watched the situation unfold.

"I thought you said the Ashfords are much too busy to host little pipsqueaks like us," Amelie said to her mother, raising an accusing eyebrow. Logan continued to try not to laugh as Lake's red face told them all that those were indeed her exact words.

"I don't usually call them that. I was just frustrated and . . . "

"Heaven knows I called the boys much worse things than that while annoyed," Morgan said to ease Lake and her flush began to subside.

"But the Ashfords aren't busy at all. In fact, what do you two say to a few fresh-made orange rolls and then a tour around the ranch?" Morgan turned and knelt so that she was at eye level with Amelie.

"Really?" Amelie asked.

"I love orange rolls," Delia added.

"Those are for the church bake sale," Lake pointed out.

"The church won't miss a few. Right, girls?" Morgan asked them conspiratorially.

"Right!" Delia and Amelie agreed enthusiastically.

Lake wore an expression of panic on her face. Logan understood it well. He often felt that way when his mother lovingly bulldozed into his life as well.

"She gets this way when children, animals, or marriage are involved," Logan explained to Lake.

Lake blinked at him. "Marriage?"

"Long story," Logan replied. He wasn't about to explain his

mom's past matchmaking attempts to the woman he had feelings for.

He cracked his neck at the thought of those last five words, feeling more than slightly uncomfortable. He hadn't been willing to acknowledge, even to himself, that he already had feelings for Lake. It was one thing to admit that one day he might feel something for Lake, but that wasn't the case. He felt for her right now —strongly. But those emotions felt much too real when Lake needed him to be nothing more than a friend. At the same time, though, it felt good. To acknowledge, even silently, that he cared for Lake as more than just a friend. For the time being that would be it. He would step back. Give her space. Be who she needed. But when the time was right . . .

"Are you okay with this?" Lake asked him quietly as Morgan ushered the girls to the kitchen island and served them each two giant orange rolls, Blue content to wait at their feet for crumbs to fall.

Lake took the empty chair next to Logan as she waited for him to answer her question.

"With taking the girls around the ranch? I'd love to. I feel badly that I've never done it before. If you'd asked me in high school, I would never have imagined playing such a small role in the lives of Fred's kids."

Or that Fred's and Lake's children would be one and the same. Logan had held out hope for far too long that Lake would come to her senses and return to him. High school Logan's future had always been with Lake. Even as he had broken up with her that summer, he'd always assumed it would be a temporary break. But when he'd gotten back from football camp, Fred and Lake were a thing and Logan could do nothing about it.

"I'd say it's about time I hang out with them, wouldn't you?" Logan asked, meeting Lake's eyes. He liked that even with his hat on he didn't have to lean back to see all of her gorgeous face. She was at just the right height for him. He wondered if she felt the same way about him?

"They are a handful," Lake warned. "And your mom is filling them up with sugar. If you thought they were full of energy beforehand, just you wait."

Lake's fingers strummed nervously on the tabletop as if she were still trying to come up with a solution, somewhere to send her kids while she worked.

Logan put one of his big hands over Lake's beautifully dainty one, stilling her fingers.

"I've got this." He sent her a wink, hoping to comfort her with his relaxed demeanor.

But the shock on her face wasn't what he was expecting.

She quickly schooled her features but Logan knew what he'd seen. How had he shocked her? And was it a good shock or a bad shock?

"These are so good," Delia said, interrupting his thoughts.

Logan smiled at the girl before warmth began emanating from his hand and he realized he still held Lake's. It reminded him of how he'd felt when she had taken his hand in Chicken and More. He was sure she'd thought nothing of it, but his racing heart hadn't let him think the same.

He lifted his hand, even though the last thing he wanted to do was let her go, knowing better than to press his luck.

"So good," Amelie agreed. "Would you like a bite, Mama? Or . . . " she looked to Logan and Holland, but Holland kept her back to the girls because she was openly smirking as she glanced from Logan's hand to Lake's. He should have known his sister wouldn't have missed that. He turned away from Holland's pointed look. It looked like he'd be ignoring her for a second time that morning.

"I'm Logan," he introduced himself to the cute little girl offering him a bite of her precious orange roll and then pointed to his sister who sat across the table from him. "And this slightly less attractive female version of me is Holland."

"What he means is very highly more attractive," Holland said. She turned quickly in her seat to face their guests but Logan hadn't missed the appalled look on her face.

"I'm pretty sure that wasn't even proper English," Logan teased.

"Oh, are we going to point out when the other is using our language improperly now, Cowboy?" Holland tilted her head impudently as she teased right back.

Logan had to admit there were many times when ease won over using all of the words he'd need to be grammatically correct. He didn't think it was a cowboy thing. It was more of a laidback thing.

"But though we thank you for the offer of orange rolls, how about you enjoy them?" Logan said to Amelie.

Amelie nodded, happily taking another bite and looking at her mom.

"I'm good too, Leelee," Lake replied, seeming to relax as the Ashfords spent time with her children. She was probably beginning to see that it wouldn't be the disaster she'd imagined or that she wasn't putting any of them out like she'd feared.

And Lake would be right about that, because what kind of sweetheart offered the delicious food she was eating to near strangers? He'd be more than happy to get to know Lake's adorable and pleasant daughters even if they were a bit rambunctious.

"You do look like a cowboy," Delia said between bites of roll, referencing Holland's comment.

"He is one," Holland replied. "The hat is just the start of it. He has the boots and I've never seen him wear shorts. He lives in jeans. I'm pretty sure he even sleeps in jeans." Holland fake whispered the last sentence and the girls giggled.

"Pretty sure you'd be shocked by what I sleep in." Logan meant to say it just loud enough for Holland to hear—she deserved to be teased after her comments—but even though he'd spoken in the direction of his sister apparently Lake had also heard what he'd said, according to her small gasp and reddening cheeks. Logan needed a swift kick to his rear. Had he really just mentioned his sleepwear in front of the new widow? He was going to hell.

Logan noticed his mom taking the last of the rolls out of the oven. This was his cue.

"Who's ready to see Blue Falls Ranch with a real cowboy as their guide?" Logan decided to play up his role.

"Me!" Both girls squealed as they raised sticky hands in the air.

"First clean up and then the ranch tour." Lake looked from her daughters to Morgan and then to Logan.

"Come on up here and wash your hands." Morgan showed the girls the way to the bathroom just off the mudroom.

"Are you sure about this?" Lake asked in a low voice. "I'm sure I can figure something else out."

"Lake, my mom being willing to go through Dad's stuff? That is huge. For some reason she's ready now that you're here when she hasn't been able to face the idea for months. If you help my mom with that, I can surely watch your kiddos."

"That's my job," Lake replied.

Logan shook his head. "Pretty sure you're doing far beyond your job if you've helped Mom get to this point. Just think of it as a thank you. And honestly I am thrilled to be doing this. I've been hoping to get to know your girls for some time now."

Logan hated to admit that his desire to meet Lake's children had grown since she'd become single. He'd met the girls and seen them on occasion when they'd come home, but he doubted they even remembered those encounters because he'd played such a small role in their lives. He should have cared more before this. But for years his heart had been aching that Lake would never be his. Maybe he'd avoided the girls and, honestly, Lake and Fred, on purpose? No, he definitely had. And it had been wrong. But he could try to make up for it now, right? Or were his motives purely selfish? He was hoping he could find a combination of both because he had to admit there were definite selfish motives behind his wanting to get to know Lake's girls now, whether he liked it or not.

"Fine. But don't come crying to me when those girls drive you up the wall," she said with a tilt of her head. But the way she looked at her daughters, her eyes full of warmth and adoration, let Logan know she didn't mean the words as a derogatory comment toward them, more as a warning to Logan.

"No crying when I'm stuck on top of a wall. Got it," Logan joked.

Lake laughed as her daughters ran to the table and skidded to a stop in front of Logan with damp hands and huge, expectant smiles.

"So where do you want to start? Tractors, horses, or the pond?" he asked, listing what had been his three favorite things about the ranch as a child.

"Horses!" Amelie said at the same time Delia declared, "All of it!"

"Sounds good," Logan said, standing and taking a hand of each girl.

He glanced back just long enough to see Lake watching them all with wide eyes.

He wasn't sure how this day was going to go, but if he could make Lake look at him with that kind of wonder and awe, it would all be worth it.

Thirteen

LAKE COULDN'T HELP glancing out of Morgan's bedroom window yet again. She'd done it at least six times in the last five minutes but she couldn't seem to stop herself. Somewhere out there Logan was caring for both of her daughters. And he'd had them for the past four hours. They were expected back soon, as it was getting close to lunch time, but four hours?!

Fred hadn't been able to manage that even when he was "babysitting" in his own home. Lake hated that term for when a father watched his children. Why was it babysitting for Fred yet the norm for Lake? They were both equally parents, were they not?

Fred had disagreed. How many times had he told Lake that because he was the breadwinner he shouldn't be expected to carry any of the home load? He believed his work was done outside of the home and Lake's in the home. And while Lake could understand that to a degree—she didn't work outside the home so she should do more where their house and the girls were concerned—it didn't seem right for Fred to refuse to do anything when he got home from work.

Lake recalled asking Fred to do the dinner dishes once. She'd made the meal, deep cleaned all four of their bathrooms, taken the girls to and from school, helped with homework, refereed at least a dozen fights, and she had a PTA meeting that night. She had been completely exhausted and as she watched Fred relaxing on the couch with the game on she'd wondered why he couldn't do it.

Lake had never witnessed a bigger temper tantrum before or since. And that was saying something, considering she'd volunteered in her girls' classrooms every year since they'd started school and taught a three-year-old Sunday School class at their church in Boise.

She had learned that night, through lots of yelling and name calling, that a man's job did not involve those kinds of things, according to Fred. Since then Lake had been wary of asking anything of him, even watching the girls. Or maybe especially watching the girls. Lake hated the idea that Fred might ever blow up at them the way he had at her.

Yet here Logan was, touring the ranch with both of them for four hours. Not only had he agreed to the plan, but he'd actually seemed excited. As if this was a fun thing for him, not an obligation he'd be fulfilling and would hold over Lake's head for months to come.

"They're fine. He may not look it at first glance, but Logan is incredible with children. He's been teaching youth Sunday School classes for the past six years," Morgan said when she noticed where Lake's attention had gone yet again.

Lake opened her mouth to argue that Logan actually looked just like the kind of man who would be incredible with children. His eyes were compassionate, his arms always open, his hand ready to hold onto or hold back whatever may come their way.

Lake closed her mouth. Um, yeah, she would not be saying any of that to Logan's mother.

Holland began laughing and Lake worried she was laughing at her until she saw that Holland was looking at Mama Ashford.

"You paint him like some kind of saint. We all know he only teaches in those classes to avoid the adult classes where some of the single females act a little too adult, if you know what I mean," Holland said between peals of laughter, giving Lake a knowing look.

After witnessing the way Avery had pawed at Logan, Lake could much too easily understand what Holland meant.

"Holland, be nice to your brother," Morgan reprimanded.

"I have to be nice even when he isn't here? Mom, that's asking too much," Holland said, dramatically falling into the pillows behind her as Blue joined her, yipping with excitement.

Holland, although she should have been studying, hadn't seemed to be able to walk away from Morgan and Lake when she realized what they'd be doing today. She'd stayed out of the way, making herself comfy with Blue on the gigantic king-sized bed in Mama Ashford's room, but she was there. Watching but not participating, as if she could sense that her mother didn't want her right in the mix of things. And Holland had seemed all too happy to comply. There were a few items that, when Lake had pulled them out of the closet, Holland couldn't even seem to look at.

So Lake had spent the morning taking things from Mitchell's side of the closet and handing them to Mama Ashford, who was seated just outside the closet. She had a plastic storage box on her right where she was placing all the things the family would keep, a brown cardboard box next to it for items to give away, and a garbage bag on her left. Lake noticed that Mama Ashford winced anytime she caught sight of the contents of the garbage bag. Lake thought of what a contrast that was to the way she'd handled Fred's things.

She'd already been through all of his stuff—she did so the day after the reading of his will—but thanks to the anger she felt because of Sachia, Lake had used the garbage bag far more than she would have liked to admit. Thankfully her mother had been there to take a few things Lake had prematurely thrown away and discreetly moved them to the keep box. Lake had pretended not to notice but deep down, even through her fury, she knew her mom was doing the right thing.

"They're back," Holland announced from her spot on the bed while Lake was in the closet gathering the last of Mitchell's shirts. After that there was only one box of things left on his side of the closet. They were so close to being done and Lake couldn't be prouder of Mama Ashford.

"They are?" Lake hurried out of the closet and dumped the armful of shirts in front of Mama Ashford. Typically she would have set them down gently or even held them up one at a time so that Mama Ashford could see each item individually.

"I'm so sorry," she gasped, scrambling to gather up the shirts. How could she have been so self-centered?

"Don't be," Morgan said as she tugged the shirts out of Lake's hands. "You go to those babies of yours. See how they fared with my baby." Morgan grinned before her eyes fell on a particular shirt and the grin faded away.

She still missed him so much. Lake couldn't help but think of how different Mama Ashford's grief was than her own. Shouldn't Lake ache with sorrow too? She felt guilty yet frustrated. Wasn't it Fred's fault she couldn't just mourn? And then she felt guilty for that. She was stuck in a miserable cycle.

She shook her head free of her thoughts.

"I guess I should. But I'll be right back," Lake promised Morgan because they still had that box.

Mama Ashford shook her head. "I think I've had enough for today."

Lake immediately felt badly. She shouldn't have acted so eager to leave.

"Don't you dare worry that you've hurt my feelings. You've been a Godsend, Lake." Mama Ashford shot Lake a fading smile. "But I'm an old woman who has pushed her emotional limits for the day and I think I'll just rest. Holland's been keeping that spot warm for me all morning."

"Now I'm going to have to scold you for that one. Calling such a young woman 'old,'" Lake replied, her smile wide, hoping she could smile enough for the both of them.

Mama Ashford laughed.

"But I completely understand. Do you want me to start cleaning the laundry room?" Lake asked. Morgan had mentioned trying to get to that sometime this week.

"How about you leave that for tomorrow? Take your babies home. Spend some of that time with them that you used to get."

"Oh, I didn't mean to complain when I said that. I am so grateful for this job. It's just different now," Lake said, her cheeks warming. The last thing she wanted to do was offend Mama Ashford.

"I know. But those girls have endured so much change these past few weeks. How about giving them some familiarity instead?" Morgan asked.

That did sound amazing, but it was barely noon. Lake felt guilty taking a half day off when she'd been working at the Ashfords for less than two weeks.

"I insist," Morgan said in her firm tone and it was decided.

Lake wasn't about to argue with Mama Ashford when her mind had been made up.

"Thank you," she said, dropping to her haunches to kiss Mama Ashford on the cheek. "See you both tomorrow." Lake looked at Holland on the bed and then back at Mama Ashford.

"See you." Holland barely looked up from her phone to say goodbye.

"Enjoy your time off," Morgan said and then added, "And bring those babies back sometime soon. It was nice to have young life in the house again."

Lake smiled as she stood, nodding her assent.

"Hey, I'm still young life," Holland said, crawling to the edge of the bed, closer to her mother.

"Of course you are," Morgan placated.

"No, seriously." Holland's voice grew distant as Lake made her way down the hallway that connected the main bedroom with the kitchen.

"Mom!" Delia and Amelie sang out in unison when she got to the kitchen. They ran to her, throwing their arms around her waist.

"Hello," Lake said with a chuckle. She hadn't been expecting such an exuberant greeting but she never turned down daughter hugs.

"It was so fun, Mom," Amelie said at top speed as Delia excitedly asked, "Can we move to a ranch with a thousand horses? Did you know they have *more* than a thousand horses here, Mom?"

Lake raised an eyebrow. She knew Blue Falls Ranch was enormous and that there were quite a few horses, more than she'd ever seen, but a thousand?

"We won't have quite so many when Austin sells some of them in the spring. And others are owned by our clients and just stabled here," Logan tried to explain.

"I'm so glad you had fun, Amelie," Lake said first and then turned to Delia. "I'm not sure about the whole ranch thing, but is it good enough for now that your mom works on a ranch with a thousand horses?"

Delia seemed to consider it as she pursed her lips.

"I guess for now," she finally conceded.

Thank heavens for that.

"Thank you," Lake said, looking up at Logan and feeling that the words were inadequate. It couldn't have been easy on him, especially considering the energy her girls still had after all those hours.

"Don't mention it. I had a blast. Really. We went to parts of the ranch I haven't seen in a hot minute and they told me all sorts of stories." Logan raised his eyebrows.

Lake blushed without even knowing what had been said. The look in Logan's eyes said it all.

What kind of dirt did her girls have on her?

"Logan is the best, Mom," Delia claimed.

"Uh-huh. We love Logan," Amelie agreed.

Logan's smirk turned to the sweetest smile Lake had ever witnessed as he dropped his gaze to her girls.

"Well, I think you two are the best and I love *you*," he said without hesitation.

Lake couldn't help the tears that immediately sprang to her eyes. The girls were longing for someone to notice them, someone to care. Fred had tried with the girls, at least more than he'd tried with Lake, but he'd never really enjoyed time with them. Fred would prefer to be at the office or with his friends and they'd all known it.

But in one day Logan had seen them. Talked to them. Found a way to connect that had her girls claiming him as theirs. But he wasn't theirs. Soon enough he'd get scooped up by some young woman without the baggage of a cheating husband who died with his ex-mistress and two darling but wild daughters.

She needed to take a step back. Have them take a step back. But how?

Logan drew the girls close as he bent down to their level. Looking at the joy on all three of their faces, Lake realized they couldn't take a step back. It was too late. And she couldn't even completely regret it. If her daughters were hurt in the future she'd feel terrible, but this moment right here, seeing how happy they all were, made that future possible pain feel worth it. And if she knew Logan, this wouldn't be the last time he'd be there for her girls in any way they needed.

"You're coming to my play, right?" Delia asked as she turned her face up to him seriously.

"And my daddy donut day?" Amelie added her request.

Lake felt her heart drop. That was . . . a lot. Logan couldn't say yes, could he?

"Of course," he said to Delia and then dropped to the ground so that he sat crisscross applesauce in the middle of his mother's kitchen while he looked Amelie directly in the eyes.

"I'd be honored, Amelie," he said so sincerely Lake could do nothing but believe him.

She felt emotion well in her throat. She couldn't cry, but it was all so overwhelming. She was scared. Scared that the girls were too attached. She was nervous. Nervous that watching Logan like this with her children would only make her fall harder for him. But most of all she was hopeful. Hopeful that Logan could fill this need in their lives, even if just for a short time until he started his own family.

Lake cleared her throat, wishing it was as easy to clear her soul of her emotions. But she'd deal with those later.

"Girls, why don't you go to the car. Mama Ashford gave me the rest of the day off, so we can go through the drive through on the way home!" Lake pulled out the big guns, knowing it wouldn't be an easy matter to get them out of the house and away from their new best friend.

"Yes, French fries!" Delia said as she ran to the door.

"And chicken nuggets!" Amelie added.

The girls fled, the slam of the door echoing behind them.

With the girls gone there was nothing else to do but face Logan. Yet she wasn't sure how to do it. Not when he'd been so kind to her girls.

Lake looked down to see him still on the ground, where he'd moved to be on the same level as her little Amelie.

"You've won their hearts for life," Lake said softly, unsure how to convey the connection the girls felt for Logan. But he had to understand, at least a little.

"There has never been a more blessed man," Logan replied. He said the words so simply. As if that was how he really felt.

So he did understand? Or at least he was trying to? Lake felt gratitude well up in her chest until it almost overflowed.

"You don't have to go to donut day," she added as Logan uncrossed his legs and stood. That was asking too much, wasn't it? She couldn't even bring herself to say 'daddy donut day' since Logan wasn't the girls' dad.

"I know. But I also know what an honor it is that Amelie asked me. I really am trying not to overstep my bounds. But if you want me here, there, wherever, I want to be here for you, Lake." Logan stood face to face with her, their toes just inches apart, their chests rising and falling in unison.

And just like that Lake's gratitude was replaced by something else altogether. She fought her body's strong urge to lean forward. She'd never been more attracted to a man, emotionally or otherwise.

She leaned back, her realization scaring her.

"Thank you," she whispered. What more could she say? She needed to leave before she reacted to all that she was feeling. Surely she'd say or do something she'd regret.

But just before she turned to leave she remembered the date. So she took a step back instead. Standing this close to Logan was dangerous, but it was time to think of him instead of herself.

"Isn't this the fifth business day?" she asked, feeling the need to be there for him the way he seemed to always be there for her.

He nodded slowly. "I've been trying to think about anything else. I still don't think my dad could have done it. But it will be nice just to know, you know?"

Lake nodded, thinking about Mitchell's past but also her own. Wouldn't it be nice just to know why that woman was in the car with Fred?

"You'll let me know when you know?" Lake asked. Logan had

been there in every way for her; this was the least she could do for him.

Logan nodded.

The sound of her car doors slamming warned Lake the girls were on their way back. She needed to head them off.

"Seriously, though. Thank you, Logan," Lake said as she backed her way toward the door.

"And thank you, Lake. Being let into all of your lives is a treasure," Logan said.

Lake's heart and stomach flipped as if they were performing a synchronized diving routine in the Olympics.

She bit her lip and fumbled for the doorknob behind her. She couldn't find it so she turned and walked out the door, unable to keep the giant smile off her face.

Logan Ashford was something else.

"I WANT TO GET THE MAIL," Amelie complained.

"You get to carry the food inside. Can I get the mail, please?" Delia begged.

Did everything have to be a fight? Lake drew a calming breath and answered.

"Delia's right, Leelee. You go ahead and take the food in and Delia will get the mail. But Delia, no complaining if Amelie starts eating before you get to the table." Lake offered a compromise.

"Okay," Amelie said.

"Yes, Mom," Delia said excitedly, and the girls took off in opposite directions. Amelie sprinted toward the house and Delia rushed to the mailbox.

Lake jogged to catch up to Amelie. She needed to get the front door open before Delia got back with the mail or she'd have an upset seven-year-old on her hands. The only reason Amelie gave in was because she loved the idea of digging into her meal before Delia could get to hers.

Lake opened the front door, a fresh citrus scent greeting her. Lake's mom had used the same lemon cleaner since Lake was a kid so the smell, in Lake's mind, equaled home.

Amelie dashed for the table, hurriedly emptying the fast-food bag, and found her chicken nuggets and fries. She shoved a fry into her mouth just as Delia came running inside with a towering stack of mail.

"Wow," Lake said but then remembered that she'd taken a while to forward things to this address. This must have been all the mail that had stacked up since they'd moved, or maybe even before that. Lake hadn't checked the mail since Fred's death, and it had now finally arrived.

Delia dumped the pile of mail on Lake before dashing to the table.

"Wash your hands," Lake remembered belatedly.

Amelie jumped up from her seat and Delia changed direction, both racing to the bathroom. Thankfully that one had double sinks or there was sure to be another fight.

Lake looked from the table with the burger and fries that she'd grabbed for her lunch to the pile of mail.

Her twisted-up stomach made her decision for her. She wasn't sure what to make of Logan's words to her. Had they really meant what she'd thought? Or was she a lonely woman and widow reading way too much into the words of the most handsome man she knew?

If it was the latter Lake needed to calm down. She was practically chomping at the bit where Logan was concerned. Hadn't she just resolved to take a step back? Granted, that was before he'd treated her daughters like princesses and told Lake he'd be there for her whenever, wherever, however.

Lake fanned her face. Hotness didn't even begin to describe Logan.

Yup, lunch would be later. It would be cold but her stomach couldn't handle the grease right now. It was hopped up on Logan.

The girls raced back, Delia hot on Amelie's heels, before they launched themselves into chairs.

"Hey, that's mine," Delia claimed the moment she saw Amelie's chicken nuggets.

"You both got the same thing," Lake replied before the fight could start, trying to hold back an eye roll. "There should be another box of nuggets."

Delia looked at Lake skeptically before checking the table and, sure enough, finding another box of nuggets. With no apologies for her accusation, Delia tore into her meal, now racing Amelie to see who could finish their meal the fastest.

Sisters.

Lake sat on the floor, once again reminded of Logan, as she began to sort through the mail, dividing her mail from her parents', putting mail to her family in one pile, junk in another, and bills in the last. There seemed to be nothing else in there. Lake wished that mail wasn't quite so boring these days.

She was almost to the bottom of the stack when a card-shaped white envelope dropped into her lap.

This wasn't the size of a normal bill. Probably a real estate invite or some such.

But when she saw that it was addressed to her, she figured she'd open it. Might as well break up the monotony of bills and fliers.

We've never met, but you know who I am.

Lake dropped the card as if it were on fire. On the front of the card had been an innocent pink flower. But on the inside . . .

The sender was right. Lake knew immediately who she was. She didn't know her handwriting, just her name. And yet Lake knew.

She closed her eyes and clutched the carpet on either side of her, hoping it would ground her.

"What is it?" Grace asked quietly.

Lake had forgotten she was home. She should have told the girls to be quieter. Grace must have been napping after her shift.

"I'm sorry they're so loud," Lake said instead of answering.

Grace took a seat on the ground beside Lake.

"I couldn't care less about that. I sleep with a sound machine and ear plugs." She glanced from Lake's pained face to the card on her lap. "What's in that note?" Grace pressed.

Lake shook her head. "I can't read it. I just know it's from her," she whispered.

"What?" Grace yelled before glancing to the girls who were still shoving fries down their throats in an attempt to win. They didn't even look up at Grace's voice. She nodded and turned back to Lake.

"How do you know?" Grace now matched Lake's whisper.

"I saw the first line and I just knew."

Lake felt a knot in her throat. Was this normal? She'd felt other sensations in the same place but this was like someone had actually taken her esophagus or vocal cords or maybe her carotid arteries and tied them together.

"Why would she . . . ?" Grace's voice trailed off before she glanced down at the card again. "Do you want me to read it?"

Lake pushed the note off her lap as if she no longer wanted it touching her. Did she want Grace to read it? Was it fair to ask that of her baby sister?

But she realized that even if she read it first, Grace wouldn't let her go before reading it as well. She'd know one way or the other what was in that note. Lake realized her only decision was whether she wanted Grace to read it to her or if she'd read it on her own.

Lake looked to her girls. Her headstrong, feisty girls. What would she want for them?

Never to be in this situation. But that part wouldn't be their choice. It hadn't been her choice. What was her choice? How she wanted to accept this.

And she didn't want to crumple at the sight of a card. She wanted to be headstrong and feisty. A small portion of her girls.

"No, but thank you," Lake said as she lifted the card once again. It was just a piece of paper. It had no power to hurt her. Maybe it would even give her some answers.

Lake slowly opened the card. She could feel Grace's eyes on her as she forced herself to read the words.

We've never met, but you know who I am. I know who you are. I know your family. I know that you hold onto some part of Fred's heart. For some reason he won't let you go. But you have to know, he won't let me go either. He might feel obligated to you, but he loves me. He wants me. But he won't leave you. He's too good of a man. Even if I'm the one he can find happiness with and with you it is nothing but drudgery.

Lake began to tremble. She could hear Fred saying those words. He must have said them to her as well. What this woman wrote felt like the truth even as Lake hated every word.

Let him go. Let him be happy—with me. He won't leave you, so please, please leave him. Give us all a chance at living our best lives. Let him love again. I know you probably won't do it. I've heard the way you cling to him, but just know I won't let go either. And maybe you have the ring, but I have his heart. I always will.

Lake flipped over the note. That couldn't be the end.

But it was. No more words, not even a signature.

Lake dropped the card and gagged before running to the bathroom. Grace followed her closely.

"Are you okay, Mom?" Delia asked.

"She's fine. Her stomach is just feeling a little funny. How about you two go to the treehouse and I'll be out there in a minute?"

Thank heavens for Grace. Lake was incapable of speech.

She threw open the toilet seat and knelt in front of it, waiting.

But nothing came. Grace watched her intently for a few

minutes before realizing the same thing. Nothing was going to happen. Lake felt sick to her stomach but she'd be okay.

Grace opened the note she'd brought with her and began to read, her eyebrows drawing closer and closer together as she took it in.

"Is it bad to want to kill a dead person?" she asked, looking over the top of the note as she tried to meet Lake's eyes.

"Probably," Lake managed weakly.

"How could she say these things to you?" Grace's face was full of concern.

Lake shrugged but she knew how. If Lake had cared more about Fred she would have had no problem saying the same words or worse back to Sachia. "She's in love. She's doing anything she can to protect what she has."

Grace pursed her lips. Lake understood it was a hard pill to swallow.

"She loved him. So much more than I did then," Lake said quietly. She wasn't going to say than she ever did. No, Lake had truly loved Fred once, but that love had faded when he'd done nothing to nurture it.

"But at least it answers my question. She was in the car with him because he was back with her. It was probably only a matter of time before he left me and the girls."

Lake hated her first thought after her statement. *It was better this way.* How wrong was that? To think that life was better with Fred dead. To think that the world was better off without the father of her children in it. She said a quick prayer for forgiveness and then thought something a bit more kind. At least her girls hadn't had to endure their parents' divorce before the death of their father.

"You don't know that," Grace replied.

Lake waved at the note.

Grace shook her head as if she wanted to argue but Lake wasn't ready to hear it. Instead she stood and walked slowly back to the living room. The couch was a better place to deal with all of this than the bathroom floor.

"Are you okay?" Grace asked, reaching a tentative hand toward her sister.

Lake hadn't ever noticed how nebulous that question was. Okay. What did it even mean? Was she going to throw up? No. Was she devastated to learn that her husband was cheating on her again? That she'd been a fool to take him back? Honestly, no. She was frustrated with herself, angry that she'd ever believed him, but no. Not devastated. She realized she'd assumed as much when she found out who was in the car. And even then she hadn't been devastated. Furious, yes, but she knew she would get over it. That she was already getting over it.

So she guessed she was okay.

"Yeah," Lake replied.

"Seriously?" Grace asked once more.

Lake nodded before taking the note from Grace's hands. "She was fighting for him. Did she play dirty? Yes. Can I blame her? No."

Lake's answer surprised even herself. But if she were fighting for the man who held her heart? She would have fought hard too. She hadn't fought harder for Fred because he hadn't held her heart. Not for a long time at least.

"You are a strong woman, Lake Johnson," Grace said.

Lake smiled at the use of her maiden name. It sounded right.

"You are a good sister, Grace Johnson," Lake replied.

Grace smiled before looking out the sliding glass door. "I'd better get out there before those girls claimed I lied."

Lake chuckled. It was one of the worst accusations the girls could hurl.

"Thank you. I just need a minute."

"Take all the time you need," Grace replied. She cast a sympathetic backward glance at her sister before opening the sliding door, walking out, and shutting it behind her.

Lake marveled that they could be out in the treehouse at this time of year. Granted, it was warm for a December afternoon and her dad had set up a heating system last Christmas, but still it had to be cold. But the girls loved that hideaway—especially when Aunt Grace joined them.

Lake leaned back into the couch, basking in the silence. She'd prayed for answers. This was probably as close as she'd ever get. And the relative peace that had come over her since sitting on the bathroom floor had been nothing short of a miracle.

She knew this much: she was ready to let Fred go.

A knock sounded at the door, startling Lake.

She glanced at the clock. Who could be there?

She thought about ignoring it but the knock sounded again. It seemed only polite to answer the door. She'd see who it was and send them on their way.

Lake made her way across the living room and checked the peephole.

What in the world?

She opened the door immediately.

"Logan?" she asked, excitement filling her.

Was this wrong? That she felt so much toward Logan and, when the dust settled, so little over what Fred had done to her?

"Hey. I have some news," Logan said, looking around behind him.

It took Lake a second but she realized she shouldn't leave Logan on her front porch forever.

"Oh yeah, come in." She opened the door wider.

Logan entered, shutting the door behind him.

He seemed nearly as shocked as Lake that he was there. Except he'd driven himself to her house and knocked on the door. He couldn't have been shocked by his appearance . . . unless this news he'd brought was causing his strange behavior. That had to be it.

They both stood in the foyer, neither saying a word or

moving for too many seconds before Lake realized what she was doing. She wanted to slap a palm to her forehead, just like the emoji.

What was she doing?

Logan was the one with shocking news. Lake needed to pull herself together. She took a step back, fighting the urge to physically shake herself. "Have a seat," she offered, gesturing to the couch in the living room.

Okay, that was nearly normal. She was getting there. Baby steps. Logan was in her living room after all, his crisp, clean scent filling her nostrils.

And that was not normal. No more sniffing Logan. Or thinking the word 'nostrils.'

"Thanks," Logan said, his long legs eating up the distance quickly as he walked to the couch, taking the seat just next to the one Lake had been in.

Lake thought about going back to where she'd been but instead took the cushion one away from Logan. She'd already stood in the foyer staring at him. And then she'd sniffed him. She didn't need to add 'creeper who sat as close as she could to Logan' to her list of things she should never do again.

"So what—" Lake began as Logan said, "We got the results—"

"You go first," Logan offered.

"Oh, no way. And?" Lake asked as soon as she registered what Logan had said, ignoring his offer for her to speak first because she wasn't about to say anything important anyway. Lake tried hard not to bounce her knee but this was big.

Logan drew in a deep breath before letting it out with a shaky smile.

"Madison is related to me. But the findings suggest her DNA isn't a match for a sibling but instead for a first cousin," Logan replied.

Lake grinned. Thank the Lord for that.

"You never doubted," she said to Logan.

Logan shook his head. "I tried not to. I didn't want to. But I have to admit I had my moments."

"How's your mom doing?" Lake asked.

"She's already started celebration baking. Be ready to eat your weight in lemon squares tomorrow."

Lake laughed. She was so happy for this family she'd come to love.

"And Madison?" Lake asked.

"Still curious. She's grateful she wasn't the bearer of bad news for our family. But now she's worried about another family she might hurt. I've told her a bit about my uncles," Logan explained.

Lake wondered how that would go. She knew a couple of Logan's uncles also had kids around Madison's age. If Madison was theirs, they'd cheated on their wives. Lake had to hope that wasn't the case. But the last possibility was Ronnie. He wasn't Lake's first choice of a father for anyone. Granted, he'd been doing better in recent years. Ronnie had been a drug addict for decades but had recently turned his life around after finding Millie, his wife. Their kids were quite a bit younger, probably just around the age of Lake's girls.

"Mom's realizing Dad probably never told her because he didn't want her to think poorly of whoever the father is. He'd basically abandoned Madison and her mom."

Lake nodded. She could see Mitchell trying to protect everyone around him.

"How are you?" Lake asked. She couldn't believe it had taken this long for her to ask that question.

"Relieved. Excited to get to know my new cousin. Worried for what she'll find when she figures out who her dad really is. A little angry at the uncle who didn't step up to care for his child," Logan revealed.

Lake could imagine.

Logan shifted in his seat, pulling out from under his leg a piece of paper that he must have sat on. *The card.*

Oh dang. How had Lake just left that lying around? The instant she saw Logan through the peephole she'd somehow totally forgotten about the card.

"Is this yours?" he asked, holding up the card.

Lake nodded, frozen in place while she considered her options. She considered grabbing it and pretending it was nothing. On the front of the card was a harmless flower, after all. If she acted like it was nothing, Logan would think nothing of it.

But Lake didn't want to say it was nothing. He'd just come to her—it had be so soon after he'd received the news about Madison—telling her something so private about himself and his family. He'd let her in.

And Lake suddenly wanted—no, needed—to let Logan in as well. Partly to see how he'd react but mostly because she was ready to open up to him.

Was this too soon?

She guessed she didn't care.

"It's a card from Fred's mistress," Lake said, weighing Logan's reaction with each word.

His eyes went from curious to furious in a millisecond.

"What?" he asked through clenched teeth, although he relaxed his jaw as soon as he'd spoken. As if he hadn't realized how upset he'd seemed and when he did notice it he didn't want to alarm Lake. But she saw that one of his hands was still in a tight fist, frozen beside him.

"I found out about it nearly five months ago now. I don't know how long it had been going on. I hadn't wanted the particulars. But he did tell me it was a nurse from his practice, Sachia. The whole thing was a mess. He promised to leave her." Lake gave a succinct summary of the facts, unsure of how else to go about this.

The card began to crumple in Logan's hands. It was only the noise that seemed to alert him to what he was doing. He dropped it on the ground.

Lake made a wordless, understanding sound in her throat, fully grasping Logan's intense emotional response. But receiving that card had done something to her. First it had made her feel sick, a perfectly logical reaction. But in the following minutes it had done something more: reached a part of her that Lake wasn't sure had existed. A part of her that had understood Sachia. A part of her that was asking Lake to let the hate go, because it was only hurting Lake. So she had done her best to release at least some of the hatred from her heart and when she had, she suddenly felt freer than she had in months. So free that she was ready to open herself up to Logan in a way she never would have imagined even hours before.

Logan watched her expectantly and she knew it was time to continue her tale.

"After Fred begged for my forgiveness, we made a second go of it. Things seemed to be getting better. At the time I thought it was enough. Looking back I know none of us were actually happy, not even the girls. But it was easier at the time just to maintain the status quo."

Logan sat ramrod straight. She wished she knew what he was thinking, but realized he didn't owe her his thoughts. This was a gift she was giving him—the gift of seeing into what had shaped her these past years. But because it was a gift it couldn't be conditional. The way Logan reacted, what he said to her—that was all up to him.

She drew in a breath. Preparing herself to tell Logan the last, hardest part. "But then the accident took him."

Lake paused.

"It took them."

"She was in the car with him?" Logan's voice betrayed how bewildered he felt as he scrubbed a hand over his face and then into his hair.

Lake nodded. "Knowing that truth had been driving me crazy ever since the accident. Fred had said one thing, that he was done with the affair, but then I found out another. I was furious, confused, sad. Completely a mess."

"That's understandable," Logan said as he scooted forward, closer to Lake. Slowly, almost hesitantly, he lifted his arm. An invitation.

Lake immediately accepted it, falling into that space between his arm and his core, welcoming the comfort.

"And that's a note from her." Lake pointed at the ground toward the crumpled card. "Cliffsnotes version: she was still completely in love with him. She was fighting for him. She wanted me to give him up, because he no longer loved me."

Lake was surprised that her eyes remained dry, her voice steady. But now that she'd lived it, told the story to others, and had a little time and space away from it, it almost felt like she was recounting someone else's life story. Maybe because she'd finally given herself permission to just let go?

Whatever the reason, Lake was grateful. She felt more like herself than she had in a long time.

"He wasn't worthy of you," Logan said into Lake's hair.

She reveled in the sensation of his breath on her head. It felt like every nerve ending on her scalp and beyond had come to life.

"It didn't feel that way," Lake replied honestly.

"I'm telling you now. You need to know the truth."

Lake nodded, believing Logan. He spoke with such conviction that she had to.

"He should have loved you. Treasured you."

"I wasn't innocent." Lake finally shared the part she'd been scared to admit. They'd drifted apart long before Fred's affair. She could have worked harder to save things long before they all went down the drain.

"No one is."

Lake figured that was the truth as well.

"I can't believe you've been carrying this." Logan's voice was filled with a mournfulness that spoke to Lake's soul. "You are remarkable, Lake."

Lake longed to believe all that Logan said to her. There had been a hole in her life for a long time, a place that had felt empty from the moment Fred had started changing, becoming a man Lake didn't recognize. When he'd chosen to pursue his career before her. Lake felt the hole fill, little by little, with the affection Logan was showing her.

"You make me feel remarkable," Lake whispered, looking up at Logan.

He suddenly dropped his head so they were barely an inch apart. Lake tried not to notice all the places Logan touched her but it was impossible. Her arm against his chest, her hip against his torso, her thigh pressed against his thigh.

A fire she'd long forgotten started as a spark. As Logan dropped his head the tiniest bit more, it became a flame.

Lake knew it was up to her. Logan didn't want to push her beyond what she felt comfortable with, but she knew the fire in his eyes matched the one in her belly. He wanted her.

And she wanted him.

Lake stretched up to close the distance between them, pressing her lips against Logan's strong ones. The flame was now an inferno and Lake wasn't sure how to quell it. She wasn't sure she wanted to.

She quickly tucked her legs under her, shifting onto her knees and making it even easier to keep her lips pressed to Logan's forever.

She wrapped her arms around his neck and felt him groan as his hands clutched at her waist, lifting her even closer.

Logan nipped at Lake's full bottom lip and she was done. She wound her hands through his hair, her eyes closed as she savored the moment.

"Little eyes are about to enter," Grace's voice called as the sliding door opened.

Lake jerked one way as Logan jerked the other, their heavy breathing showing they'd been equally effected by the kiss of a lifetime.

But rational thought filled her mind at the same rate air filled her lungs. She hadn't worried about either while kissing Logan but now they were impossible to ignore.

Oh heavens, no. She'd kissed Logan. Her boss. Her ex. Her friend. Fred's friend.

What had she done?

Fourteen

LOGAN HAD KISSED LAKE.

Dreams of his lips lovingly meeting hers had filled the ensuing night and although he'd read the regret on Lake's face when her daughters had almost caught them mid-kiss, Logan didn't regret it. Not one bit.

After hearing what Fred had done to Lake . . . Logan had been forced to control his emotions in front of Lake. He was reeling from the knowledge that this man—Logan's friend—had stepped out on the most amazing woman on the planet. Logan had been a fool. Not as much of one as Fred had been, but a fool all the same.

He tried to imagine having Lake in his life and then doing something so ridiculously idiotic, but it turned Logan's stomach even to consider the idea. He stopped imagining. It would help no one.

When the kids had run back into Lake's parents' home, he'd seen the emotions flash across Lake's face. Panic, guilt, and finally regret. She'd nearly shoved Logan out the door as Grace had eyed him carefully, probably wondering about his intentions toward her sister. And Logan had wanted to shout from the rooftops that they were nothing but noble. If he had a chance with Lake, he already knew he wanted it all. All of her. When he'd awakened that morning the ghost of what could be had been with him, the idea of Lake in his arms as they slowly greeted each new day together, her girls and maybe a few future children jumping into bed with them.

But alas, reality had struck and that image drifted away. But not before Logan had gotten a taste and knew that this was all he wanted.

So he knew he'd have to work for it. Winning Lake would be an uphill trek. One he'd already kind of messed up when he'd kissed her. But again, he didn't regret it.

Because that kiss.

He blew out a breath. Their kisses in high school had been great. Magnificent, even. After Lake was no longer in his life, Logan had used those kisses to judge every other kiss he received. But those were nothing compared to the night before.

The physical part of the kiss had been hot. Logan could use no other word to describe it. He wouldn't be surprised to still see steam coming off of his lips, the kiss had been that fiery.

Yeah, he needed to stop thinking about that.

But the kiss had been so much more than physical, at least to Logan. He'd always believed that physical intimacy was an outward display of what was happening between the souls of two people and that's exactly why that kiss had been so incredible. He'd felt their souls coming together in a way he'd never experienced. He was sure he'd never experience it again even if he kissed hundreds more women. There was something about Lake. She was it for him.

If his brothers could read his thoughts . . . he didn't even want to think about the taunts he'd receive.

Logan looked over at the clock in his kitchen to see that it was nearing nine am. He'd gotten to sleep in a bit that morning since it was his day off.

Cowboys didn't often get time off, especially those just starting out or those running ranches on their own. But Logan was lucky. Not only was their business stable, but he had six brothers to manage the workload with him.

It had been one of the things his dad had been adamant about when they'd started working for him. Days off. A rancher could literally work twenty-four/seven if they allowed themselves. The work never stopped. Foals came into the world in the middle of the night, caring little that ranchers wanted to sleep.

So Mitchell Ashford had sat down with each of his boys and told them that the ranch would demand everything from them. But it was up to them, as men, what to give the ranch. If they gave their heart, soul, breath, light, and life to the ranch, it would take it. And it would probably thrive.

But then what else would they have? If the ranch had all of them what would be left for their family—the Ashford family or, one day, their own wife and children?

Mitchell had let them know that could never happen. His priorities in life had been God, his wife, his children, and then the ranch. In that order. Never changing. And it was only because he'd stuck to that hierarchy that he felt okay with leaving the world when he had.

So that's why Logan had a day off today, on a random Tuesday. The brothers had set up a simple system where they could request certain days off. They tried to have the majority of them working each day if they could, but because brothers like Memphis always wanted Saturdays and Sundays off it was easier for Logan just to find a day in the middle of the week to rest. Honestly, as long as he had time for Sunday services he didn't really care if he got weekend days off.

At least for now. He wondered if Lake's girls played soccer the way she had. He could imagine himself pulling up in his truck to those games on Saturday mornings and Memphis would just have to suck it up and take a different day off.

Okay, his thoughts needed to calm down. It was one kiss. A kiss Lake clearly regretted.

But then again, Logan wasn't deterred. If it weren't for her girls running into the house he knew in his soul that Lake would have felt differently after that kiss. The regret was solely because her daughters had almost caught them. He'd felt it as she kissed him that it was right. For both of them. As much as the timing may have seemed unwise to everyone else in the world, when it came down to Lake and Logan, that kiss was timed perfectly. And that was why Logan couldn't regret it. But he could also understand why Lake had.

Her regret just meant that he'd have to work that much harder to let her know how much he cared, how much she deserved from life. And Logan welcomed that challenge. He'd never been one to stay away from something just because it would be hard work.

And proving himself was actually what he was supposed to be doing right now, instead of reminiscing over that kiss. He'd woken up determined to figure out a good excuse to get into the old ranch house and then had tried to plan what he would say to Lake when he had the chance. He thought about apologizing—not for the kiss, never the kiss—but for putting her in a position that made her uncomfortable. But then again, apologizing after a kiss never worked out for the heroes of the romcoms Holland made him watch.

So no apologizing.

What Logan really wanted to do was start bashing Fred. Lake needed to know she'd done nothing wrong. After what he'd done to Lake, she deserved to move on from her marriage as quickly as she wanted.

Or as slowly, a small voice from the back of Logan's mind pointed out.

Logan wanted to squash that voice but that wasn't right. The voice was correct. If Lake wanted more time, Logan needed to give it to her. She deserved that and so much more from him.

So should he just go hang out at the house? Let Lake take the lead? That didn't seem like working hard to win her over.

But sitting patiently did sound like torture. Maybe waiting for Lake would be the hardest work of all?

Thankfully the sound of a truck rumbling up his drive saved him from his own thoughts. He'd know the sound of that truck anywhere.

Sure enough, when he looked out his kitchen window he saw his mom parking and climbing out of her cherry red truck, the truck his dad had gotten her a few years back on her birthday. She'd squealed and leapt into Mitchell's arms. She'd wanted that exact truck forever and the smile on Mitchell's face when he'd gifted it to his wife was a moment Logan would carry in his heart forever.

"Come in," Logan called out before his mom could knock.

He'd told her she didn't have to knock—he never did at her house—but she insisted. She kept saying this would one day be home not just for him, but for his wife and their family. They deserved privacy even if Logan didn't feel the need for it now.

"Good morning," his mom called out, not as cheerily as normal, and the sound of Logan's front door closing followed her greeting.

Logan was going to return the sentiment with a little more enthusiasm than his mother but was cut off by her entrance into the kitchen.

"What did you do?" Morgan asked, a frown prominently featured on her face.

Logan kept his mouth shut as he eyed her warily. He'd fallen into that trap a dozen too many times. His mother would ask him what he'd done and he'd admit to something she had no idea about, getting him in trouble for two things instead of just one.

Nope. Logan had learned his lesson. He'd wait until Morgan gave him a clue about his supposed crime.

"I know it's because of you that she's quit," Morgan continued, eyes snapping.

Logan felt his eyes go wide.

"She didn't," he said, shaking his head. Lake wouldn't do that. Even if she was uncomfortable with their situation, she wouldn't leave Morgan in the lurch. "She wouldn't strand you like that."

"Of course she wouldn't. You should know the woman you love better than that," Morgan replied.

Logan's mouth dropped open. Could a man have no secrets?

"You're easier to read than any of those studs when they strike a fancy for one of our mares," Morgan said with a dismissive wave of her hand at his shocked look. She took the stool next to Logan and lovingly patted his arm.

Logan wasn't sure how he felt about being compared to a horse. At least there were worse animals.

"She called and asked how I was doing after the news about Madison. She was thrilled for me. And I told her it was reassuring, but I'd known deep down my Mitchell wouldn't have done that and then left the world without a word about it."

"Dad wouldn't have done it, period," Logan had to interject.

"No man is perfect, Logan. I would hope your father wouldn't have done that, but every marriage is tough work. We all make mistakes . . ."

"But never that mistake," Logan interrupted again.

"I've learned two words that are smart to kick out of any marriage: never and always. You put too heavy of expectations on your partner and yourself when you use those words."

Logan thought about it and acknowledged the truth of that statement.

"But Dad wouldn't have gone to any other woman. It wasn't in him," Logan insisted.

"It's in all of us. If we entertain the idea of other people for too long, if we fantasize about what could be, if we allow that devil even a sliver of our minds, he can creep in and before we know it vows are broken. I'm not saying if your father had had an affair it would be okay. I would have been crushed, and I'm not sure if our marriage would have survived it. But it's dangerous to believe that you or your partner is above anything. We are all susceptible to temptation. It's just up to us to fight it with all we've got."

Logan's stomach turned. He couldn't be capable of such a thing, could he? But he supposed his mom was right—to think he was above ever being tempted of such a thing would be the pride before a fall.

Morgan seemed to understand Logan needed time to digest those words before speaking more on that same subject, so she moved on.

"Lake asked if, now that Madison had some answers about her paternity, she'd be going back to Oregon. I let her know I didn't think that was the case, and I was pretty sure she'd be coming to the house for the foreseeable future. She wanted to stick around and get to know her family. I told her we'd even discussed Madison moving in for a bit. It was then that Lake sighed, the sigh so full of meaning I could have written an entire love song with its intentions and this is how I knew you were involved with why Lake was quitting. She followed the sigh with saying that she was grateful I had Madison because she was pretty sure she needed to stop working here. So I'm going to ask you again, what did you do?"

Lake was running. Logan shouldn't be surprised. Their kiss had been a lot. Her emotions had to be all over the place. She was probably wanting to find a place of peace and calm and working at the ranch surely wouldn't bring that for her. He shouldn't begrudge her that.

Still, all he wanted to do was chase after her.

"I kissed her," Logan confessed. She'd find out anyway. His

mom could be a bloodhound when it came to figuring out things that were happening in her children's lives.

"Oh," Morgan said as she leaned back on her barstool, surveying him thoughtfully.

"Is that all you're going to say?" Logan asked.

He was sure there would be follow up. Either in the vein of *now what are you going to do?* Or *you'd better not be messing with that sweet girl.*

But Morgan said nothing. Just watched him.

"Am I right? Do you love her?" Morgan asked.

Logan nodded wordlessly. It felt good for someone to know the truth. He couldn't be telling Lake anytime soon without risking that she'd run for the hills. She'd already run to a new job. Wait, she had a new job, right? She needed the money; that's why she'd come to Blue Falls Ranch in the first place. And if Logan had driven her away without another alternative? He'd get her back. Promise he'd never go to the old ranch house while she was there. Let her know this was a safe place for her even if she doubted it.

"I have go to after her. She needs this job," Logan said, standing.

His mother grabbed the sleeve of his Henley and yanked him down hard. So hard that Logan decided to sit once again.

"She has a job lined up. Lottie got her one at the B&B. Apparently the timing is perfect because they just opened a bunch of new positions now that the renovation is complete," Morgan explained.

Logan nodded but couldn't help his accompanying sigh. Now that that was taken care of there was literally no reason for Logan to go see Lake.

Because if she'd run, he should give her space, shouldn't he?

"People are going to say it's a little soon after the funeral for love," Morgan said slowly.

Logan nodded. He understood that. But he didn't care what people said, just what Lake felt.

Besides, Fred deserved none of Lake's loyalty to him after death, especially when he hadn't even been faithful during their marriage. When he'd held Lake's heart and callously broken it.

Logan felt a twinge of guilt for wishing Fred was alive just long enough for Logan to put him in some pain. Maybe a punch or two to the gut, a jab in either eye.

"Fred wasn't—" Logan stopped, knowing he couldn't tell Morgan any of what Lake had told him. Yet he wanted his mother to understand.

"I picked up on things. Watching Lake live the Madison and Mitchell situation with us opened my eyes to a few things. Don't reveal her secrets."

Logan hadn't been about to but he was grateful his mother knew without actually knowing. He guessed her crazy, spot-on intuition was good for something.

"But I'm guessing her girls know nothing?" Morgan asked.

Logan shook his head. And it had to stay that way.

"So if they see their mom dating some guy right after their father's death?" Morgan pressed.

Oh, when she put it that way. Logan had understood that Lake's hesitation and regret after their kiss had been because of her girls. But he had honestly thought it was a bit of an overreaction, especially considering that her girls had welcomed Logan into their lives with open arms. What he hadn't considered was that it might not continue to be the case if they knew Logan wasn't just their mother's friend. That Logan wanted a permanent place in their lives. And while Logan couldn't have cared less if people in the town thought they were disregarding Fred if they dove into a relationship so soon, how it would appear to Lake's girls did matter. So much.

How could he have been so blind?

"I need to give her space," Logan decided even as his heart sank.

Morgan nodded.

Logan bit his lip. "No way around that?"

"Oh, there's always a way. You could push your way in and see where the chips fall. I'm pretty sure that girl is just as head over heels for you but she's scared to death. And you'd push her past that fear, for better or worse. You'd push her into making a decision—maybe before she's ready to make one."

"And I could lose her."

"Or you could have her, but then lose her later when she realizes you didn't respect her needs right now."

Ouch. His mom was right.

Logan had to leave Lake alone. But how in the heck was he supposed to do that? With her just across town?

He knew he'd do all in his power to run into her by "accident" at the grocery store. Good grief, his thoughts were bordering on stalking. He needed to take action.

He should get out of town, at least for a bit. It was the only thing that made sense.

He'd never taken a real vacation since starting at the ranch. His dad had encouraged him to, but something had always come up. Maybe now it was finally time? All of his brothers had taken vacations. They wouldn't begrudge him one.

He gazed at his mother. His mother who had likewise endured a devastating loss. Thanksgiving was over, but Christmas was a couple weeks away. Maybe a distraction right now was exactly what they both needed.

His mom loved traveling and because of that his dad had taken her on babymoons before each of their children. In fact, they'd named their kids based on their vacation destinations.

They'd been pretty poor when Logan had been born so a vacation to a town in north Utah, a few hours south of Blue Falls, was all his parents could afford. They'd upgraded to Jackson Hole,

Wyoming for Jackson and had ended with their only out-of-the-country destination, Holland.

They'd gone on a few more international trips over the years since Holland had been born, but looking at his mom and realizing he needed to get out of town, the idea of one of his mother's bucket list trips came to mind.

A Caribbean cruise.

His dad had been the type to love destinations where they could be on the go, exploring and active, but his mom loved the idea of relaxing on the sandy white beaches in the Caribbean.

And just like that his decision was made. He needed to get out of town and his mom deserved this treat.

"I'll give her space," Logan promised.

Morgan smiled.

"But it will nearly kill me if I stay in town."

Morgan's smile dropped.

"So do you want to go with me on a Caribbean cruise?" Logan asked.

His mother's eyes sparked with immediate unshed tears.

"Are you sure?" Morgan asked. She knew leaving town was a sacrifice for Logan. But they both knew it needed to be done if he wanted to honor Lake.

"I'm sure."

Logan would step away. Give Lake some time. Hopefully when he got back from his trip it would no longer be so hard to stay away from her. He'd let her grieve, let her children grieve. He'd give them all the time they needed to figure out their lives without Fred.

And then when they all were ready, Logan would be there.

Fifteen

"I can't believe you rehired her!"

Lake froze in the hall. The yelling sounded like it was coming from the very room she had been directed to by Mabel at the front desk.

It was her first day working at Blue Falls B&B and she was a little nervous. And to be honest, the yelling wasn't helping her to feel any better about the decisions she'd made in the past seventy-two hours. She hadn't wanted to quit her job at the ranch but it had been the only thing that made sense after she'd been stupid enough to kiss Logan.

Holy cannoli, that kiss.

Lake waved a hand over her face and remembered where she was. In a hallway that led to the office of Charlie Brown, Lottie's mom and one of the owners of the B&B. An office where she'd heard someone yelling.

Should she hurry forward and see if Charlie needed help? The woman was older but then again she did have Lottie's spunk. Honestly, maybe Lake should get up there to save whoever was idiotic enough to yell at Charlie. Or should she go back to the front desk and alert Mabel to what was going on? Although

Mabel was at least twenty years older than Charlie, so Lake wasn't sure how she would help.

"Brandon."

Lake paused at that name. That's why the yelling had sounded somewhat familiar. It was Lottie's brother, Brandon. But why was he yelling at his mom? That wasn't like him at all. She'd only seen the younger Brown sibling a couple of times, even though he worked at the ranch as well, but each time he'd been ready with a smile. He was usually so calm and easygoing. But something had him worked up.

"Brandon, I wish you would lighten up on the poor girl. She's had a hard time of it," Charlie said.

Lake began to backpedal. She really shouldn't be listening to this.

"Maybe life would be easier on her if she didn't con people." Brandon's voice now lacked any anger; Lake swore he was just sad.

She had been apprised of enough town gossip from her mom and sister that she knew exactly who Brandon was talking about. Alice and Allie, the cute twins who'd worked for the Browns a few years before, hadn't been entirely honest. Alice, in fact, had straight up stolen from the B&B in order to perpetuate the feud that had begun brewing between the Heathcliffs and the Browns. Lottie, a Brown, and her now-husband Leo, a Heathcliff, had been caught in the middle of it all and although it had all ended up wonderfully, things had gotten hairy for a while. Especially because Brandon had started dating Allie, the twin who wasn't stealing but was keeping her sister's secret. According to Lake's mom, Allie had been against the whole thing and had begged Alice to come clean, but she hadn't been able to completely turn on her sister by letting the Browns know what was going on.

It had been quite the muddle but apparently Allie was back now, working at the B&B.

"Can you imagine how hard it was for her to come back to us?" Charlie asked.

"Yeah, because she shouldn't have." Brandon's voice was firm.

Lake couldn't say she blamed him. He'd been bamboozled. But Lake also felt sorry for Allie. Neither of them deserved what had happened to them.

"It's done, Brandon. And I'm not sure why you're so upset. You don't even work here anymore."

Lake heard an indignant huff and the office door began to open. She hurried back to the hall entrance so it would look like she'd just gotten there.

"Sorry for trying to protect my family," Brandon said bitterly before leaving the office and storming down the hall.

He was so upset that he barely acknowledged Lake with a nod before escaping the area. Poor guy.

Lake eased her way down the hall. It wasn't very long but she didn't want to show up at Charlie's office before Charlie was ready for her.

"Don't need to lollygag out there on my account," Charlie called out.

Lake looked around. How did Charlie know she was in the hall?

She suddenly looked up and spotted a camera.

"We had them installed with the remodel," Charlie explained.

Lake must be practically making eye contact with Charlie through the camera.

"So you know I heard all of that?" she asked, wincing a bit as she paused in the office doorway.

"At least you made an attempt to leave. Most in town would have put their ears to the door," Charlie joked as she stood, rounding the desk, and hugged Lake warmly.

"Welcome home," Charlie greeted her.

Lake breathed in Charlie's comfort and hugged her right back.

"Not the best circumstances to come home in but we're mighty glad to have you," Charlie said.

Lake nodded as Charlie let her go.

She was grateful Charlie hadn't mentioned Fred. She wasn't sure if Lottie had warned Charlie that things had been strained in Lake and Fred's relationship or if Charlie's get-to-the-point manner was what drove her, but either way Lake was glad. The last thing she wanted to do was receive condolences for Fred. Especially because the reason she was here was because she'd kissed a man just days after Fred's funeral.

Okay, that was an exaggeration. It had been weeks. And considering Fred's double betrayal, she didn't even really blame herself, but her feelings were complicated at the moment. So it was nice that Charlie hadn't said anything to complicate them more.

"Thanks for starting on a Friday. I know it's a bit strange, but we needed you to start as soon as we got your paperwork together. Did Lottie say what we need you for?" Charlie asked.

Lake nodded. Lottie had told her a bit. Mabel was getting on in years but refused to give up her job at the front desk. She did allow others to work shifts but she still wanted at least forty hours a week where she manned the desk.

"Mabel's been having a hard time learning the new reservation system?" Lake ventured. She didn't want to assume, but that was pretty much what Lottie had told her. Lottie's exact words had been, "I wish Mabel would just admit to herself this is one new trick she can't quite master."

Lottie had said the words fondly. It was easy to see her love for Mabel, as well as her frustration since the reservation system was vital to business.

"That's the understatement of the year. But she's determined to keep at it. Thankfully most of our guests can check in virtually so we don't need Mabel for that. But sometimes a guest comes to the front desk and needs information from the system. Mabel, sweet as she is, just can't find it. And our guests have been lodging complaints. Not that I could ever tell her that. It would break her heart."

"So I need to either get on the computer to find the information or appease the guests while Mabel does so?" Lake asked. That didn't sound too bad.

Charlie nodded. "We've had the hardest time filling this position. We weren't sure anyone could do it. Lottie thought about coming in, but she's got her hands full with those adorable grandbabies of mine," Charlie said. "But when she said you needed a job . . . you've always had the kindest soul. If anyone can walk this tightrope it's you, Lake."

Lake felt her heart swell with the compliment. Charlie might be buttering her up but Lake didn't care. It was such a generous thing to say and her poor battered heart needed all the compassion it could get right now.

"My dad is still insisting on working in the kitchen. I was worried about him as well but we've hired an incredible chef to help him. So Mabel was my final concern, but with you here I know it will all be fine. It's been intense trying to find enough new hires after the remodel. We added onto the B&B since we were already doing so much work to the existing parts. With the remodel we've nearly doubled our capacity—thus hiring Allie. I'm sure I can trust you to keep that conversation you heard under wraps?" Charlie asked.

Lake nodded. "Of course."

"Thank you. I feel badly for Brandon. I really do. But he had no idea what Allie is enduring right now and we really needed her as well. I know we can trust her again, and if Brandon would give her a chance he'd see that too. But . . . "

"It's different when love was involved."

"You hit the problem on the nose." Charlie sighed.

"Sounds like a lot to juggle," Lake said sympathetically.

Charlie nodded. "You could say that again. But I have a feeling, now that you're here, that it won't be quite as difficult to manage it all."

Lake nodded again. She would miss the ranch. She'd miss Morgan, Holland, and Madison more. Logan most of all.

But she felt a peace come over her. She was supposed to be here. The B&B needed her. And she needed the B&B.

Now that she no longer worked for Logan, things would be a little less complicated for them. Fred, her girls, her family, and his family all popped into her head. Okay, still complicated but less so.

But maybe with one less complication she and Logan at least had a chance. Because if she pushed away her worry, guilt, and frustration at Fred, she could see that real feelings for Logan were developing.

Did she and Logan really have a chance?

"How was your first day of work?" Lottie asked.

She'd insisted on meeting Lake at the B&B's restaurant for dinner that evening and since it was a Friday night Lake had seen no reason not to. Her parents had even encouraged her to take some time to herself, volunteering to babysit.

"It was pretty incredible, as far as first days go."

Lake knew she'd been blessed with her jobs since Fred had passed. So many would have still been floundering but her support system, Blue Falls, had sustained her and brought her not just one but two extraordinary jobs.

"Mabel figured out why I was there in about zero-point-two seconds. She quickly let me know she didn't need my help and then felt guilty for the way she spoke to me. After that we kind of fell into a rhythm. I gave her a couple of minutes to try to figure out an issue while I entertained the guest or did whatever aside from the computer I could to help out the staff member with an issue. She usually got the job done, but if she couldn't she'd turn it over to me."

"Really? It was that easy? She's been fighting Mom on this for months," Lottie said with a sigh as she looked over to the front desk that was now being manned by the night shift manager.

Mabel was somewhere in the back of the B&B where the family had its residence. She had a studio apartment next to the space where Charlie lived with Rodney, Lottie's grandpa.

"I think she felt sorry for me. I may have pulled the young widow card," Lake said, biting back a smile.

"You didn't." Lottie appeared shocked.

Lake didn't blame her. It was a pretty low blow.

"You are a genius," Lottie said as her shock gave way to a giant smile.

Okay, not the reaction Lake had been expecting but she'd take it.

"I mean, Fred does owe you. It's the least he can do from the afterlife after all he's put you through." She whispered that last sentence even though they were seated a few tables away from the nearest party. Lake was sure those tables would fill soon but Lottie had seated them, waving off the restaurant's host, and she'd selected the most private table the place had to offer.

Lake guessed Lottie was right about Fred owing her, though. And Lake wouldn't have said anything but when Mabel had snapped at her, Lake had really been about to cry. She was sure that if Mabel knew why she was there she would insist Charlie fire her. And then Lake would have to go back to the ranch. That would be so much more embarrassing than if she'd just gone back to work after the kiss. All of those thoughts had been swirling and the tears had started.

Mabel had taken Lake into her arms and immediately apologized, saying she couldn't believe what a snark she'd been to the poor young widow.

Lake hadn't corrected her or explained the true reason she

was crying. And after that things had gone swimmingly, so Lake had gone with it even though she felt some pretty immense guilt.

Leave it to Lottie to smooth things over and make that guilt disappear into thin air.

"I'm not sure about that, but I'm glad things are working out with Mabel. Although things have been pretty nuts with all the new hires around." Lake explained the biggest difficulty of the day. Well, other than the moment she thought Mabel was going to fire her.

"I'm sure. Most of them have experience in their jobs, right?" Lottie asked.

Lake nodded. "But even then. There are just little things, you know? And so many of those little things involve us."

"Yeah, the front desk really is like the control center of the B&B. Especially with Mabel there," Lottie said, obviously remembering her time working there.

It was nice to have someone who not only understood Lake's new job but all of her coworkers as well. She was feeling more and more grateful that Lottie had insisted on this dinner.

"Speaking of new hires, how's Ruby doing? I'm pretty sure she's been working for a few days now," Lottie added, remembering the other hire she'd suggested to her mom. Ruby, Madison's best friend, had decided to stay in town as long as Madison did. That was true friendship right there. But Ruby evidently didn't have the same nest egg as Madison, and didn't want to live off of her friend's money. So she'd started hunting for a job as a waitress, which was what she'd done back in Oregon. When Lottie had heard she needed a job, she'd offered her one at the B&B's restaurant and Ruby had started working sometime that past weekend.

"I think she's doing just fine. Although I heard that she had to help escort a diner off of the premises last night. She came over to tell us the story, distracting Mabel while I helped a guest with an urgent matter. I meant to get the details later today but it was so crazy busy through my whole shift. Oh well, I'm sure I'll hear them soon."

"That sounds intense. I always miss all of the good gossip now that I'm home all day with my babies. Any idea who the diner was?" Lottie asked.

Lake shrugged. "I figured it was a tourist. None of our own would behave so badly."

Lottie nodded.

"But other than that she seems to be doing amazingly. We've gotten no complaints about her. And believe me we've heard plenty about some others. Speaking of which . . . " Lake nodded in the direction of a server on the other side of the room. Ruby's striking blonde hair was hard to miss.

Even from where they sat it was easy to see the smiles on the faces at the table Ruby was serving. Granted, it was a table full of men and Ruby was gorgeous, but either way it spoke well for her that her customers were happy during her first week of work.

It was then that their own server brought their drink orders, a caffeinated soda for Lottie—she was sure she would be up most of the night with her baby; she said he liked to punish her whenever she left him behind—and a water for Lake.

Their waiter took their order and as he left Lake recognized another blonde from her day. Allie was cautiously making her way to their table.

"I'm sorry to interrupt," Allie said, her signature smile absent.

At least that was what Lake had been told. Mabel's exact words had been, "It's a shame that girl left her smile at home today. It's a good one."

"Not a problem," Lottie replied.

Lake took a long swig of her water and sat back discreetly, trying not to intrude on a conversation that obviously didn't concern her.

"I just . . . I have to apologize to you," Allie said, her eyes brimming with tears. "I can't believe your family took me back. I tried applying at the Heathcliff resort first but the manager remembered me and didn't even give me a second glance. I was sure your family would do the same."

Lottie's eyes had become slits. "Who did you say wouldn't even give you a chance at the resort?" Lottie asked.

Lake smiled. Of course her friend's anger was at the person who hadn't given Allie a chance, not at Allie. Although from what Lake had heard, Lottie had plenty of reason to hold a grudge against Allie.

"Oh, I didn't mean . . . that guy did what I expected. I just meant to say that your family is—I can't—" Tears began streaming down Allie's face and she fiercely swiped them away. "I've done so much wrong. And I promise I wouldn't have come here if things were any different. But I have to be back in town and I have so few skills. Housekeeping is pretty much all I can do. Oh man, I'm babbling. You all are incredible and I am so, so sorry. If I could take back what Alice did, and my part in letting her do it . . . "

"You caught that, right?" Lottie looked at Lake and then back at Allie. "What Alice did, not what Allie did." Lottie looked meaningfully at Allie, hoping the young woman would understand her point. "I'll admit I was angry for a bit. What happened made it hard for me and Leo in the beginning."

"I know. I am so sorry." Allie looked on the verge of sobbing.

"But it all turned out fine. Incredibly magnificent, in fact. Leo and I are stronger for what we've gone through and when I really thought about it, I realized I might have done the exact same thing you had. If Brandon was doing something wrong, could I have turned him in? I wasn't sure I could. So how could I judge you for the very thing I might have done if I'd been in the same situation? That wasn't fair."

"What I did to you all wasn't fair," Allie said.

"What your sister did to all of us wasn't fair. You were a victim too. When I began to look at it like that I realized how terribly we'd all treated you, but you were long gone by then. So I have to say I'm sorry as well."

Allie shook her head.

"I should have tried to help you out back then. You needed someone and we all turned on you."

"As you should have. You didn't know you could trust me. You still don't and yet your mom gave me a job." Allie once again wiped away her tears.

"Okay, how about this?" Lottie offered. "We both said we were sorry, and we both hated how things went down. Let's start over?"

Allie looked up toward the ceiling, blinking away more tears.

"You can't mean that."

"I can and I do," Lottie said with a genuine grin.

Allie brought her gaze down, looking at Lottie with awe-filled stars in her eyes.

"Thank you," she said brokenly before throwing her arms around Lottie.

Lottie returned the hug immediately.

"I promise your faith in me won't be misplaced ever again," Allie vowed.

"I know," Lottie replied as Allie pulled away.

"I'll let you both get back to your dinner," Allie said, still blinking and wiping at the remnants of tears on her cheeks.

"See you tomorrow," Lake said to her coworker, who smiled at her gratefully. Now Lake could totally understand what Mabel meant about that smile.

"That was beautiful," Lake said to Lottie.

"It was, wasn't it?" Lottie said, looking in the direction Allie had left. "Forgiveness is powerful."

Lake almost dropped her glass, but caught herself in time to set it down carefully before letting her hands drop to her side, where they trembled slightly.

"Did I say something? Your face has gone white," Lottie said to Lake.

Forgiveness is powerful. That was what she had to do. Lake had to find a way to forgive Fred. Until then she'd never be able to move on.

But Fred didn't deserve her forgiveness. He hadn't even been repentant. He'd been with that woman on the day he died. With his last breath his actions had told Lake how much Sachia meant to him and how little their marriage mattered. How was Lake supposed to forgive that?

And yet she'd seen forgiveness in action. She'd been the one to say it was beautiful. She'd seen it heal not only Allie but Lottie as well.

But with Fred it was different, wasn't it? She just needed time, not forgiveness, to get over her complicated past with Fred and be able to one day give her all to Logan. Because the only reason she was even considering forgiving Fred was if holding that grudge would hurt her future with Logan. But after enough time that guilty, worried part of her would be appeased. Forgiveness wasn't necessary. And then she would be ready to give all of herself to Logan. No part of her would be hesitating the way it was now.

Yup, that was what she needed, time. Forgiveness was for other situations. Like Lottie's and Allie's.

"I'm fine. Just thought of something, but I'm okay now," Lake responded.

"Are you sure?" Lottie asked.

But Lake didn't get a chance to answer.

"You *are* here," Grace called from about four tables away.

From the determined way she and Holland were approaching Lake and Lottie they had come to find them. Or more likely just Lake.

"Better question is, what are the two of you doing here?" Lake asked when the girls grabbed two chairs from nearby tables, dragging them over to join Lake and Lottie.

The restaurant at the B&B wasn't the fanciest in Blue Falls—there were a few high-end dining establishments that could beat it in that category—but it wasn't anywhere near casual dining either. Not a place where guests grabbed their own chairs from other tables to join an already seated party. But that didn't deter Grace or Holland in the least.

And while the fanciness of the restaurant could be beat, the food couldn't. Even the cuisine at the Heathcliff resort might come second to this one.

"You know this isn't some diner that you can just stroll into and pull up a chair?" Lake asked since her first question was being ignored.

"She owns the place. You don't mind, right, Lottie?" Grace asked.

Lake rolled her eyes but Lottie laughed. "As long as you keep reminding my brother that I own the place, you can do whatever you'd like."

"See?" Grace asked Lake triumphantly.

Lake elbowed her sister in the ribs. Since the table was meant to seat two, they were all within easy reach of each other.

Their server brought Lake's and Lottie's entrees. Lake had ordered the fish special of the day and Lottie the carbonara, but he quickly registered the new guests, asking for their drink orders.

"Are you just having water?" Grace asked Lake.

Lake nodded. It was her beverage of choice. She knew others liked fancy drinks and such but Lake never felt better than after drinking plenty of H2O.

"Booooring," Grace declared. "We'll have what she's having." She pointed to Lottie's drink. "Oh, and her pasta too."

"I'll take the steak," Holland ordered, closing her menu.

Lake realized Holland had been uncharacteristically quiet. What was going on in that pretty head of hers?

"To answer your initial question, we're here because you're here. You didn't come home and we wanted to see how your first day went," Grace said to Lake.

That was actually really sweet.

"Your first day of running," Holland amended Grace's statement, directing a raised eyebrow at Lake.

Now Lake was wishing Holland would go back to being quiet.

"What she said," Grace agreed.

"I wasn't—" Lake started.

"Don't think you can hide anything. I already told her that I caught you and Logan," Grace said, tipping her head toward Holland.

"Wait, caught you with him?" Lottie's eyes went wide.

"Not what you think," Lake protested frantically. This situation was getting out of control.

"But not *not* what you think either," Grace said with a shrug.

"What does that even mean?" Holland asked, turning to Grace.

Lake was wondering the same thing.

"That's why you quit the job at the ranch. You and Logan were . . . " Lottie asked.

"Kissing!" Lake burst out before any other insinuations could be made. She looked around uneasily at the other diners. She'd said that far too loud.

"That's what I was saying," Grace said.

"Me too," Holland added.

"Definitely all I was implying," Lottie finished.

Lake was going to scream.

Especially because her declaration had drawn the attention of most of the tables near them.

"Yes, I kissed Logan," Lake hissed quietly. "Yes, I quit because of that kiss. And yes, I'm running. My first day of running was great. Thanks for asking."

She leaned back in her seat and crossed her arms over her chest defiantly.

"We didn't mean to make you upset," Grace said in a softer voice, watching her sister carefully. "It's just . . . I want you to be happy. And it seemed like kissing Logan made you happy."

"Kissing Logan would make anyone happy," Lake murmured in response.

"Ugh, not me," Holland responded immediately.

"Nor me," said the very married Lottie.

"He's a little old for me," Grace put in.

Lake gritted her teeth. "You know what I mean."

The women at this table were some of the few singles in town who wouldn't have been pleased as punch to exchange places with Lake for that kiss.

"So if kissing Logan made you happy, why did you run?" Holland asked. Her voice was filled with curiosity, but thankfully no accusation.

Lake could understand if Holland was upset with her. She was the one with the most invested if Lake hurt her brother. Was Logan hurt? She hadn't heard anything from him so she figured he was as freaked out as she was and hadn't even considered that possibility. She'd feel terribly if he was hurt.

"Fred just died," Lake whispered, pushing away the possibility that Logan was hurt. She had enough to feel guilty about at the time being.

"So?" Grace asked.

Lottie nodded in agreement with Grace.

Only Holland seemed hesitant to do or say anything.

"He doesn't deserve your concern for preserving his memory," Grace spat.

Lake got it. She'd felt the same way. But then . . .

"But don't his daughters deserve their mother to honor their dad's legacy?" she asked. She knew the girls had asked Logan to join them for family things, but that wasn't the same thing as Lake dating Logan, letting him take a place only Fred had held. Surely they'd feel their mother was pushing their father out too soon if she tried to replace him so quickly.

Grace dropped her gaze.

Lottie nodded again.

"He understands," Holland said gently.

Lake was confused. Fred understood? What did Fred have to understand? And how on earth would Holland know what he'd thought?

"He didn't tell me everything, but he gets it. He's taking my mom on a cruise. I think it's so he can give you space."

Wait, she was talking about Logan. Logan was leaving?

"What? For how long?" Lake couldn't help but ask. Logan couldn't leave her.

Her breathing became rapid.

"Well, I guess there's no question in my mind about your feelings for Logan," Grace smirked.

Why was no one answering her question?

"About a week? He'll be back soon," Holland finally responded.

Thank heavens.

It was only after Lake got the answer to her question that she had a moment to think about her response.

Logan's leaving had sent her into a panic. And as much as she wished she could go after him, to tell him how she felt, she couldn't. Because feelings weren't enough, at least for the time being. Lake's girls needed her to keep her distance. To figure things out for them, for herself, to be the best Lake she could be on her own. And then if and when the time was right, she'd find a way to be with Logan.

She found herself praying, pleading, that one day the time would be right for them.

Sixteen

LOGAN COULDN'T IMAGINE a place on the cruise he wanted to be less than in the bar with his brothers. Yep. Memphis and Jackson had joined Logan and his mom on their vacation. Morgan had been thrilled at the idea of sailing with more than one of her sons so Logan had acquiesced. Honestly, he couldn't have cared if the whole town came with them as long as he had the space he needed from Lake.

He fought the urge to close his eyes and relive that kiss once again. It really was a good thing he'd left Blue Falls when he had. There would have been no way on this green earth that Logan could have stayed away from her had he been in the same town. As it was, he reached for his cell at least once a day, ready to cave and text Lake, since that was the only form of communication at sea.

Usually his phone was either wrestled away from him by Jackson or Logan came to his senses and deleted the text before it was sent. He was a little embarrassed to admit the former happened far more often than the latter.

But they were now on night six of the cruise—just one night left—and Logan was getting used to steering clear of Lake. He eyed his cellphone, lying on the bench next to him in the open booth he sat in with his brothers. His fingers itched to grab it. Okay, he was totally lying to himself, Logan was used to nothing. Would it be so bad to text Lake? Just to see if she was thinking of him as well?

Ack! He'd become the punchline to a sappy love song. And yet he honestly didn't care as long as in the end he and Lake were happy . . . together.

Now he was writing his own personal romcom in his head.

He needed help.

He threw his phone toward Jackson, who grinned as he caught and pocketed the offending piece of technology.

"This is the life, isn't it boys?" Memphis asked, lounging back in his seat and propping a foot up on the coffee table between the couches that made their booth.

They were in an upscale sports bar, so on one side of the room stood the dark wood bar with a cluster of TVs behind it, playing what looked like every football game that had been aired in the past week. Where they sat was a more open area of plush brown couches arranged into semicircles to create booth-like seating. Jackson had insisted that if they had to come to the bar tonight he was at least going to sit on a seat that didn't feel like it was imprinting itself on his behind.

Logan noticed a replay of Phoenix's game on one of the screens behind the bar so he'd been watching it on and off for the past fifteen minutes, although he'd already seen the full game earlier that week.

"Sailing in the middle of the Caribbean. A drink in each hand. Gorgeous women eyeing us from the bar," Memphis added after a few moments of silence when no one responded to his comment on 'the life.'

Logan raised an eyebrow toward his little brother. He was the only Ashford who had a drink in his hand, much less two. Logan and Jackson were steering clear of the hard stuff on and off of the cruise.

Logan's mom had been raised by a violent alcoholic. Mitchell had had to protect his wife from his father-in-law on more than one occasion in their marriage. And even if Logan hadn't witnessed firsthand the dangers of alcohol as he'd watched his grandfather scream and raise his hand at his mother for what seemed like no reason at all, his dad had warned his sons against the dangers of drinking to excess from the time they were wee things. Between his grandpa and his uncle Ronnie, Logan knew alcohol addiction ran in his family, on both sides, and he didn't care to have anything rule his life, especially something as fickle as alcohol. So while he wouldn't always turn down a single drink for a special occasion, Logan rarely touched the stuff. But he didn't judge those who did. Except maybe Memphis, because he was already beginning to slur his words. How could two drinks have done that to him? Or had he started drinking before they'd gotten to the bar?

That worried Logan. Memphis hadn't mentioned anything about drinking beforehand. Was he hiding it? It was never a good thing when someone hid their drinking habits. Logan would need to keep an eye on his little brother.

"Pretty sure those women are eyeing the men in the group over there," Jackson said as he leaned back, raising his arms and resting them on the back of the couch. "That puts you right out of luck, Memph, since you're still just a boy."

"I'll show you a boy," Memphis said, slamming both glasses down on the table harder than necessary. The glasses rattled as he stood, albeit shakily.

"Stupid rocking ship," Memphis mumbled, although Logan didn't think the ship was at fault for his brother's lack of steadiness.

"Don't wait up for me," Memphis snapped as he strode across the room toward the women whom he claimed were eyeing them.

By the way they smiled flirtatiously at his approach, Logan had to say that Jackson had been wrong. The women were obviously interested in Memphis.

Jackson chuckled as he watched the interaction.

"Did you say that just to get rid of him?" Logan asked with a raised eyebrow.

"You're not the one who's been rooming with him for the past week. After you've spent six nights in a tiny room with that one, you can judge."

Logan raised his hands. "No judging here. If anything, I'm impressed."

Jackson laughed again, partially because of Logan's words, but mostly because Memphis, apparently thinking he was being discreet, was waving his hand behind one of the women's heads to get his brothers' attention, gloating about where he was sitting.

Of course they could see him. As could the friend of the woman Memphis had chosen to sit next to.

The friend was watching him quizzically before she said something to the woman next to Memphis and got up to sit at a booth instead of at the bar where Memphis had joined them. She seemed to keep a watchful eye on her friend who'd stayed back with Memphis as she ordered another drink.

Logan was pretty sure Memphis wouldn't be allowed to chat up the woman much longer with her friend so wary of him.

"Do you think we need to worry about him?" Logan asked seriously, shaking his head as their brother ordered yet another drink from a passing waitress. At least Logan hoped it was just one more.

"He seems like he didn't hear Dad's speeches the way the rest of us did," Jackson said.

Logan nodded. But it was more than that. Memphis had always liked having a good time, but this much drinking was out of character even for him. Thinking back, he realized it had started around the time of their dad's death. Was Memphis still mourning? Or was it even more than that?

"Should I be worried about him?" Logan asked again because Jackson hadn't really answered his question.

Jackson watched Memphis receive the drink he'd ordered and immediately down it.

"Maybe," Jackson said thoughtfully. "But there's nothing we can do tonight except make sure he stops soon and get him into bed."

Logan agreed. Although if their mother was there, Logan knew she would have done something. The right thing. She always knew how to handle her boys, but she'd already headed to bed for the evening.

Logan considered talking to her in the morning but hesitated. He knew it would hurt his mother's heart to see Memphis behaving in such a manner. Memphis, sensing that, seemed to save his heaviest drinking for whenever their mom wasn't around.

So Logan wouldn't present this side of their brother to their mother unless he had to. To protect both of them. The rest of them would just have to make sure Memphis didn't do anything too stupid.

"The one at the booth is still eyeing you," Jackson said, nudging Logan as he glanced toward the woman who'd left Memphis behind.

"Or you." Logan didn't even look in the direction of the booth. He honestly didn't care who the woman was looking at.

"Nope, definitely you," Jackson said from his nearly reclined position, his eyes shifting from the games to the woman and back again. "But I'm guessing you still have eyes for just one woman?" he teased.

"It hasn't even been a week, so yeah, I'm still pretty hung up on Lake," Logan shot back.

Jackson cleared his throat. "This isn't like a passing fancy?"

Logan turned to look at his brother. "I'm pretty sure I've been in love with her since I was fifteen."

Jackson's head jerked back as if he'd been punched. "Whoa."

"Yeah, whoa," Logan agreed. He'd never admitted that out loud.

"Even though Fred was a friend?" Jackson asked.

Logan would never reveal what Lake had told him. Even though he knew it would make him look bad to his brother, he couldn't betray Lake's trust or cause her any further pain.

"Fred wasn't much of a friend when he asked Lake out right after we broke up." Logan gave the best excuse he could. "Besides, it's not like I ever acted on those feelings."

"Until now."

"Until now," Logan agreed.

"So why sit back and wait, if you're in love with her?"

"She needs time. She's got kids who also need time. I may not still feel any allegiance to Fred, but I want what's best for Lake and her girls."

"You really are in love."

Yeah, Logan really was.

But reflecting on that fact was doing nothing to lift his mood, so Logan decided to change the subject.

"What about you?" he asked.

"What about me?" Jackson countered. He sat up from his slouched position and shifted uncomfortably.

"You sure jumped on the opportunity to join us as Memphis's roommate. I thought for sure Austin would be our fourth but it felt like you were just as anxious to get out of town as I was."

"Did it?" Jackson asked, avoiding his brother's gaze as he leaned forward to grab his water and took a gigantic gulp.

Oh yeah, there was a story there.

"What happened, Jacks?" Logan pressed.

Jackson blew out a breath. "I guess you'll probably hear about it through the town grapevine anyway. I went on a date with Avery."

Logan had followed Jackson's example of drinking water, lifting his glass to take a gulp as well. At just the wrong time.

Water squirted out of Logan's mouth with Jackson's revelation.

"You what?!" he spluttered, coughing as he tried to clean up his mess with a tiny napkin.

"It's not what it sounds like," Jackson said.

"So you didn't go on a date with Avery?"

"Oh no, I did. I didn't mean to but I did."

"That makes absolutely no sense."

"Give me a minute to explain."

"Fine," Logan said, leaning back as he propped a foot on his other knee.

"So you know we're working on the land deal with the Hartfields."

Logan nodded.

"Avery has actually been really helpful with everything. I thought for sure that after you shot her down at Chicken and More we were screwed, but she didn't seem to let it affect anything professionally and I was impressed."

Logan groaned as Jackson sighed.

"She got things moving and we were going to draw up a deal when Avery suggested that maybe we should go to dinner with the Hartfields. Make this personal for them. Remind them that I'm their neighbor, Mitchell's son. We've been friendly for years."

Logan bent forward to grab his glass of water. He felt like he needed something to hold onto. His heart raced as if he were about to walk into Avery's trap.

"I thought, why not?" Jackson continued.

"Why not? Why would you? You could have had Mom invite the Hartfields to dinner and cut Avery out of it." Logan was trying to save past Jackson to no avail.

"I know this now. But she'd been so cool. I thought she'd actually be an asset at dinner. And this way Mom wouldn't have to be involved. She hosts everyone for us. It was my way of taking control of things."

"By letting Avery take control?"

"You said you'd let me speak."

"Sorry." Logan bowed his head, truly repentant.

Jackson was already feeling stupid and apparently things had gone so badly that he'd had to run away. Logan didn't need to add to that.

Jackson dipped his head once in acknowledgement.

"So we got to dinner. Avery had insisted on picking me up, telling me that's what she normally did for clients."

"Ugh." Logan groaned again.

Jackson glared and Logan slammed his lips shut.

"We went to the restaurant at the B&B."

"Nice place." Logan changed up his approach. He was now being supportive of past Jackson to let present Jackson know that he wasn't judging past Jackson.

"Yeah," Jackson said through gritted teeth.

Wait, the restaurant had been the problem?

"We show up and they take us to a table for two. I'm about to point out to the hostess that we need two more seats when Avery grabs my arm. It startled me so much that I didn't say anything. I just sat. Avery sat on the other side of the table and then smiled. You know that smile."

Logan did his best not to physically shake off the willies that Avery's winning smile caused. If Avery was winning it meant whoever was with her was losing.

"She let me know the Hartfields had 'cancelled.'"

"What?" Logan couldn't help but ask.

"My thought exactly. I told her if they cancelled why were we there? She said why not just enjoy a meal, the two of us? No need for our evening to be ruined just because the Hartfields didn't show."

Logan's mouth hung open. He knew Avery was capable of doing just about anything to get what she wanted, but this was low.

"Do you think the Hartfields were ever invited?" Logan asked.

"No," Jackson said with a defeated sigh, letting his head fall onto the couch behind him.

Yeah, Logan would have felt the same way.

"But it gets better. Not only am I there on a forced date with Avery, but you know Madison's friend, the one that came with her, Ruby?" Jackson asked.

"Yeah," Logan replied.

"She's our server."

Logan frowned, unsure how that made things any worse. Being manipulated into a date with Avery felt like rock bottom.

"So she comes to our table and asks for our drink orders. My mind is still spinning from what Avery has done to me so I don't even register what is happening, I'm just staring down at my plate, trying to figure out a way out of this mess. And then Ruby clears her throat and tells me she already knew I was rude but my treatment of her that night was just ridiculous. She leaves, without taking our drink orders, and even bumps my arm with her hip as she storms away."

That did kind of make things worse. But he was still stuck on a date with Avery.

"So then Avery asks who that was. I tell her she's Madison's best friend and Avery doesn't believe me. She insists we have a past. I tell her we do, the one I just explained, and then I wonder why I'm trying to explain things to Avery like she's my girlfriend. It feels like I'm in this alternate universe where up is down and crazy is reality."

"How have you kept this from me for so long?" Logan wondered, wide-eyed.

"It's not a night I relish reliving," Jackson replied grimly. That made sense.

"So I clamp my mouth shut. Avery says, see, that proves I'm guilty. Guilty of what I'm not sure. Ruby comes back with two glasses of water, the first she gives to me, spilling some on my pants in the process. Not enough to even see or feel, but just enough to say 'screw you.'"

Why did Ruby hate Jackson so much? Logan could see why his brother felt so lost.

"Then Ruby warns Avery away from me. As if she thinks I'm on a real date. And why shouldn't she? It looks like a date and Avery acts like a jealous date. Everything lines up except for the fact that I wouldn't have ever come if I had known it was going to be a date."

Logan cringed. This was somehow getting worse.

"So as soon as Ruby leaves, Avery asks why Ruby is telling her to run while she can if Ruby isn't an ex and I've finally had it. In the calmest tone I can possibly muster, I tell Avery that this isn't a date. She has no right to be jealous. If Ruby is an ex, that is between me and her. This was supposed to be a business meal, and she should have told me the Hartfields weren't coming because if I had known I would have never come tonight. I had not and would not ever have any interest in going on a date with Avery."

"Ouch," Logan muttered.

"Yeah, she took it even harder than that. Avery gets up, finishing the job Ruby started by throwing the rest of my glass of water on me before storming away. It's then that I remember she was my ride. I'm looking around the restaurant for a solution when Ruby brings the host over, demanding that I be removed from the premises after causing such a scene. So I'm bodily lifted from my chair by the two of them. It takes me a minute to register what is happening because my mind is still back at the moment where Avery threw my water at me. I finally figure it out and shake them off."

"This happened when?"

Logan wasn't sure why he'd heard nothing about the incident before leaving town. This was the juicy stuff that Blue Falls lived for.

"The day before we left. I'd come home straight from that dinner, in an uber since Avery had abandoned me, when you told us about the cruise and I jumped on it. We booked our flight and the passage close to midnight, remember?" Jackson asked. Of course Logan remembered; it had only been a week before. But he had a feeling this was more about Jackson getting things off his chest than telling Logan what had happened at this point. "And then we left Blue Falls early the next morning, flying to Miami to get on this cruise."

"But why has no one from home texted me about this? I could see no one contacting me for the first few days after the incident; it would have taken some time for the news to spread. But I'm sure everyone in town knows by now, right?" Logan asked as he extended his hand, a silent request for his phone.

"Um, I might have stolen yours and Memphis's phones and put them on do not disturb mode right before we got on the cruise," Jackson said, squirming, as he returned the device.

"Bro . . . " Logan shook his head. That was pretty underhanded of Jackson.

"I just needed this week without being reminded of that night. You know I'll be bombarded with it when we get home."

That was true.

"But Mom knows?" Logan asked.

Jackson nodded. "I told her on the plane. She said that if you boys caught me messing with your phones she would deny, deny, deny, but she also said that she understood what I was doing and why."

Logan understood as well so he couldn't really be mad. Had

the situation been reversed, he would have totally done the same thing.

Wait, his phone was on do not disturb? What if Lake had texted?

Panic overwhelmed him as he hurried to change the settings on his phone and waited as text after text chimed its way through.

He should have been wise to what Jackson had done, considering he hadn't gotten a single text while out at sea. But he'd only worried about Lake texting him and it had made sense that she hadn't. Maybe he'd subconsciously assumed everyone else in his life was giving him a break while on vacation? He really hadn't cared.

But as he read the names on the texts he didn't see the one he was hoping for.

Logan sighed.

"Nothing from Lake?" Jackson asked.

Logan shook his head.

"Would you have killed me if you'd missed a text from Lake because of what I'd done?"

"Probably not killed. Definitely maimed."

"So is it okay that I'm glad that she didn't text?"

Logan shrugged. His hope had flared like a beacon when he'd heard that his phone had been blocked from receiving texts. But then when no text from Lake had come through, his hope had fallen from that high place and it was like hitting the pavement, hard.

"Just give her some time. I've seen the way some of the older guys on this ship do a double take when they see Mom. She hasn't noticed any of it. And if it's too soon for Mom it has to be too soon for Lake, right?"

But Jackson didn't know what Fred had done to Lake. The reason why Lake should have no problems leaving thoughts of her douchebag husband behind.

But then again, hadn't his mom been concerned that their dad might have done the same thing? It would have been years before so maybe not quite as hard to swallow, but still.

These thoughts had Logan's mind wandering back to the moment he'd found Lake with that note. She'd felt like she now knew what Fred had done, that he'd surely chosen his mistress over his marriage, but she couldn't be sure, right? He thought about how his mom had felt when she hadn't known for sure. Even though she was pretty sure Mitchell would never do that to her, she still had that tiny doubt. And it had seemed to drive her crazy. Now Lake was pretty sure Fred had been back with his mistress—he probably had been, considering the signs—but shouldn't she get that same closure? For better or worse, didn't she deserve to know the truth?

"You know she's into you, right?" Jackson said.

Logan was startled out of his thoughts and turned to look at his brother.

"The way she looks at you. Almost like it's painful but she can't look away. It's obvious. Not as obvious as when you look at her, but close." Jackson's quip at the end kept from the moment being too serious.

"It'll work out. You two—don't ever quote me on this—you're meant to be. Each trial and stumbling block will just make your story that much better. So when you're finally together you'll be much more sure that you have exactly what you want, because you've had to fight for it."

Logan grinned wider than he had all week. His brother, his very unromantic brother, was speaking things Logan had only ever dared to hope for and to hear Jackson say it solidified Logan's hopes in his mind. Because if someone as reality bound as Jackson thought this all to be true, it had to be. So it was. Logan's truth.

"That was incredibly poetic. Thanks, Jacks." But because Logan was Jackson's big brother he couldn't let the tender moment continue. It was time to add a little bit of ribbing to the mix. "And they say you're all brawn and no brain."

"Who says that?" Jackson asked, his eyes narrowed in offense.

Logan slapped his brother on the back without answering, knowing it would drive him nuts. But Logan had moved on to more important items of business. Now that he and his mother had gotten their truths, didn't Lake deserve hers as well? Logan had to find it for her.

"I'm serious. Who says that?" Jackson asked again.

No one had actually said that, but it was fun to mess with his brother. And the best way to continue messing with him? Change the subject.

"How has Memphis not figured out that his phone is on do not disturb? Mr. Social has to be wondering why he's gotten zero texts in the last week." Logan wondered aloud the question that had bothered him since Jackson had told him about their phones. It was one thing for Logan not to realize his phone was on do not disturb; he'd been preoccupied and easy to distract. But Memphis lived for his phone.

"My phone is on do not disturb?" asked an outraged voice.

Oops. Logan hadn't realized his brother had come back and was right behind him.

Jackson groaned.

"You did this?" Memphis accused Jackson as he fumbled with his pocket and finally got to his phone. "You told me we can't get any reception out at sea."

Logan chuckled. That was a smart move on Jackson's part. They all knew Memphis hadn't read any of the material the cruise line gave them at check-in. So Jackson had made up his own rules.

"I've been missing texts this whole time?" Memphis fell onto the couch and frantically swiped at his phone. It began chiming, many more times than Logan's had.

Logan was pretty sure all of his own texts had been from

people telling him about the Jackson situation. He'd told Brandon to only contact him about ranch stuff in case of an emergency and everyone else important to him knew he was on this vacation to get away from it all. Memphis had to be getting all of those texts about Jackson plus others from his friends and the women he was seeing. Logan really doubted Memphis had made the effort to tell anyone he was leaving town.

"This one is from Annabelle. She's not happy here. Jackson! She's telling me she heard I'm seeing Pam too. This came THREE DAYS AGO and I wasn't able to defuse the situation. I'm going to kill you." Memphis launched across the booth toward Jackson, who easily caught and then flipped his brother onto the couch so that now Jackson was on top of him, holding him down. Although Memphis would be considered large by all standards at nearly six-foot-five and long lean muscle, thanks to his years on the ranch, Jackson had nearly thirty pounds of pure muscle on the kid, despite being two inches shorter.

"Night," Logan said as he stood. He noticed cruise security heading their way.

"You can't just leave me with him," Jackson said, his muscles taut as though he were holding down a calf. Thankfully, drunk Memphis wasn't all that hard to subdue.

"Consider it payback," Logan said with a wink. Jackson had to have known Logan wouldn't let him just get away with messing with his phone, even if he had given him advice about Lake that had made him hopeful.

"Logan! Get him off me!" Memphis called out to Logan's back as he walked out of the bar.

He wasn't worried about either brother. Memphis would calm down the minute security stepped in and Jackson wouldn't have to do much more than walk Memphis back to their room. Honestly, Jackson was getting off easy for what he'd done to Logan.

Well, getting off easy with Logan. What had happened back in

Blue Falls sounded like a version of hell. So Logan would be there for Jackson when they got back into town, when he'd really need him. Not now when it wasn't necessary.

Logan chuckled as he imagined the scene that was surely unfolding back in the bar. Memphis as stubborn as a mule, Jackson frustrated beyond belief.

But the scene faded away as images of Lake once again filled his mind. It was two hours earlier back in Blue Falls. Probably right around bedtime for her girls.

And a thought suddenly squeezed Logan's heart. He wanted to be a part of it. All of Lake's life. Even those mundane moments like helping with the bedtime routine. Or he could do the dishes while Lake was with the girls.

Logan had thought that when his life came to this point he'd be scared of the unknown. That he'd back away from things like bedtime routines, school drop-offs, ending every day and night with the same woman by his side.

But Logan now found that he wanted to leap forward. He wanted to embrace all of that, as long as it was with Lake.

But before they could consider any of that, something had to be done for Lake. A plan had begun to form in the last few minutes. Surely a private investigator could find out the truth. Fred's dad had to know more than he was letting on, and others who worked with Fred and his nurse. Maybe the PI could even access traffic cameras. Logan wasn't sure about that, but he did know with absolute certainty that he was going to find the person who could figure out what had happened on the day of Fred's death. He was going to give Lake the peace she deserved.

After that maybe she would be ready for Logan to step into her life. But then again, maybe she wouldn't.

Another surprising thought hit Logan. He wasn't doing this to gain anything personally. Maybe Lake wouldn't be able to heal until she got this closure, but it might just be the start of her healing. It might be months or even years before she considered another man. And although Logan planned on being that man, helping her find closure wouldn't necessarily speed up his timeline. He desperately hoped it would, but it wasn't what really mattered. He realized as long as the truth made Lake's life better, that was all he cared about.

Would Logan have ever done something like this without an ulterior motive for a woman in his past?

He doubted it. And for that he felt badly for his past girlfriends. But he liked that he was changing, bettering himself for Lake.

People said the right woman would change him. He'd never believed it.

But they were correct. He was wrong.

And for maybe the first time in his life, he was just fine with being wrong.

Seventeen

"You'd think people would no longer be interested in an incident that happened over a month ago," Ruby said to Lake as she leaned against the front desk.

"Welcome to Blue Falls?" Lake offered, looking up from her computer screen with a sympathetic half smile.

Ruby laughed.

"People are still asking me if I was fighting with Avery over Jackson. As if I'd ever be attracted to that man." She huffed and folded her arms.

Huh. Lake wondered what that was all about. Ruby's reaction seemed rather strong toward Jackson, considering they couldn't know one another very well, could they? She guessed maybe Jackson had somehow rubbed her the wrong way. That was all that made sense. But it didn't seem to matter how Ruby really felt about Jackson. The town had already placed them as two points in a fateful love triangle.

It had taken a few days for the Blue Falls rumor mill to get ahold of information surrounding the dramatic meal centered around Jackson, Ruby, and Avery, but once it got going it went full steam ahead. And apparently wasn't stopping. Poor Ruby.

Lake had heard all the rumors about the big showdown in their dining room. She'd even heard some of it from Ruby's mouth herself. Not that Lake had asked Ruby for any details. Lake had let her tell what she wanted to in whatever way she wanted to in the weeks that had passed since the fateful meal. But it sounded like the other Blue Falls residents hadn't given her the same consideration.

Lake pursed her lips. If it had been that long since the waterfall dinner, as some were now calling it, it had also been several weeks since Lake had kissed Logan. That kiss. She'd begun to think of time in terms of 'before the kiss' and 'after the kiss.' Maybe that was terrible, considering her husband had just died and for most that would be the big event that they measured time against, but when she pressed guilt and all other emotions aside, that kiss was what she chose to remember. It was joy in a time of intense turmoil. Light when Lake could have been lost in darkness.

She'd seen Logan once during those weeks. They'd been at the grocery store where Logan stood, in his tanned post-vacation glory, in front of the avocados as Lake had turned her cart into the produce section.

She'd frozen, watching him, wanting to go to him, to be close to him, but her feet wouldn't move.

Logan had gazed at her, every part of him welcoming, but he waited, allowing her to move at her own speed. No pressure, just a sweet smile.

But even as Lake adored Logan, her fear hadn't allowed her to move. She knew she had so many reasons for concern when it came to starting a relationship with Logan. Her trust had been broken by Fred. Her girls couldn't be ready for another man in her life. She was a cheated-on widow. And yet she knew she could move past all of those things—if she put her mind to it, she could and would. It wasn't fear of those things that had held her back. But as she'd dug for her true fear she'd come up empty. She wanted to cry into the air that it wasn't fair. What was keeping her back from starting her life with this incredible man?

But because she hadn't known, she'd had to walk away, telling herself it would all be okay one day.

"I know what you're thinking. He's good-looking, funny, loyal, honest . . . but do we really know that's who he actually is, when we dig down deep?" Ruby asked, leaning into the desk so that her head was now just inches from Lake's.

Oh right, they were talking about Jackson. That hadn't been at all what Lake had been thinking but she was grateful Ruby had assumed so. Did Ruby know Jackson deep down? What had happened in Jackson and Ruby's past?

"Anyway." Ruby seemed to shake off the conversation as she stood, drawing attention from every male in the lobby. The poor bellmen looked ready to jump at Ruby's very command. The woman was gorgeous and—it was the craziest thing—she seemed to have no idea.

"I guess I have to try to play nice, since he's Madi's cousin and she's now living with the Ashfords," Ruby said as she glanced around the B&B with a reluctant smile.

Jordan, the bellman, beamed as if Ruby's smile had been just for him.

Ruby turned back to Lake. "And I really do love this place. If Madi had to find her family in any small town I'm grateful it was this one. It's just too bad this town and her family aren't Jackson-free."

And there he was again.

Lake was just about to question Ruby's feelings toward the man when Ruby moved the conversation in another direction.

"Where's Mabel?" she asked, her eyes bouncing to the space behind Lake, where Mabel typically sat on a high seat.

Oh well. Lake was sure she'd have another chance to ask about Jackson later.

She chuckled. "Last I heard, yelling at Rodney about something or other." Those two were worse than cats and dogs. But their dramatics did help to keep Lake entertained. Mabel was forever yelling at Rodney and the latter secretly loved it, though he'd never admit it.

"Those two argue like an old married couple. Wait, have they been married in the past?" Ruby whispered her question.

Lake wasn't surprised by the query. If she didn't know Mabel and Rodney's past she would have wondered the same thing.

Lake shook her head, glancing around before responding. This wasn't exactly her information to share, but since the whole town knew the story, Lake didn't feel badly about passing it on to Ruby. She deserved to be in the know, if for no other reason than to keep from saying anything unknowingly hurtful to Mabel or Rodney. "Mabel and Rodney's wife were best friends. His wife passed about ten years ago."

"Oh." Ruby's mouth rounded.

"Yeah."

"So it's complicated?" Ruby asked.

"To say the least."

"Because they have chemistry."

"Lots of it," Lake admitted.

Ruby leaned her hip against the desk as she pondered. "You know, though, I think Rodney's wife would be okay with it."

"You do?" Lake asked, curious for more than just Rodney and Mabel. She knew it was silly but she couldn't help but compare their story to her own circumstances with Fred and Logan. She wasn't sure it was wise, since the two situations couldn't be any more different. Fred and Logan hadn't been close in the end, whereas Mabel had been the last person to talk to her best friend besides Rodney. And it wasn't like Ruby knew Fred. She couldn't assure Lake that he'd be okay with her moving on with his friend. To be honest, Lake didn't even know if she cared what Fred thought. The idea of hurting him, even in the afterlife, was actually kind of pleasant. Did that make Lake a horrible person?

"The people she loved most. Wouldn't she want them to be happy? Even if that happiness was together?" Ruby asked.

Yeah, that made sense. Except not for Lake. Logan wasn't one of the people Fred had loved most. Heck, Lake wasn't even sure she'd been one of the ones Fred loved most.

"As long as those on earth are okay with things, like Rodney and Mabel's families, the rest are heavenly issues. In God's hands. And if things are in God's hands, I'm pretty sure they'll all be handled perfectly."

"Isn't that the truth," Lake agreed.

Lake wished that God would come down and fix her situation for her. Remove her paralyzing fear, make sure that her girls were okay with Logan in her life. Because even though it had been months since Fred's passing, she just wasn't sure where her girls stood. They'd cried a lot in the week or so before and after the funeral but once they moved to Blue Falls it was almost as if their mourning period had ended. They had moments of sadness but for the most part they seemed just fine.

However, Lake realized she shouldn't take their actions at surface value. She should do some digging.

She hadn't dug before because she'd thought feelings would resurface on their own, especially during Christmas. It had been the first real reminder that Fred didn't just have some extended business reason for leaving the family behind, he was really gone.

Lake had done all that she could to fill the hole Fred's absence might leave. He was always great about buying a big, expensive gift for the girls, something that put even Santa to shame, and for some reason he only ever put his own name on the tag even though Lake was sure to let the girls know the rest of their presents were from both Mom and Dad. But whatever, that didn't matter now.

So Lake had made sure their best presents—the touchscreen educational pad Amelie had been dying for and the electric scooter Delia had heavily hinted for—were from Fred.

And with Lake's extensive preparations, Christmas Day had gone off without a tear. There was the occasional mention of wishing Dad had been there, but Lake had expected more.

Lake wasn't really sure why she'd been expecting more of a reaction from her girls, considering Fred had missed parts of their last Christmas celebration even when he was alive. And then Lake had begun to realize that her girls were too used to life without their dad. So little had actually changed for them since his death. During the time when they had mourned, the girls had been sad about the loss of the idea of their father, not the actual man himself. Because he'd been so absent so often.

And now, a couple of months later, life without Dad was completely normal. Or so it seemed to Lake.

But she should talk to the girls. Make sure they weren't secretly mourning. A better mother would have already done this.

You have plenty on your plate. They know you love them. You are a good mother, her conscience tried to reassure her.

"I should get going," Ruby said, glancing toward the restaurant where she worked. "It was nice to chat with you."

"You too," Lake said honestly, even though her emotions were still churning thanks to her many thoughts. But it really had been easy and fun to just chat and relax with Ruby. There was something about her that made Lake feel lighter and brighter in her presence. Lake was guessing she wasn't the only one who felt that way, considering how Jordan, all of the other bellmen, the restaurant's host, and Malcolm—one of the B&B's maintenance men—gazed after Ruby.

Lake had a feeling that as long as Ruby stayed in town, the Blue Falls gossip would be well-fed.

"Pizza!" the girls cried out in unison when Lake asked them what they wanted for dinner.

Her girls seemed to disagree on so much these days. Lake was more than grateful that their favorite foods aligned.

Lake tried not to eat out too often, now that they were saving every penny for a home of their own. Lake really wanted to buy a house, to give her kids the security that Fred hadn't provided when he'd passed, but saving enough for a down payment that would keep her mortgage low was proving to be difficult. Especially with the housing market the way that it was in Blue Falls. As soon as a property came onto the market it seemed to sell.

But they were doing it. Pinching pennies and saving dollars. Lake could see her goal in sight. Well, like a year down the line, but still in sight. And that meant eating home-cooked meals for the most part.

But tonight Lake was breaking their rule. She'd been working so much and the girls were growing up so quickly. She wanted to make a fun memory with them . . . and maybe butter them up a bit before asking them how they were doing.

Luckily for Lake, the pizza parlor in town was one of her favorites as well. She'd been told that a person's hometown pizza always held a special place in their heart and she believed that to be true for The Pizza Shack. The place had been named when a certain Hut was at its peak and may have been a bit of a copy, but Lake believed the Shack deserved to be known by more than that. She'd take their pie over the Hut's any day.

"Can I have olives?" Amelie asked from the middle seat of Lake's minivan. The girl loved a good olive but hated almost every other pizza topping.

"But I want pepperoni," Delia complained from the far back. Lake wasn't sure why Delia had placed herself back there when there was another seat next to Amelie, but if Amelie wasn't complaining, Lake wasn't about to point it out.

Enough arguing was happening over pizza fixings. Too bad her girls' similar tastebuds didn't go as far as toppings.

"We can do half olives, half pepperoni," Lake conceded. She

figured she'd one day have all the margherita (her favorite pizza) she wanted. For now peace between her girls was more important.

"Yes!" Amelie celebrated, pumping her fist down and accidentally driving her elbow into her side.

Delia just smiled.

They pulled up into the parking lot of The Pizza Shack and the girls jumped out barely after Lake put her car in park.

"Look out for cars!" Lake called after them as they hurried to the sidewalk along the front of the Shack and darted through the door. It was a chilly, dark January evening and Lake wanted to get in those doors ASAP as well.

She locked the car and followed behind, shivering even after she got into the warm dining area. Almost every table was full; apparently half of the town had also realized that Tuesday night was great for a family pizza night.

"Can we sit there?" Delia pointed to an open table.

The Shack's hostess, Jess, was busy seating another family but nodded in Lake's direction, so Lake led the girls to the empty table.

Delia immediately pulled out the menu that sat behind the red pepper flake and cheese shakers even though they'd already decided on their order. Lake worked hard to keep Amelie's attention on anything else since there was only one menu and Lake didn't want to referee another fight.

"Do you know this song?" Lake asked her younger daughter.

"No, but I like it," Amelie said cheerfully, her foot tapping in time to the song's rhythm.

Lake was about to ask Amelie about her day at school when a very harried Jess bustled up to their table.

"Sorry, we're swamped tonight," Jess said. "Thanks for seating yourselves."

"Not a problem," Lake returned with a smile.

"We got the table I wanted," Delia added.

"I'm so glad." Jess beamed at her.

"I'll be right back with waters but I'm helping take orders tonight since we're understaffed. Do you want anything else to drink?"

Both girls looked to Lake. But a pizza night was stretching her budget enough. Drinks would have to be a treat for another day.

"Water's good," Delia said, reading her mother correctly.

Amelie nodded.

Jess seemed to understand and kept up her smile as she said, "There are some special straws back there we give to little girls who ask for just water."

"Really?" Amelie asked, jumping to her knees.

"Really," Jess assured.

"Thank you," Lake mouthed to Jess.

She nodded at Lake and although Lake had never been close to Jess, she did know that Jess was a single mom as well. She probably understood Lake's daily battle.

"While we wait for our special waters, I have a question for you guys," Lake said, ready to get this portion of the meal done. She wanted to enjoy her night with her girls, but right now she was too worried about what this conversation could unearth to relax.

"Yeah?" Delia asked.

Amelie was moving the shaker that held the red pepper flakes.

"Can you look at me please, Amelie?" Lake asked.

Amelie let go of the shaker and looked at her mom.

"I've been thinking about Dad today."

Delia nodded. Amelie grasped the edge of the table.

"Did you think about him?" Lake directed the question to Amelie.

Amelie nodded, her eyes on the table.

"Do you miss him?"

She nodded again.

"What do you miss about Daddy?" Lake asked.

Amelie looked up and the confusion in her eyes was enough to break Lake's heart. The little girl knew she missed her father but couldn't say what he'd done to make her miss him. He'd been so absent in recent years. Even though he'd made a little effort in the last few months, there hadn't been enough time to repair those years he'd practically been missing.

"I miss the way he called me Lia bug," Delia said.

Lake smiled. Delia had a few more memories of her dad since he'd been more involved during her early life.

"I miss when he would let me ride on his back," Amelie spoke up.

"Dad didn't do that," Delia interjected.

Lake didn't remember that occasion either, but she wasn't okay with Delia calling Amelie out on it.

"Delia," Lake reprimanded as Amelie doubled down. "Yes, he did!" she insisted, tears springing to her eyes.

"No, the kids in that book you like, *Brenda's Happy Family*, ride on their dad's back. Our dad didn't do that," Delia insisted.

Amelie's bottom lip jutted out as she realized that Delia was right.

Oh heavens. Amelie hadn't meant to lie. She'd honestly attached that memory to her own father, apparently wishing that her dad was like the one in the book.

Lake blinked hard. She would not cry. Not right now.

"But maybe Dad did that in your dreams?" Lake offered gently.

"No," Amelie shook her head, gaze on her lap. "It was just from the book."

Reality hung heavy over her.

Lake pressed her eyes closed. She had to fix this.

"I don't think we really miss Dad. Not as much as we used to," Delia said, too wisely considering she was only ten. "I don't like that he's dead, but he was always gone so much before. It's not really that different. I only get sad when I realize I won't ever see him again."

"On earth," Lake amended because she had nothing better to say. She'd had no idea her girls were so intuitive. They saw exactly what she had.

"Yeah," Delia replied as if what Lake had said didn't matter much. Lake guessed to a ten-year-old it was hard to imagine ever not being on earth, so time after this life was the same as forever.

"Dads work a lot," Amelie said, as if she was trying to cope with her memories versus what she'd heard about dads.

"Your dad is home a lot," Delia pointed out to Lake.

And that had been a Godsend. Lake's dad had been there for the girls in a way that Fred never had been.

"So just our dad worked a lot?" Amelie asked. Her lip trembled.

Come on brain, think of things, Lake willed her mind but came up blank.

"Are you guys ready to order?" Jess was back, carrying the special waters with light-up straws.

They were perfect. And Jess's timing had been perfect as well. The girls squealed as they turned their straws on and off. Lake was just as happy with her gift from Jess—the reprieve.

"Can we get a half and half?" Lake asked.

The Pizza Shack only had one size of pizza. Gigantic.

"Sure," Jess said, pulling out her pad and clicking her pen.

"Olives on one side and pepperoni on the other."

"Yum. Those are some of my faves," Jess said as she licked her lips dramatically.

She walked away and with her went the carefree feeling of their last few moments. Lake's reprieve was over. She knew she had to resolve her girls' worries or at least try. They might always have concerns when it came to Fred, but Lake had to let them know they were cared for, by her as well as him. And that when they did worry about their dad they could always come to her.

"Dad loved you both," Lake started.

"We know," Amelie said as she drank from her straw.

Delia didn't seem convinced as she eyed Lake.

"Then why did he work so much? On the shows that I watch only the dads who want new families work that much," she stated.

Lake needed to look into these shows Delia was watching, but until then . . .

"He wanted to provide the best life for our family." Lake gave her girls the excuse she told herself. And she hoped it was at least partially true.

"We did have a nice house," Delia conceded.

"Not as nice as the ranch house, though. They have horses," Amelie said.

"And a dog," Delia added.

"Can we get a dog?" Amelie asked. She and Delia both turned expectant eyes on their mother.

Wait, how were they here?

"And next time you find us a dad, maybe get one who doesn't work so much," Delia added.

Lake held back a gasp as she clutched the table for dear life. She surely would have toppled right over otherwise.

"Next time I find you a dad?" Lake asked, her voice strained.

"Everyone says you're too pretty not to get married again," Delia said. Clearly her little ears were taking in much more than they should. "If you get married again it means we'll have a new dad."

How was she so matter-of-fact about this?

Amelie scratched her head. "I don't think I want a new dad."

"Don't you want Mom to be happy?" Delia turned to her sister.

Amelie nodded vigorously.

"Then Mom should get married. To a good and handsome man."

She sounded so much like Lake's mother that Lake knew she had to have a conversation with her. Had Delia overheard her grandma?

"And he should be funny," Amelie added.

Now Amelie was okay with this too?

"For sure funny. And have a nice house, like the ranch house."

"I know!" Amelie gasped. "Mom can marry Mr. Logan!"

The words were said so loudly that many in the crowded restaurant looked their way.

Lake's face burned and she took a frantic gulp of ice water.

"I thought you might need this immediately," Jess said as she rushed over with their piping hot pizza.

Yes, something to stuff their mouths sounded just perfect.

"Who's ready for pizza?" Lake asked with way too much pep. But it was all she could do. She was still in shock over what her girls had been saying.

"Me!" both exclaimed, seeming to forget their conversation.

Lake put slices on two plates, careful to get the toppings right for each girl, and passed them to her daughters. Then she put a piece of pepperoni on her own plate. She needed some good old comfort food right about now.

The girls were confused about their feelings when it came to their dad, but beyond that? They were fine with her finding love again. In fact, they were pushing her in that direction. They *wanted* a new dad.

Lake hadn't even considered that the way they'd want to fill the hole Fred had left in their lives was with another dad. One who actually wanted to spend time with them.

"So will you marry Mr. Logan?" Amelie asked around a mouthful of pizza. Apparently it was Lake's wishful thinking that the girls had simply forgotten the idea. "I can ask him at daddy donut day on Friday."

Was that this week already? Lake had nearly forgotten Amelie had invited him. She'd done it the same day Lake had kissed

Logan. And that kiss had driven everything out of her mind but Lake's concerns. So she'd hidden behind the idea that the girls weren't ready . . . but they'd just proved to her they were. They'd each asked Logan to be a part of their lives. But then again, Lake hadn't equated Amelie wanting Logan at daddy donut day and Delia inviting him to her play with wanting him as a dad. It wasn't the same thing.

But now . . . the girls were ready to propose. They knew in such a short time what Lake had been scared to admit. Logan was the right man for all of them. They didn't care that others would say it was too soon. They wanted a good man for their mom and one who would love them too in their lives. And they saw that in Logan.

Lake saw that in Logan.

So what was holding her back?

She took a bite of pizza, savoring the warm, salty flavor as it hit her tongue. And with only a moment's thought she had the answer to her question. All of the other obstacles had been moved out of her way and the path to her answer was finally clear.

Her. Lake was holding Lake back. She was scared of so much. There were small fears, like what the town would think of her, or that people would think Logan was too good for her . . . but more importantly, she worried that her girls would one day look back and judge her, that Logan would realize he was too good for her. But there was something else, a fear worse than all of the others, nagging at the back of her mind.

It suddenly came to her, as if it had been blocked but something in Lake's consciousness had finally set it free. The thing that had stopped her from going after Logan, that big fear.

Her big, insurmountable fear was that Lake had been the problem in her last marriage. That she'd driven Fred to his decision. That because she was the problem, the same thing would happen in each and every one of her relationships. That one day she'd find herself in the same situation with Logan if they were together. And that would truly break her.

"You can't ask Mr. Logan to marry Mom. He has to ask her. With a ring." Delia pointed out Amelie's errors, interrupting Lake's scary thoughts.

Even just the idea of Logan breaking their vows had Lake shaking.

"Oh. But how will Mr. Logan know to propose?" Amelie asked.

"He asks her after they go on dates. They have to go on dates first."

As her daughters planned out her love life Lake realized that although her fear still had her trembling, she now at least knew what it was. She'd jumped a huge obstacle. And if she tackled that one she could tackle the rest.

It all had to start with finding the truth about that day. She deserved the truth. She'd pushed that idea away for months now because she was afraid of the repercussions, but it had to happen. She had to face her past before she could pursue the future she wanted. So she'd dig into the day that Fred died. Why was he with Sachia?

But more than the truth, the only way to fight that fear was to understand that Lake wasn't some cursed woman. That should be easy, considering there was no such thing. People made mistakes. Fred made his choice. Lake wasn't at fault for that. And she had to make herself believe that.

But how?

By loving yourself. The answer came swift and sure. Of course. She had to love herself. As much as Lake loved her girls, her family, and friends and cared so deeply for Logan, none of them could fix her. If she didn't love herself, how could she believe anyone else's love for her was real?

So how did she begin?

She toyed with her pizza crust as she looked at her daughters. How was her love for them so sure?

And then she knew. She had to allow or maybe force herself to see the parts of her that made her deserving of love. To remind herself that she was worthy. A work in progress but worthy.

Okay, Lake believed that. She truly did . . . now. At other points in her life she hadn't, but today she did. Maybe because she'd been in the embrace of her family, the town she loved, her girls, and Logan. Always Logan. They helped her to see herself in a way that she hadn't for a long time. She was hard-working, loyal, and genuine, and she tried her best to be all she could for those she loved. That was a woman worth loving, right?

So if that were the case, if she were worthy of love, that put her in the same category as all of the other incredible women in her life. She'd never believe that her daughters, Mom, Grace, Lottie, Holland, Mama Ashford, or any of the women she loved were bound to be cheated on by every man in their lives because she loved them. She knew their worth. And she was starting to understand her own.

So she would continue that journey. She knew, deep down, that Fred's actions were on him. What Lake had done in the marriage wouldn't have mattered. So she pulled that truth up. Repeated it in her mind. She would until she believed it.

Fred chose to destroy our vows. I didn't deserve the way he treated me, Lake said in her mind and then wrapped her arms around herself, feeling a little more love for the woman who had lived through so much. Who was still battered and bruised but was finding herself, loving herself.

She knew this change wouldn't come overnight, but she felt different. Just finding her fear and then putting Fred's decisions back on him had started her healing, opened a space for love for herself in heart.

She had a feeling she'd fill it soon. Lake was a loving woman, after all.

"So how do we get Mr. Logan to ask Mom on a date?" Amelie asked, tapping her cute pointer finger on her pizza sauce-covered chin.

Now to manage her girls' expectations. Although if their kiss was any indication, Logan wanted to ask Lake out. He just needed the all clear.

And she'd give it soon. When she was ready to be the woman with an open heart that Logan deserved. But more importantly, when she loved the woman she was. When she was on her way to being the woman that she deserved to be.

Eighteen

"I've got some news for you," said Celia, the private investigator out of Boise that Logan had hired to look into Fred's activities. She'd called with what felt like an important update just a few weeks after he'd hired her.

It had taken Logan two weeks after the cruise to locate a PI whom he felt he could trust with Lake's situation. He'd spoken to a few duds, but when Logan had first interviewed Celia it had felt right.

The woman had started as a police officer thirty years before but found that she enjoyed all of the investigating and none of the bureaucracy. She also liked the fact that she could cross a few more lines as a civilian than she could when she was a cop. She'd told Logan she hated seeing a solution to a problem just across the line she was told never to cross and having to walk away.

As a PI she worked hard not only to find information, but when Logan had said he might want the information she found to disappear forever, so that Lake's girls would never find out about their dad being with another woman at the time of his death, Celia had said she could make that happen.

Logan had hired her on the spot.

"Great," Logan replied into his phone as he jumped up from the couch. He'd been at work all day and then to the old ranch house for dinner and was just about to start winding down for the evening, but this call had him unable to relax. "Do I come to you? Meet you somewhere? Verify anything?"

Verify anything? Logan needed to shut his mouth and let Celia talk.

"Nope, no verification needed." Celia's voice still had her typical dry, raspy tone, but Logan could have sworn she was biting back a laugh. "Typically I just tell you what I found over the phone and you let me know how you'd like me to proceed."

"Excellent," Logan replied, deciding to keep his answers brief.

"Stanley, Fred's father, seems to have put a tight lid on most sources of information. Good news for us, if the point is that his granddaughters never find out the truth about that day. After Stanley, I looked into Sachia's family. The only ones who she seemed to be in contact with in the years just before her death are a grandmother and brother. The grandmother gave me nothing. Not even an inkling of knowing about Fred. She just said her granddaughter died in a horrific car accident and to leave an old lady alone."

Logan's chest tightened. Poor woman. She'd not only lost her granddaughter well before her time but had surely been bullied by Stanley after Sachia's death. She deserved to be left alone. Hopefully Celia would be the last one bothering her. As long as things went according to plan, she would be.

"The brother tried to refuse to see me but I found a way."

Logan could imagine Celia hiding behind the man's car after he left the office, by his trashcan when he took out the garbage, or really anywhere. Celia wasn't the type of woman to let anything get in her way.

"He threatened to call the police. Didn't even admit he'd had a sister. I had a feeling they wouldn't share what they knew, especially after Stanley pushed and bribed them both into signing NDAs, but I had to be sure."

Logan nodded. He was grateful for Celia's thoroughness. He knew Sachia's family was probably unhappy with the intrusion, but if they knew that Celia's one-time pushing would be the end of questions about Sachia's death they would be grateful as well. Logan was positive about that.

"There was a leak I was able to exploit. Stanley's worked hard at covering Fred's tracks. He checked on every name at the accident scene to see if they had had any association with Fred in the past. None did. He checked the names of the hospital staff that worked on Fred and Sachia. Only two knew the pair but Stanley talked to both of them and let them know that the two were together for professional reasons. He made up a whole fake story about visiting an elderly patient, painting Fred as a saint. It was so good even I believed it. When he heard the press was interested in running an article on the death of a prominent young citizen, Stanley handpicked the guy to write the story and fed him the information he wanted him to share. The journalist didn't even know Sachia was in the car. I also found out that very few people knew about the affair. Only those who worked at the medical office, Sachia's grandma and maybe her brother, Stanley, and Lake."

"Hm," Logan replied, disgusted. Fred knew how wrong his actions had been. It was why he'd hidden them so well. How could he have put Lake through that?

"Sachia had a close group of friends that I worried my source hadn't known about. Sure enough, when I spoke to them they knew nothing. They talked about Sachia's secret boyfriend but they didn't even know his name. They also told me about the car accident but indicated she'd been driving and alone."

"So Stanley made sure that this looked like two different accidents," Logan interrupted.

"Exactly. I checked into official records and he somehow

managed to change the location of Sachia's accident. I don't want to know the underhanded lengths he had to go through to do that, but it's obvious Stanley has friends in high places."

"But who told you all of this?" Logan asked. Someone had spilled their guts to Celia and that person was a liability for all of them. If they told Celia this much would they tell others? And would word get back to Lake's girls?

"Stanley's assistant. The very woman typing up all of these NDAs for others to sign—Stanley didn't even think to have her sign one as well. She was hired fifteen years ago, maybe before Stanley had skeletons in his closet? I don't know. But he seems to trust the woman, and didn't force one on her."

Logan shook his head. Stanley's life seemed like a mess. But that wasn't his business. All he cared about was if the assistant would share her info with others.

"So our next step is making sure his assistant stays quiet?" Logan asked.

"If your goal is to keep this under wraps forever, then yes," Celia replied.

Logan nodded absently before realizing Celia couldn't see him. He wasn't exactly sure what his endgame was because it wasn't up to him—it was up to Lake. But Logan wanted to be sure that if Lake wanted no one else to know the truth of what had happened that day, no one ever would. Then it would be up to her to tell who she wanted and when. Especially the girls. Maybe they should never know. Maybe Lake would tell them in ten, fifteen, thirty years. But that decision should be up to Lake, not a concern in the back of her mind that if she didn't tell her girls someone else might do so at any time.

"What do you think it would take for her to sign our NDA?" Logan asked.

"The money we discussed earlier should more than cover it," Celia replied, ever the professional.

"Perfect. Then please get that signed. Are we sure there are no other possible leaks of information?"

"None," Celia assured.

Logan breathed out a sigh of relief.

"And I'll get all of this to Lake. She'll know the information came from me but she'll never know who hired me."

"Thank you." Logan was grateful Celia was fulfilling each of his requests. His final requirement may have seemed a bit strange, but the last thing Logan wanted was for Lake to feel indebted to him. If she knew that he'd been the one to hire Celia, that would be the case. And he didn't want her to feel any pressure from him or toward him because of what he'd done. So keeping his identity a secret seemed to be the only solution.

"And now to the main reason you hired me," Celia continued. "Why was Sachia in the car with Fred?"

Logan stopped his pacing and braced a hand against his countertop. This was the information he'd been dreading but also longing to have.

His breath was coming way too quickly and he imagined how Lake would feel when she heard this.

Lake. This was all wrong.

Logan shouldn't be the one receiving the news. Lake should know first. Maybe she should be the only one to know. She could tell Logan when and if she wanted to . . . even though it might drive Logan insane to never know the truth. But it was Lake's truth. Not his.

"Just send that info on to Lake," Logan said before he could give into temptation. And it was strong. But he would withstand it for Lake.

"Are you sure?" Celia asked.

"Yup," Logan replied quickly. He needed to get off the phone before he did something stupid like beg Celia to tell him after all.

"It was good working with you, Logan. I'll let you know if there's anything else I need."

"You are even better at your job than you indicated. And that's saying something," Logan said as he dropped onto a barstool, emotional exhaustion claiming him.

But it had been worth it. Lake could now move forward with no fear of her past returning to haunt her. Every possible leak had been plugged—even Celia had signed a contract with Logan that she'd never discuss this case with anyone else.

"If you have any more PI needs," Celia offered.

"I'd go nowhere else."

"Good to know." Celia hung up.

Logan had expected as much from the gruff woman.

He set his phone down on his countertop and breathed a sigh of relief. Lake was safe. In every way.

Logan wasn't sure what that meant for them or for their future, and honestly right now he didn't care about that. As long as Lake was safe and happy, he could feel the same way. Knowing she had her truth would be enough for him.

Nineteen

LAKE WATCHED in the mirror as her reflection hugged herself once again. A ritual she did every morning now.

It was hecka cheesy but it was helping. It was an outward representation of what she felt for herself. People kissed their significant others; why not take a moment to hug themselves?

"Lake! You've got a package!" Grace called down the hallway to the bathroom Lake shared with her two girls.

Lake would have never thought after moving into the home she and Fred had inhabited, the home with six bedrooms and nearly as many bathrooms, that she would ever be back to sharing a bathroom . . . and with her daughters. But she actually kind of loved it. This morning all three of them had been in there, getting ready for their days. Delia couldn't stop talking about her dress rehearsal that would be happening that evening and Amelie was still enamored with Logan a full week after daddy donut day. Without sharing a bathroom Lake would have missed these conversations. Although having some counterspace to herself would have been nice.

Donut day had come and gone. Lake's hands had shaken as she'd texted Logan to remind him about it. With how strained things were between them—no, strained was the wrong word; maybe just weird—Lake hadn't been sure how Logan would respond. She hadn't spoken to him since she'd basically kicked him out of her house. But Amelie had her heart set on taking Logan, so Lake put on her big girl pants and did what her daughter needed.

Logan's response may have been the sweetest thing Lake had ever read. *I already have it on my calendar. I even have my pink dress shirt steamed because Amelie told me it was her favorite color.*

If Lake hadn't already been in love, that would have done it. The only thing keeping her from running to Logan immediately had been that she really did feel the need to keep healing herself, loving herself. And she was getting close to that moment. She could feel it in her heart and soul.

Although she was discouraged that she still hadn't gotten any closer to finding out why Sachia had been in the car with Fred that day. She'd tried to talk to Stanley but he'd stonewalled her. She'd then moved to the nurses who'd worked with Sachia and Fred and while they'd been sympathetic, they'd told her that not only would Stanley have their jobs if they talked to Lake about that day, but he'd also be able to sue them because of the NDAs he'd forced them to sign. So Lake had begun to wonder if she'd ever be able to completely close that chapter behind her. But maybe it wasn't meant to be? And because she'd been able to continue her healing throughout that process she figured maybe the truth wasn't necessary. Even without it, she was so close to where she wanted to be.

But was she close enough? She wanted to be sure that she was in a place where she and Logan would have their best chance of success. Considering she wanted to make things work with Logan . . . forever.

Forever? The thought should scare her but it didn't. At all. Did that mean she was considering marriage? With Logan?

Why not? The man was the best she'd ever known.

But it was too soon, wasn't it? Or too late, considering they'd had their chance twenty years before.

"Lake?" Grace called again.

Oh right, the package.

"Be right there," Lake called back, wondering why Grace was so insistent Lake open this package right now. Lake didn't get much sent to the house since she'd put herself on a shopping ban for anything other than necessities—another way to help save for their own place—but a package wasn't so important that she needed to drop everything and come immediately, was it?

Lake tied off the French braid she typically wore for work and looked over her outfit before leaving the mirror. She wore hunter green wide leg dress pants with a white collared shirt tucked into it. Over the shirt she had put on a dark pink sweater vest. The weather was still chilly, but the color of her vest once again reminded her of donut day.

Amelie had gushed about the pink flowers Logan had brought her. All of her friends had wanted to smell them and Amelie let them but then asked her teacher to put them up high where no one could hurt them. Those flowers were still sitting in a vase on her parent's tabletop, a little worse for the wear. Logan had worn his pink shirt and they'd both chosen pink donuts even though Lake knew for a fact that Logan was a chocolate guy. He'd pulled out Amelie's chair for her and according to the seven-year-old, Logan was the most handsome dad in all the school.

Lake had smiled even as she worried. Amelie understood Logan wasn't her dad, right? Was Lake hurting her daughter by holding back? But then again, she couldn't start dating Logan just so her girls could have the dad they wanted.

How had the pendulum swung so far so quickly? Even just a couple weeks before, Lake had worried that the girls wouldn't be ready for her to date again. Now Lake wondered if she should jump in before she was ready, just for her girls. Unless she was already ready?

She laughed at herself and tried to release some of her anxiety. This would all work out. She'd figure it out. She was okay.

With that she walked out of the bathroom and down the hallway, dogged by the thought that Logan would not only make the most handsome dad in all the school but Lake was pretty sure he'd win for the whole world.

Grace thrust a brown box into Lake's hands as soon as she walked into the living room.

"Aren't you supposed to be napping?" Lake asked.

"Not until you open that box," Grace replied. She stifled a yawn but her eyes were bright with interest.

Lake saw that her parents were likewise hovering. Her dad's head peeked out from the hall where the main bedroom was and her mom's from the kitchen. She had probably been helping the girls get their breakfast before school.

Lake was incredibly blessed by the help she had. But why were they all so curious?

"Open it," Grace urged.

"Why? It's just a package," Lake said.

Grace pointed to the top left corner of the box. "From Celia Bradbury, PI?"

Lake looked at the box more closely. Why would a PI be sending her a box? Come to think of it, it was too early in the morning for mail to have come and there was no kind of postage on the upper right side of the box.

"Do you think it's a bomb?" Lake asked, suddenly concerned. She had a bad habit of jumping to worst-case scenarios, but weren't unmarked boxes something everyone was warned about?

"No, I don't. I think it's information," Grace replied. She gave her sister an impatient glance. "Why would she leave her name on the box if it was a bomb?"

Oh. That made sense. Unless it was a fake name.

"Open the box, Lake." This time it was her dad who spoke.

If Dad was encouraging her, it had to be safe.

Lake tugged at the flaps of the box but they were taped down securely.

Grace was ready with a pair of scissors.

Lake slid the blade through the clear tape in the middle of the box and then did the same to the edges.

"Please just open it up. I'm tired, cranky, and hangry," Grace nearly wailed. "But there's no way I'll be able to sleep until I see what's in there."

Lake wasn't even frustrated at Grace's dramatic response because she too was starting to feel anxious and just wanted the box open.

She pulled up the flaps and at the top was a note.

I was hired to find the truth in this situation. Here is the truth. I was also hired to keep all evidence of who your husband was in the car with at the time of his death from surfacing ever again. That has also been dealt with. If you want what happened that day to stay forever buried, it will. The information will only surface in the way you want it to.

Lake let out a stuttered breath. This couldn't be true. This had hung over her head since the moment she heard about Sachia being in the car with Fred. Would her girls find out? Would they be devastated to know their father's actions? Would they be told long before they were ready to know the truth?

This was too good to be true. It couldn't be true. And yet there it was in black and white, right in front of her.

Lake dropped the note, a hand covering her mouth as the most intense and beautiful relief filled her body. Celia had given her the ability to protect her girls. A priceless gift. But Lake doubted it was from the kindness of Celia's heart, whoever Celia was. Someone must have hired her. But who? Although she felt gratitude toward Celia, she knew the real hero was the person behind all of this.

"Oh my gosh," Grace uttered.

Lake hadn't noticed her sister and parents picking up the note and reading it together.

"Oh Lake," her mother said, throwing her arms around her, sandwiching the box in the middle of their hug.

"I can't believe it," her dad said, handing the note off to Grace.

"What else is in the box? She said you'd find the truth." Grace motioned urgently at the package.

Right. There was more in here than that note. Lake lifted the next paper but as soon as she touched it she could feel it wasn't just typical printer paper. There was weight to it. She turned it over and saw that it was a black and white photo. Of Sachia and Fred.

Lake dropped the picture as if it had burned her, tears welling in her eyes. The note had stirred up her emotions and now they were spilling over. She had a feeling that the further she got into the box the more she'd find.

"Fred looks angry," Grace said, speaking quietly since the girls were in the next room.

She was studying the picture in a way Lake couldn't.

Had he looked angry?

Lake felt a strand of her hair slip from her braid and she pushed it back impatiently. She had to get into more of this box. She was about to dig further when Delia's voice caused her to pause.

"Mom, we need to go to school!"

Right, school. Work. Lake had a life to live. But this box.

"I'll take the girls to school. You should maybe consider calling into the B&B and letting them know you need a personal day," Lake's mom said.

Lake shook her head. She couldn't. "Thanks for taking the girls, but I should do it. I have to go to work. I can't take a personal day so soon after starting a brand-new job." She moved to stand, but her knees buckled and she flopped right back onto the couch.

"You won't be of any use to them today," her dad pointed out.

He was right. If Lake couldn't even stand up straight, what could she do? Her brain was too muddled to think. Even her mouth seemed to have forgotten how to move quite right.

"Let me do it," Grace offered, taking Lake's phone.

Lake wanted to protest but her limbs felt too heavy to lift, her lips too awkward to form words.

"Hello, Ms. Brown?" Grace said before Lake could do anything.

"Yes, she's okay. But she needs to take a personal day if that's alright with you?"

Lake felt terribly for leaving the Browns in the lurch. They'd been so good to her. But this was probably for the best.

"See you soon," her mom promised before calling for the girls to get their coats and backpacks.

Lake glanced around the room frantically. The girls could never see that picture.

She realized Grace already had it facedown in her lap.

"Thank you," Grace said into the phone. "I'll take care of her."

Grace hung up and looked at Lake. "She said to take all the time you need. Mabel will love the opportunity to prove that she doesn't need you."

Lake let out a single bark of laughter. Okay, good. She'd unfrozen, if just for a moment.

The kitchen door that led into the garage slammed, letting Lake know that the girls were out of the house, and soon the sound of the rolling garage door closing filled the room.

"I need to head out to work as well. I'm sure you all can fill me in on this later. This changes nothing about you, Lake," her dad said as he moved to the back of the couch so that he could lean over and kiss her head.

Count on her dad to be so matter of fact about this. Unless he already knew what was in the box because he'd hired Celia. Of course they'd hired the private investigator. Her parents must have seen the way not knowing the truth was eating away at Lake.

"Dad!" Lake called out but was greeted with the sound of the garage door closing once again.

How had so much time passed? Lake could have sworn he was in the room a split second before. She'd have to thank him later.

"I think they're arguing," Grace said, joining Lake on the couch with the picture still in her hand.

Sachia and Fred. From the picture. Had they been? Was it a lover's quarrel?

Lake's stomach rolled and she closed her eyes to keep her nausea at bay. The only lover Fred should have ever had was her.

She opened her eyes to see Grace watching her closely. Grace, who should be sleeping because she'd have to be back at work that night.

"You can go take your nap if you'd like," Lake offered, feeling badly that this box had not only taken over her life for the time being but her sister's as well. She needed to give Grace an out.

"And leave this to you on your own? Heck no," Grace said with a sassy tilt of her head.

Lake loved her sister.

But her attention quickly went back to that box.

"Why would they be arguing?" Lake finally asked but her stomach rolled again, telling her she didn't really want the answer to that question. She didn't really want to dig into that box.

But didn't she need the truth?

She'd have to push aside her wants because right now her needs and her wants warred with one another and her needs—her girls' needs—had to win.

Grace didn't answer Lake, silently waiting for her next move.

It took everything in Lake to once more look into that box and take out the next item.

A folder. A very thick folder.

What was in it?

She cautiously lifted it, its weight surprising her. She caught it as it nearly slipped out of her hand. Lake opened it slowly, afraid of the secrets that folder could hold.

But it was just a bunch of legal documents. Lake scanned the first one, not understanding much but realizing these were nondisclosure agreements.

She handed it off to Grace.

The next document was the same thing.

"These are all assurances that these people won't speak to anyone about Fred and Sachia or tell anyone that they were together in the car that day," Grace said.

Lake nodded. She'd gathered the same.

Wait, could this have been Stanley? He would totally have covered up for Fred, to keep Fred's legacy (or more like Stanley's own legacy) unmarred. But no, if this were Stanley he wouldn't have taken the time to have Celia send Lake the info nor would he have paid for someone to find out the truth. Stanley had literally told Lake he didn't care why Fred was with Sachia, only that no one else find out about it.

Lake closed her eyes. She was stalling. She had to dig in further. The truth was right there; she could feel it.

As she glanced back into the box, sure enough, brown cardboard was almost all there was to see. The only thing left in the box was a black flash drive.

The couch next to Lake sank down and she looked up to see Grace. When had she left? And she was already back? Lake shook her head, still feeling so strange in every way, as she carefully lifted the flash drive from the bottom of the box. Grace took the box, offering Lake her laptop.

Wow, Grace had acted quickly. Or Lake was still moving in slow motion. She wasn't sure which.

The computer was already on so Lake simply lifted the lid and plugged the flash drive in.

A folder immediately appeared on the home screen, labeled 'Fred Hollowell.'

Lake was grateful that was all it said. No association to her and especially no association with Sachia.

The fact that she'd had to share her husband with that woman in life had been hard enough but he still wasn't Lake's now. She had to share him even in death.

"Ahhhhh!" Lake screamed out suddenly.

Grace sat stoically beside her.

"I HATE her!" Lake screamed again.

"I know," Grace replied quietly.

"I hate him even more!" Lake shouted at the top of her lungs. Her throat was already scratchy from the strain she'd put on it.

"I know."

"He was supposed to love me. This isn't how it was supposed to end."

Lake wondered at her dry eyes. Maybe she'd already filled her quota of tears for Fred.

"I know," Grace said for a third time. Her voice and presence were a constant comfort.

"I should have been able to mourn him. To accept condolences without feeling the need to share them with his mistress. The woman he'd chosen that last day he'd lived. Because even if the affair was over, he'd gone to her that day. He lied to me and chose her. In the end none of this matters because he chose her."

Lake was filled with a rage that scared her.

She screamed again, allowing that rage to blow up and out of her. She didn't want to hold onto it.

"So choose you," Grace said softly.

"What?"

"He didn't choose you, but you can choose yourself."

Lake looked at her sister, understanding dawning. Lake could choose herself. Her family. Her girls. Their future.

Looking into herself, she found that was exactly what she wanted to do. She wanted to let go of Fred and what he'd done and choose herself. Because she loved herself. She was worthy of being chosen.

Lake smiled as the tears began to fall. She was crying these tears for herself. Not because of what Fred had done, but because of the way she felt. She was sorry for herself and herself alone; none of this emotion was for Fred. She'd done enough for him for long enough.

Taking in a shuddering breath, Lake clicked on the folder, now knowing she could accept whatever the truth was. The truth didn't change her, as her dad had said. Fred had stopped loving her. Maybe not fully, but his love for her hadn't been enough. He'd always said he still wanted her and their family even after the affair, but his love had only been partial, conditional, difficult to actually feel. And that had broken her.

But now Fred's lack of love wouldn't affect her. Because Lake loved herself enough.

Fred chose Sachia. That was the truth. Lake was about to find out why he'd chosen Sachia. Whatever the reason, it wouldn't make his decision okay. He should have talked to Lake. Maybe if he'd never gone to Sachia he'd still be alive.

But none of that mattered now. None of that could be changed. Lake would find out Fred's why and then move on. Because she was choosing herself and what she wanted.

Business Cam One, the first file read.

Lake clicked on it.

She recognized Fred's luxury car immediately. Sachia was at the passenger door, leaning over to speak into the car. Fred didn't look happy. He kept shaking his head.

And the video ended.

Lake didn't wait. She clicked on *Traffic Cam One*.

The video began to play. Sachia leaned over, her body draped across the console as Fred stared straight ahead. She put a hand on his arm and he angrily shoved it away. The video restarted and Lake closed it.

There was one last video before an audio file. *Traffic Cam Two.* Lake recognized the coordinates of the traffic camera. It was one street over from where the accident had happened.

Sachia looked distressed. Fred was yelling at her. He looked forward again, almost as if he wanted the traffic cam to catch his words.

You lied, Lake swore she saw Fred say.

And the video was over.

Lake closed the video, not processing, just taking it all in.

She moved onto the audio file that was titled, *Deleted voice message from Fred Hollowell's phone.*

Lake knew it had to have been a message from Sachia. She had called Fred. Fred had listened to it, even after promising he'd never have contact with Sachia again. And Fred had deleted the message. To hide it from Lake.

Before her thoughts ran wild Lake pressed play.

Fred. I know I promised never to call you again. But I'm scared. I need you. You promised me that if I ever needed you you'd be here. There's this guy who lives in my building. He's been following me and I'm pretty sure he's the one that left a bloody note on my doorstep. I think I need to file a police report. But I can't do it alone. I need you. Please come, Fred.

The message ended.

That's why Fred had gone. He had obviously told Sachia to stop contacting him. For that Lake was proud of him. But still, when she did reach out, he'd gone to her. And maybe he should have, if she really had no one else. But he should have come to Lake. Told her the truth.

The words *you lied* came back to Lake. Had Sachia lied during the message? Tricked Fred into going to see her?

And it hit Lake. This was as much as she would ever know. She was pretty sure Fred wanted to be recommitted to the family at the time he'd died. Yet he'd still lied to Lake. He'd still gone to

Sachia. A part of him would always belong to Sachia because he'd given it to her. So maybe he hadn't necessarily wanted Sachia, but that didn't matter to Lake anymore.

Fred was gone. And Lake had finally come to the point where Fred no longer had any say in her worth. For better or worse.

Lake was worth loving even if she hadn't believed that for a long time. And she'd found that love for herself.

She handed the computer back to Grace.

"Are you okay?" Grace asked.

Grace was right to be concerned. Lake had been through the gamut with this box.

But the rage had gone with her screams, not only her anger at Fred and Sachia but her anger with herself.

Fred hadn't cheated on her again. She was sure of that much. That was what his frustration at Sachia in the car had told her. He hadn't wanted to be there. He'd felt tricked.

But Lake realized that didn't change what truly mattered. She had the truth. She was so grateful her girls would only know when they were ready, if they were ever ready to know the truth about their father. Lake had a feeling she'd never tell them. But this snippet of truth was all the box had brought.

Lake was still the same woman, before and after this truth. Whether Fred had cheated or not didn't reflect on who she was or what she was worth.

Those things were never changing. And she was worth so much more than fear.

Lake Johnson was a strong, smart, kind, loyal, and intriguing woman. She loved fiercely and worked hard. She deserved to go after what she wanted in life.

And after opening that box, she knew exactly what she wanted—or rather, who. She was worthy of him. To him she'd always been worthy and because of that, and so much more, he was dear to her.

There would be mistakes, heartaches, and even fear. But she

knew Logan was the right man for her to press through that fear with. To explore the unknown. He was worth the biggest risk of all—giving her heart.

So she was going to do it.

"I'm better than okay," Lake finally said to her sister.

"Really?" Grace asked, surprised etched across her face.

Lake nodded. "This box helped me realize that the puzzle of emotions and concerns that I wanted to finish before I gave my heart to Logan was complete. Not with this box, but before. This information just helped me to know how little I needed to know it."

Grace cocked her head.

"Fred made his choice. Now I'm going to make mine."

"Oh yeah?" Grace asked with a grin. "Does your decision have anything to do with a tall, dark, and handsome cowboy?"

"It has everything to do with him," Lake acknowledged, her own grin somehow wider than Grace's.

Twenty

LOGAN WALKED out of the stables, drawing in a deep breath. Unlike many, he loved the smell of a stable, maybe because to him that smell meant their livelihood and, more importantly, home.

But there was nothing like fresh air and sunshine. Although they were still smack dab in the middle of winter—the crisp air against his skin was a constant reminder—the sun was shining, the sky was blue, and the mountains were heavy with glistening snow. This kind of day gave Blue Falls a majestic feeling and there was nowhere else Logan would rather call home.

Logan's serene, solitary moment was abruptly broken as what felt like every hand on the ranch rushed past him, pressing toward the old ranch house. *What was going on?* But because Logan didn't move with them he was quickly left behind. As the ranch hands neared the house he saw Jackson, Austin, and Land exiting from the office. Brooks came up behind Logan.

"Mom just called down and said she's doing second breakfast today," he said as he walked past his brother.

"But it's Thursday." Logan was confused. Second breakfast was strictly a Monday thing.

"I know. But none of us are going to look this gift horse in the mouth." Brooks cringed as soon as he heard the words escape his mouth. "Please don't ever tell Mom I just called her a horse."

Logan chuckled, slapping his brother on the back. "Your secret's safe with me," he promised as Brooks picked up his pace.

"You coming?" Brooks called back.

"Be there soon," Logan said, taking his time in the cool mid-morning air.

"Don't take too long. You know how Dave likes to hoard the sausage," Brooks said with an annoyed grunt.

Logan nodded as Brooks left him behind as well.

And then it was just Logan, the cool air, and the mountain view again.

Logan would never admit it to anyone—he loved his family too much to let them know the truth—but the old ranch house hadn't had the same appeal since Lake had gone. He still loved the place. It was his childhood home, still the home of his mom and siblings, and the heart of the ranch. But it just didn't seem full. A piece was missing. And he knew that piece was Lake. She had filled the hole Logan hadn't even realized the old ranch house had. That his life had had.

But with her gone again, that hole gaped, sometimes threatening to swallow the rest of Logan's joy. So he needed a minute to think about Lake out here, to deal with it so that it didn't consume him in there.

Lake must have gotten the news from Celia by now. Celia had said she would leave a box on her doorstep the day before. The truth would be inside it.

Whatever the truth was.

Logan had thought he would go crazy thinking about it, but he found that he was much more worried about Lake's feelings on the matter than whatever the truth was. The truth didn't matter to Logan, only how that truth affected Lake.

How was she doing? Did the fact that her girls would never

have to find out the truth about their father at least give her a small amount of peace? Logan hoped so.

He'd held an inkling of a wish that Lake would call or text him as soon as she heard the news, that she'd want to share it with him, but he knew that was unlikely. She had to process this, he was sure, and figure out how to move forward. If she wanted to move forward. And only after all of those questions were answered could she even start to imagine if it was worth it to her to trust another man again.

But one thing Logan knew was that Lake had plenty of love in her heart. Loving Logan, once she put her mind to it, would be no issue.

He opened his texts to their last communication. She'd seemed touched by his attention to Amelie. She'd even texted afterwards, thanking Logan for being so attentive to her daughter. And as much as Logan wanted to impress Lake, none of what he'd done for Amelie had been for that reason. He knew what it was like to lose your dad. How lost he'd felt. These poor little girls should have had dozens more years with their father and yet he was gone. No, with Amelie it had been all about making that little girl's heart hurt a bit less.

Logan drew closer to the old ranch house and gazed in the direction of the pond and his own home. The home he'd dreamed of sharing with Lake. He'd realized that back when he'd built the place, long before there was even a distant possibility of Lake being in his life, he'd hoped to share it with someone just like her. He'd added a huge picture window that overlooked the pond because he'd known she would love it. He'd done a few coastal finishes because Lake had always loved the beach. He'd even added a tire swing like the one she'd swung on in his backyard when they were kids.

It might have been strange at the time, but now Logan wondered if this was all meant to be. Could all of the disappointments simply be the long and winding path that led them to be together now? Logan could hope. He couldn't help but think that he'd been too young and dumb to have really appreciated Lake back then. The fact that he'd broken up with her proved that. He hated that he'd hurt her in the process and would have taken the hurt on himself if he could have. So maybe it was all Logan's fault they'd taken the long way to finding one another. But he'd spend the rest of his life making that up to her. If she'd let him.

"The bacon is almost gone, Logan!" Holland called.

That put a little pep in his step. It was one thing to run out of sausages, but bacon too? Logan opened the back door, turning to carefully close it behind him instead of slamming it the way he had as a kid. If he had a dollar for every time his mom had yelled at him about slamming that door . . .

"Grab a plate," his mom instructed.

Logan turned to take in the crowd. With how many of the hands were there that day there probably wouldn't be a place for him to sit.

But any concerns over seats and food—heck, any thought other than one—fled as soon as his gaze landed on a face. One gorgeous face that lit up that kitchen.

"Lake," he whispered, a little worried his thoughts had conjured her up. First he thought some kind of serendipity had brought them together, but then he worried that he'd started to hallucinate and was just imagining her in his home with his family.

Logan might need another vacation.

"Hi," Lake replied softly.

Her lips moved with the word. The lips he'd kissed.

She was here. In that kitchen. With his family.

Logan grinned. He wasn't hallucinating.

"Breakfast is done," Morgan called out as she began shooing men out.

Ranch hands tried to bring their plates into the kitchen but Madison collected them, helping her aunt shoo everyone out.

"Don't blow it this time," Jackson whispered to Logan with a grin before his mom smacked his shoulder and pushed him out the back door.

"We'll give you two a moment," Madison said as she and Holland dropped plates into the sink before the three women finally slipped out.

And it was just Logan and Lake.

"I have so much I want to say," Lake began.

Logan took a seat at the island and patted the stool next to him.

Lake smiled at the familiar gesture and sat, this time without hesitation.

"I missed you," she said.

"Darling, not nearly as much as I missed you."

Lake grinned.

"So first, I have a question," Lake asked, sounding much more sure of herself than she had in a long time.

Lake had always been gorgeous, but this confident side of her made her the sexiest woman on the planet.

Logan was in trouble.

"Shoot," Logan offered.

"Did you like our kiss?" Lake asked, looking him right in the eye, which told him she already knew his answer.

He'd better start talking or his mouth would do something else of its own accord.

"I'm pretty sure you know the answer to that, but yeah. That kiss was mind-blowing."

"Mind-blowing. Huh, I would have used life-altering, but okay," Lake teased.

Logan laughed.

"I'm sorry I pushed you away like I did," Lake said, her voice turning serious.

Logan shook his head.

"I know you understand why. But I could have explained

more. Been more open with you. And from now on I promise I will be."

"And I promise I will be as well. For you, Lake, I'll always be an open book. I'll admit my faults and probably take too many accolades when I do something right."

Lake threw back her head and laughed. Oh, Logan loved that laugh.

"That means everything, Logan. I'll try not to hold Fred's mistakes against you but I can't promise it won't come up. I'm still a little battered. Even though I've been working on healing myself."

"I'm grateful you're letting me in on that process."

Lake nodded. "And there's one thing I should warn you about. I've come to love myself. Like a whole lot."

"I've noticed. It's sexy," Logan said as he leaned into Lake.

Lake turned the prettiest shade of pink and Logan had to wonder if Amelie was onto something with her choice of favorite color.

"I have a lot of baggage," she warned.

"I'm pretty good at carrying heavy stuff." Logan flexed.

Lake laughed but he noticed the way she eyed his arm muscles appreciatively. That was a definite bonus to his job. He'd never "worked out" other than for sports but he always had a six-pack and some killer biceps, if he did say so himself.

"Fred was in the car with Sachia but I don't think he wanted to be there. He really had broken things off," Lake said out of nowhere.

"Oh," was all Logan could muster.

"Did you already know that?" Lake asked.

He realized he'd promised to be an open book but was still keeping this secret. His motives had been good—he hadn't wanted her gratitude to push her to him or make her feel obligated to him before she was ready to let him into her life. But staying quiet was not keeping his end of the deal.

"I didn't know. I asked Celia to tell you alone that information," Logan replied and then added, "I'm sorry, Lake. I shouldn't have kept it a secret that I hired Celia. Here I am promising to be better but messing it up within seconds."

"Wait, you aren't perfect? You'll be making mistakes?" Lake stood and turned as if she was going to leave.

She paused and looked over her shoulder with a big smile on her face, then turned back toward him. "I guess that's only fair since I'll be making mistakes as well. And admitting what you've done wrong, saying sorry, that's all I need. Especially when the reason for keeping your identity a secret was for my sake. But let me decide what's good for me, please."

Lake got back onto the stool. But this time she was on her knees so her face was just in front of Logan's.

"I can do that." He heard the frog in his throat as his heart raced.

He'd messed up. Lake was still here. They were figuring things out. They were fighting for their happiness. Because happily ever afters didn't just happen—they were made.

"And I'll let you decide what's best for you. As long as I'm okay with it," Lake teased.

Logan chuckled and felt their breaths mixing. He could smell the sweet mint on hers.

"So now I guess all that's left is the kissing?" Lake asked.

That was all the invitation Logan needed. He tugged Lake off of her stool. She yelped in excitement as he pulled her into his lap.

"Better kissing position," he explained.

"Right," Lake stammered but was cut off when Logan pressed his lips against hers.

Lake none too gently grabbed his neck as she pressed her chest against his.

How was this even better than before? Logan felt fire run

through his veins and heat emanate from his body as he began trailing kisses down Lake's neck.

"I think we gave them more than enough time," Holland's voice came from somewhere much too close. It was the only warning the couple got before Madison, Holland, and Morgan re-entered the kitchen.

Lake pushed Logan away. He would have been fine kissing her in front of an audience but her rosy cheeks advised him to take it a little slower.

Logan and Lake were still breathing hard as his mother eyed them.

"So you've figured things out?" she asked as she pointed first to Logan and then to Lake.

They nodded.

Logan was just glad Lake was still on his lap.

"Then I'd like for you to put my employee back on her own chair during work hours," Morgan said with a smirk.

"Employee?"

"I thought—I helped the Browns find someone to take my place at the B&B. So I'm working here again. If that's okay with you?" Lake asked softly.

This shy side of her was pretty damn sexy as well.

"I think I can manage to deal with that."

Lake grinned.

"But Mom," Logan said, pulling Lake back into his lap as she tried to slide down.

"Lake is first and foremost in this house my girlfriend. Anything else comes after that," Logan said, smirking right back at his mother.

Morgan laughed.

"Fair enough," she said, her smirk morphing into a beautiful smile as she took in her son and his girlfriend. Logan could see in his mother's hopeful eyes that she was already imagining their future, complete with a ring and babies. And for once in Logan's life, he'd anticipated all of those things before his mother had.

"Girlfriend. I like it," Lake said.

"But not too much, I hope," Logan whispered into her ear. "I plan on changing that title soon."

Logan felt Lake shiver in his arms, and another smile grew on his lips.

"I think I can handle that change," Lake assured him as she met his eyes.

Logan knew this was a view he'd never tire of. That it would just grow dearer to him with time.

Lake bit her lip before sliding off of Logan's lap, gripping the stool next to her to keep herself from tumbling to the ground.

But she didn't have to do that. Logan had held her steady through the whole process. The way he always would. As long as he was around, he'd keep Lake from falling. And he knew she'd do the same for him. But in those rare times he couldn't stop her fall, he'd be there to pick her back up. Always.

Twenty-One

LAKE STRUMMED her fingers against the fabric of her dressy slacks, waiting anxiously to watch Delia perform in her class's play. On one side of Lake sat Amelie, Lake's parents, and Grace. On her other side were Logan, his mom, Holland, Madison, and four of his six brothers. Phoenix was still in Salt Lake and Memphis had a date.

But other than those two, Logan's whole family had shown up to support Delia. It might have helped a little that Delia had asked each member of the family personally if they'd be there . . . with flowers. Delia really wanted to be the actress who was given the most flowers at the end of her performance.

But Lake had been concerned. She was still concerned. She and Logan hadn't even really been out in public before this night. Now not only were they here, but so were their whole families, as if they were announcing some big merger to the town. And Lake was fine with people knowing. She knew some would judge but there would also be supportive friends who would stick up for Lake and Logan. This town was made up of good people . . . mostly.

So yeah, Lake was just fine with whatever gossip, good or bad came her way; she just didn't want it to interfere with the cute play. These kids deserved all of the attention tonight. She wanted none of the spotlight but she worried that bringing everyone here would turn that spotlight on full blast.

But Delia wouldn't hear of it when Lake had asked if maybe Logan and his family should come to some later event. She'd declared she wanted all of them in the front row so that every time she looked out into the audience she would see a familiar face.

So, for better or worse, here they were. In the front row.

Logan clutched Lake's trembling hand and pulled it into his lap.

She bit her lip as her heart flipped. Would she ever get to the point where his touch didn't thrill her? She doubted it.

"It'll be fine," Logan assured her and Lake tried to believe him. He would never knowingly lie to her. So Lake tried to believe that this night would go well. They'd all have fun, and Delia would get a dozen flower bouquets. All would be well.

"You're right," Lake said, relaxing into her seat but keeping her hand in Logan's lap. It wanted to live there and who was she to stop it?

"Mom. I need to pee," Amelie said from beside Lake, a little too loudly for Lake's taste.

"I can take her," Grace offered.

Lake shook her head. Her kids needed to know that even when Logan was around they were her priority. As much as it would be nice to pawn her daughter off on her sister and leave her hand in Logan's lap, it was important to show her daughter on this first excursion with Logan that she would choose helping her over staying by Logan's side. Amelie might not even notice the gesture. But Lake would.

Grace nodded as Lake ushered Amelie down the row. Since they were in the first row there was plenty of space for them to walk down the front aisle, but they'd have to hurry. The play was about to start and Lake wanted to be back in their seats well before the curtain was raised.

"Mom, I like Logan," Amelie said as she skipped up the aisle that took them to the back of the middle school's auditorium. Delia was still in elementary school but part of the fun of their class play was that it was going to be performed where the older kids went to school.

"I'm so glad, Honey," Lake said, making sure she had a firm grip on Amelie's hand. The girl tended to move a little faster than Lake and when she took off she was hard to catch up to.

"Do you like Logan?" Amelie asked.

Lake looked around, less than thrilled that they were having this conversation in public. But no one seemed to be noticing them. And honestly, Lake needed to get over these concerns. She was dating Logan. People could know that she liked him.

"I do," she responded with a smile.

Amelie looked satisfied as she skipped right into the women's restroom and let go of Lake's hand to do her thing.

"But her husband just died," Lake heard a female voice say as the door to the restroom opened once more. "You'd think she'd be a little more discreet."

"Hey, with a catch like Logan Ashford on the line, you do anything to keep him," a responding voice replied.

Lake had to smile. The first person was being a little judgmental. But nothing more than she'd thought about her situation. Of course that woman had no idea what was going on behind the scenes and should have kept her thoughts to herself, but Lake wasn't going to hold any grudges when the people speaking came into view.

In walked two of the moms of Delia's classmates and they froze when they saw Lake standing by the stalls.

"I'm—" Lake recognized that as the first voice. She smiled at the mom she'd seen at school pickups and drop-offs.

"I'm Lake. I don't think we've ever officially met," she said, extending her hand.

The second mom took Lake's hand immediately. "I'm Helen and this is Marge. My daughter Paisley is friends with Delia."

"Of course. Paisley. We are fond of Paisley in our house." Lake shook Helen's hand.

"And we love Delia. I've heard she's playing the lead tonight. Paisley couldn't be prouder."

"Neither could Delia," Lake said in an exaggerated whisper.

Both women laughed.

Good, Lake had been hoping to ease Marge's embarrassment.

"About what I said," Marge began.

"I'm done!" Amelie announced as she ran out of the stall and toward the sinks to wash her hands.

"Little ears didn't hear, so no harm done," Lake replied lightly. Maybe a little harm. It did hurt to have her concerns validated, especially by a woman who seemed like she wasn't typically the type to bash someone else, but Lake would get over it.

"It really is none of my business," Marge said.

Lake shrugged. "It isn't. But in a town as small as Blue Falls we sometimes tend to take on the business of others even when we shouldn't."

"Amen to that," Helen agreed.

Marge nodded.

"I'm sorry," Marge said, dropping her voice since Amelie was tearing off a paper towel to dry her hands and would join them any moment.

"You're forgiven," Lake said with a grin and realized that she really did forgive Marge. Her unpleasant feelings had washed away with Marge's apology.

And Logan had been right yet again. Even when things had gone a little awry, it had all ended up fine.

"We'll have to get Paisley and Delia together for a playdate," Helen added.

"I'm sure Delia will enjoy that. She'll be going through withdrawals with no play practice after school." Lake beamed, feeling like she may have made a couple of new friends.

"Enjoy the play," Marge added, her smile just a little too wide. She was coming on a little strong in the friendly department but Lake didn't blame her. Lake would have done the same thing if she'd just stuck her foot in her mouth. Lake had been right as well. This town was made up of mostly good people.

"Can I give Delia her flowers after the play?" Amelie asked as she skipped back to their seats.

Thank goodness her stall had been far enough from the door that she hadn't heard Marge's words. Would Amelie and Delia hear those kinds of comments? Thankfully they were still young and it would hopefully go over their heads, but Lake had needed the reminder that even good people would be speculating about her choices. She'd need to make sure she asked Delia and Amelie their thoughts on the situation often so if there were any issues, they could be brought up rather than festering.

"Of course," Lake said. "Oh, quick, it's about to start."

Lake noticed one of the fourth-grade teachers on the stage so she and Amelie hurried to their seats.

The play was an adorable story, a very simplified version of *Alice in Wonderland*, but Delia killed it as Alice. She remembered every line and had the entire audience in stitches at one point.

When Delia came back out onto stage for her moment to bow in front of the audience, she beamed at her family and then at Logan and his family as the audience clapped loudly. Lake brushed away the tears of happiness she couldn't keep from leaking onto her cheeks. After Fred's death, life had looked so bleak. Lake hadn't been sure how she was going to accommodate for her daughters' physical needs, much less their emotional, social, and spiritual needs. But here they were. Delia was thriving with her peers. Amelie had managed to steal Lake's seat and was now proudly sitting by Logan. Both of her girls adored the man in her life, and judging by the way Logan cheered for Delia and then lifted Amelie onto his shoulders so they could cheer together, he felt the same toward them. God had been good to them.

The actors came down from the stage, each finding their way to their families. Delia ran straight to Logan, jumping into his outstretched arms.

"Did you see me?" Delia asked Logan hopefully.

Lake wondered how Fred would have answered that question but pushed the thought from her mind. Comparisons would help no one.

"How could I miss you? You were brighter than any star," Logan replied.

"Even the sun?" Delia asked cheekily.

"Is the sun a star?" Logan countered.

"Yes, the best one!" Amelie chimed in.

Logan smiled.

Delia turned to collect her flowers from her grandparents and aunt. "Logan said I was brighter than the sun."

Grace popped a pair of sunglasses from her purse. "Why do you think I brought these suckers?" she asked as she slid them on.

Delia laughed in delight.

She received quick hugs, congratulations, and even more flowers from each of Logan's brothers. Even Memphis had sent a bouquet with Land.

"Thank you," Delia said as she'd received every bouquet. So even though Lake was still a little embarrassed about Delia asking for the flowers, at least she politely accepted them.

Amelie stood just behind her sister, ready to take on the surplus of flowers. There was only so much one ten-year-old could carry.

Soon the crowds faded and it was just Lake, Delia, Amelie, and Logan still in the front row.

The girls chattered excitedly about the best parts of the play and then which bouquet was their favorite. They both settled on the one from Logan.

"They're already falling in love with you," Lake said, needing Logan to know how fast and hard everything was happening. Lake might be able to tell herself to take her time, cautiously feel things out, but with the girls, there would be no holding them back. And Lake didn't want them to. She wanted them to love unabashedly.

"You make it sound like that could be a problem," Logan replied, turning toward Lake and taking her in his arms.

Lake didn't even look around in concern to see who was watching. People could think and say what they wanted to. She was sure of her decision and blissfully happy. That was all that mattered.

"I just worry for them. They already lost Fred. And not just with the accident." Lake whispered the last part.

"And you want to make sure they are putting that sweet, adoring love into the right source."

Lake nodded, feeling a little ashamed. When Logan put it that way, it sounded like she was calling him out and he had done nothing even remotely wrong. In fact, he'd been the picture of perfection when it came to being there for the girls. But she had to bring this up. For their sake. And maybe a little for hers.

"Well, let me see if I can help you with that one. First off, I love them. No falling happening here—I already fully love those girls. I don't know what it feels like to be there in a delivery room, but I do know what it's like to have the cutest little girl hand you her heart. Ever since that moment, I was gone, Lake. There is no coming back. Delia and Amelie are in my heart forever."

Lake blinked back tears. How had she been so blessed?

"And second. I'm in love with their mother as well. I love you, Lake," Logan said, causing goosebumps to erupt all over Lake's body.

"I know it's fast and maybe too soon for you. I didn't say it so that you would say it back; I just needed you to know I'm all in. I'm going nowhere." Logan gave her his assurance, the sweetest gift he could have ever given Lake.

"I love you, Logan," Lake replied.

He began shaking his head and Lake lifted her arms, still within his, to hold his head still.

"I mean it. I felt it that day of our kiss. I ran from it, but I felt it."

Logan chuckled.

"But no more running. No more worrying. I'm all in too," Lake promised.

"What are you all in, Mom?" Amelie asked from the outskirts of Logan's hug where she stood with Delia.

They'd left Delia's flowers behind to join Lake and Logan.

Logan glanced down at Lake and smiled before letting her go. He bent down, lifting Delia in his right arm and Amelie in his left and then gathering Lake right in the middle.

She could get used to dating a strong, rugged, and handsome cowboy.

"I'm all in this," Lake said, putting her arms around her girls as well.

"This family?" Amelie asked.

Is that what they had become?

"Exactly. This family," Logan said with a broad grin. "And once I get a specific piece of jewelry worked out, I'll make it official."

Lake gasped.

"Too soon?" Logan mouthed.

Lake shook her head. No, it felt just right. Not only could she not wait to be Mrs. Logan Ashford, she knew deep down it was meant to be.

"Really?" Delia asked, her eyes wide. "We'll officially be a family?"

Logan looked at Lake.

She was about to explode with giddiness.

"It looks like that's the plan," she replied in a shaky voice.

"Well, you'd better get that jewelry worked out, Logan," Amelie said.

They all laughed. Amelie and Delia weren't completely sure why they were laughing; they just knew they were all exceedingly pleased. And in this together. They were all, all in.

Epilogue

JACKSON DROVE down the nearly deserted road that led to the ranch. He was technically outside of town limits and already driving along his family's land. He was still a couple of miles from the main entrance but it was deeply satisfying to drive past beautiful, green acreage and know that it was all Ashford land.

Granted, he couldn't see that it was green. Not at nearly eleven pm. Between the lack of streetlights on the country road and the fact that the moon was waning on this cloudy night, Jackson could basically only see what his headlights illuminated.

He'd enjoyed his evening out with friends but had called it quits early. His friends were still at the bar, but Jackson hadn't found much to interest him that night. Typically, even though Jackson didn't drink, he'd have fun playing pool, dancing with a pretty woman, or even just catching up with old friends.

But tonight it just hadn't been the same. Jackson couldn't put his finger on it.

His evening had started delightfully at Delia's cute school play. Seeing the pride in her eyes as she performed her little heart out and then the way she'd run to his brother? It had made Jackson's cold heart warm a bit.

He wasn't used to seeing happily ever afters play out. Sure, his mom and dad had had the kind of marriage people wrote songs and poetry about but even then, his dad had died too young, leaving their mother a beautiful young widow. And then Madison had shown up, almost destroying his dad's legacy. Yeah, life was usually more of a mess than the beauty he'd witnessed that night.

Watching Logan hold onto the little girl who would surely soon be Jackson's niece, Jackson found himself brimming with an emotion he'd hidden away for a long time, at least since his father's death. Hope.

And he wasn't sure how he felt about hope's reappearance.

Now that Logan was settling down, did it mean Jackson should consider doing the same? It wasn't that he was against marriage—he'd thought about dating just one woman a few times, but those relationships had never worked out and it was always easier to go back to his old surface-level ways of just dating around. That's what he called it. Holland called it womanizing.

But it wasn't that Jackson used the women. They all knew what Jackson was like. He plainly stated that he was still dating other women at the same time and told them they should date other men as well, and his system typically worked well.

Jackson slammed on his brakes, his truck lurching forward even after the tires had stopped.

"What in the heck," he muttered as he threw his truck into reverse and found what, or rather who, had caused him to stop.

Someone was parked on the side of the road, hood up.

And in Blue Falls, when someone was in a predicament like this one, neighbors helped out.

Jackson pulled up a bit, parking his car just in front of the stalled car before stepping out into the cold night air.

"Oh my gosh. Thank you so much," a familiar voice gushed, her car door opening at the same time Jackson's shut. "I don't know what happened and my phone doesn't get any reception out here and—"

Ruby's mouth slammed closed when she recognized who had pulled over to help her.

"You!" she said, pointing an accusing finger. As if all of this was somehow Jackson's fault even though all he'd done was stop to offer aid.

"I believe you were just thanking me?" Jackson couldn't help but push her buttons.

Ruby was obviously the most beautiful woman he'd ever met, with her striking, almost silver-blonde hair, green eyes so light that one would swear they'd just beheld precious gems instead of a pair of eyes, and her long, lean figure.

Jackson perused that figure even though he knew it would drive Ruby up the wall. Actually that was maybe why he did it.

His eyes lingered over her curves. Nope. Annoying Ruby was just a bonus. Jackson was doing this all for himself.

"Ugh!" Ruby screeched before stomping back toward her car.

"Not quite sure that's the best way to ask for help, darlin'," Jackson drawled, crossing his arms over his broad chest. He knew that position showed him to an advantage. And as much as Ruby loathed him he knew she appreciated his figure as well. They had a mutual admiration that was just skin deep.

The rest, well . . . he was sure Ruby hated him. She just had yet to say the words.

"I don't need help," Ruby ground out as she got back into her car.

Jackson made quick work of the ground between him and Ruby's car door and held it open as she tried to tug it shut.

"You're like a mammoth of a man."

"Thank you," Jackson said with a grin.

"That wasn't a compliment," Ruby snapped.

"The way your eyes eat me up say otherwise."

Ruby's eyes widened in outrage, the green lighting up the dark night sky. "Of all the . . . I hate you!" she screamed.

Well, there came the words. At least Jackson now knew just where he stood, although he had no idea why. Maybe he hadn't been completely welcoming of Madison when she'd come into their home, claiming to be his father's long-lost child, but he'd behaved like any man would have. Besides Logan. But Logan was a freak of nature who'd had complete faith in their father's loyalty. Jackson couldn't be that sure of anyone. Everyone made mistakes. Sometimes really big ones.

"Let go of my door," Ruby seethed.

"I can't let you stay out here all alone." Jackson spoke for the first time without teasing or drawling. He'd just stated a fact.

"Then let me use your phone. I'm guessing because you live on this Godforsaken land you get reception?" Ruby asked, putting out her hand.

Jackson readily handed his phone to her.

"Although I'm not sure who you'll call. Tony's the only one in town with a tow truck and his shop closes at six. He's open for emergencies until ten," Jackson said.

"And what about emergencies after ten?" Ruby said through her teeth.

"They wait until morning."

Ruby pursed her lips.

"I'll just call Madi. She'll be happy to come out and pick me up," Ruby said as she began dialing.

Jackson scowled. What was the point in Madison driving all the way out here at nearly midnight when he was already standing right there with a perfectly good truck? But he let Ruby continue her call, although his scowl deepened.

"Hey Mads?" Ruby said after Madison answered the call. "I was on my way to visit you when my car broke down. I'm stuck out here in the middle of nowhere."

Ruby paused.

"It's Jackson's phone."

She paused again.

"Yeah, he's standing right here."

She paused yet again.

"Because I don't want to."

"I get that it doesn't make sense; just come and get me!" Ruby demanded.

She hung up the phone, her scowl rivaling Jackson's.

"Madison says you should just jump in my truck and get a ride home?" Jackson guessed.

"She hates driving out here in the dark," Ruby muttered.

Ruby threw Jackson's phone at his chest. Thankfully years of playing all kinds of sports made his reflexes quick and he caught the phone before it could fall.

"I'll just wait it out," Ruby muttered, looking around her car that did not look equipped for winter camping.

"All night?" Jackson asked with a raised eyebrow.

"Someone will be by sometime."

"Our ranch is really the only reason for someone to be on this part of the road," Jackson replied. "As far as I know, the rest of my family is at home. Memphis might still be out. But he might stay out the whole night. Who knows with that one."

Ruby lifted her chin.

"Then I can sleep in my car."

"The temperatures are dipping into the subzero range. Sure you want to chance that?" Jackson asked. Even with his rancher jacket that got him through the worst of winters he was still a bit chilly out here. Ruby had to be freezing.

But he could see that her pride wouldn't let her give in. And what kind of man would he be if he let her freeze out in this, even if she did hate him?

"You know, I'm sure you'd only make Madison feel guilty if I went home without you. Then she'll come out here even though she's scared to death. And some of these roads are probably still a little icy from the last storm. If she isn't paying attention and something happens to her . . . "

Even in the dark Jackson could see Ruby's features drop.

She looked around, trying to find any other option. Her eyes finally landed back on Jackson, resigned.

"Don't think this means I hate you any less."

"Wouldn't dream of thinking something so silly." Jackson knew the way he worded his sentence would let Ruby know just what he thought was silly.

She bit the inside of her cheek.

"And don't try any moves on me. We might be in a dark truck together, but don't you dare force your attentions onto me. I'm not like all of the other women in this town who fawn all over you."

Jackson narrowed his eyes. Just what kind of man did this woman think he was? He may not be in a committed relationship, but that didn't mean he'd throw himself on an unsuspecting woman. In all of his days Jackson hadn't so much as held a girl's hand unless she'd wanted him to.

"Don't worry your pretty little head on that account. My hands won't be coming anywhere near you," Jackson spat.

Ruby looked taken aback by his reaction, but what had she expected after her implication?

"Fine," she said, gathering her things and slamming her door behind her before stomping over to Jackson's truck.

It took everything in Jackson to stay put, not to hurry ahead and open her car door for her, but he was sure he'd be accused of something unsavory if he acted like a gentleman.

Ruby hopped into his truck and Jackson fought the thought that she looked good jumping into his ride. Who cared what a woman looked like when she acted so vile?

Jackson followed. Thankfully he'd kept his truck going, so the cab would be nice and toasty when they got in.

He opened his door and saw Ruby eyeing his keys.

Had she really considered taking his truck and leaving him here? He wouldn't put it past her.

He hauled himself into the driver's seat and sent Ruby a warning glare. No one would be driving his truck besides him.

Jackson put it into drive and they were off, Ruby watching the landscape as they drove past and Jackson's eyes never leaving the road.

A few seconds later, the tense silence was killing him. He wasn't used to people hating him. In fact, Ruby was the first to ever tell him so—besides his siblings when they'd fought. But they'd never meant it. Ruby . . . well, Ruby had.

He turned on the radio to a station that always helped him relax.

"I hate country music," Ruby said sullenly from her spot where she leaned against the truck door as if she moved a millimeter closer to Jackson he'd what? Attack?

"No one hates country music. They say they do until they really listen to it. The stories that country music tells are unlike any other."

"I grew up on country and could probably sing more of the classics than you can. And I hate it," Ruby reiterated as she crossed her legs, moving herself even closer to the door.

The mournful love song played for a few more seconds until suddenly Ruby was no longer pressed against the door. She was reaching across the cab, toward Jackson.

To turn off his radio.

Silence once again filled his truck.

Jackson's eyes went wide. She did not just do that. This was his danged truck. If he wanted to play music to cover the tense silence in the car, he could play music to cover the tense silence in the car.

This was too much. Ruby was too much.

"I'm not sure what's happening here. I hardly know you and apparently you hate me."

"Hardly know me?" Ruby scoffed.

What in the heck did that mean?

"Do I know you?" Jackson asked with a raised eyebrow.

Ruby watched him, taking in his frown, and finally shook her head.

That's what he'd thought.

"So where do you get off acting like you know me, like you have some reason to despise me?" Jackson asked as he steered along the long drive that would take them up to the old ranch house. They were almost done with this torturous ride.

Ruby seethed. Jackson could almost see the steam coming out of her ears. He'd hit a nerve and as always with Ruby he had no idea what that nerve was. "You might not know me. But I know you, Jackson Ashford." She threw open the truck door even though Jackson hadn't come to a complete stop and jumped out, looking like a nimble fairy. A tall, beautiful fairy.

Jackson shook his head. Talking to this woman was like trying to solve a riddle. He didn't know her but she knew him? In what world did that make sense?

She must just be saying it to mess with his head. She didn't know him. She couldn't know him. Jackson hadn't seen Ruby until she'd followed Madison into the old ranch house a few months before.

Right?

Julia Keanini

Julia Keanini is just a city girl living in a country world (and secretly loving it). She loves the mountains and would adore the beach, if it weren't for all the sand and salt (wait, that is the beach?). A good book, a great song, or a huge piece of chocolate can lift her mood, but her true happiness is found in her little fam. She writes about girls who deal with what life throws at them and always about love, cause she LOVES love.

Made in the USA
Las Vegas, NV
24 May 2022